SWEET REVENGE

Books by Fern Michaels:

Mr. and Miss Anonymous
Up Close and Personal
Fool Me Once
Picture Perfect
About Face
The Future Scrolls
Kentucky Sunrise
Kentucky Heat
Kentucky Rich
Plain Jane
Charming Lily
What You Wish For
The Guest List
Listen to Your Heart
Celebration
Yesterday
Finders Keepers
Annie's Rainbow
Sara's Song
Vegas Sunrise
Vegas Heat
Vegas Rich
Whitefire
Wish List
Dear Emily

The Godmothers Series:

The Scoop

The Sisterhood Novels:

Deadly Deals
Vanishing Act
Razor Sharp
Under the Radar
Final Justice
Collateral Damage
Fast Track
Hokus Pokus
Hide and Seek
Free Fall
Sweet Revenge
Lethal Justice
The Jury
Vendetta
Payback
Weekend Warriors

Anthologies:

Snow Angels
Silver Bells
Comfort and Joy
Sugar and Spice
Let It Snow
A Gift of Joy
Five Golden Rings
Deck the Halls
Jingle All the Way

FERN MICHAELS

SWEET REVENGE

ZEBRA BOOKS
KENSINGTON PUBLISHING CORP.
http://www.zebrabooks.com

ZEBRA BOOKS are published by

Kensington Publishing Corp.
119 West 40th Street
New York, NY 10018

All Kensington titles, imprints and distributed lines are available at special quantity discounts for bulk purchases for sales promotion, premiums, fund-raising, educational or institutional use.

Special book excerpts or customized printings can also be created to fit specific needs. For details, write or phone the office of the Kensington Special Sales Manager: Kensington Publishing Corp., 119 West 40th Street, New York, NY 10018. Attn. Special Sales Department. Phone: 1-800-221-2647.

ISBN-13: 978-0-8217-7879-1
ISBN-10: 0-8217-7879-X

First Printing: October 2006
10 9 8

Printed in the United States of America

SWEET
REVENGE

Prologue

Isabelle Flanders walked out of her apartment, careful to lock the door behind her. She sniffed the cold February air, then drew a deep breath. The fresh air smelled wonderful. It was mid-morning and it was Valentine's Day. Always a romantic, she smiled. She wondered if she was too old to hope for a special valentine from a special someone. Yep, she was too old. She took another moment to savor the crisp, cold air.

She'd been confined to her apartment for the last three weeks with a gruesome case of the flu. It had all started at New Year's with both Myra and Charles coming down with the miserable bug. Then, one by one, the sisters had all gotten the flu. She was the last to recover and she knew her colleagues were waiting for her at Pinewood to start her mission, which was already five weeks past schedule.

While she was in a hurry to get to Pinewood, it was still Valentine's Day, and she had something she had to do. Something she had done on this day every year since the accident that had rendered her helpless for longer than she cared to admit.

Isabelle started the engine of her Honda and waited for the heater to kick in before she slipped the car into gear. She knew she was punishing herself by driving past her old office today of all days. So what if fellow architect, Bobby Harcourt, her one-time fiancé, bought into her downfall and then dumped her after the dark stuff hit the fan? So what if Bobby ended up marrying the very woman who brought about her downfall? So what? That was then. This is now. Now, with the aid of the Sisterhood, she was finally going to get her revenge for what Rosemary had done to her. Bobby, too.

She was driving now, mindful of the time and how long it was going to take to drive out to Pinewood in McLean, Virginia. First, though, she had to rub her nose in her own stupidity one more time.

How could she have been so wrong about Rosemary and Bobby? Back then, she'd been on top of the world with her business, her engagement, and the rosy life that lay ahead of her. Being Architect of the Year gave her every right to expect things to progress accordingly. How wrong she'd been.

Isabelle pulled the Honda to the curb and parked. She stared out the window at the building where she'd labored eighteen hours a day to build her business. It was now a real estate office. She wondered if any of the employees of that real estate office ever slept there at night the way she used to sleep on the sofa when she was under the wire. Did it matter? Those days were gone.

Still, she didn't move, her mind wandering back to what she called her lost years. Years spent trying to earn a living, trying to forget Rosemary Hershey's betrayal—Bobby's, too. In the beginning, after the trial, after Rosemary Hershey, she'd cautioned herself to take it one day at a time. But that hadn't worked so she'd taken the physical route—exercising, running, hiking and biking. She knew now that all those things had kept her going, kept her sane, kept her alive to fight another day. And always in the back of her mind was the hope, the desire, the determination to get her license reinstated so she could go back to the work she loved.

Now, if things went the way she hoped they would, she'd climb back to the top. She had the guts to do that. She was prepared to claw her way back if she had to and, in the end, she'd make Rosemary Hershey and Bobby Harcourt sorry they had ever tangled with her.

Revenge was going to be so sweet. Her eyes sparkled with what was to come.

The next stop was St. Andrew's Church where she had expected to marry Bobby Harcourt on Valentine's Day. A lifetime ago? Damn close.

Isabelle watched an elderly lady wearing a black shawl over her head trying to maneuver the steps with her walker. Isabelle opened the car door and sprinted forward to offer help. The woman smiled up at her.

"What a sweetheart you are for helping me. I can do it but it takes me forever. I come here every day as I live just around the corner."

The steps safely conquered, Isabelle returned to her car. Sitting here wasn't going to do anything for her. Right then, she made a promise to herself that she would never go down this section of Memory Lane again.

Her eyes still burning, she turned on her signal light and moved slowly into the traffic. An hour later she cruised through the open gates of Pinewood and pulled up next to the row of parked vehicles. All of the women were here. Parked next to Alexis's Mini Cooper was Kathryn's eighteen-wheeler. Next to Kathryn's rig was Nikki's BMW and beside that was Yoko's nursery van. All present and accounted for. Well, almost. Julia wasn't here, would never join them again. And yet she *was* here; her spirit was with them all.

The kitchen door opened. A grin blossomed across Isabelle's face when she saw Myra and the rest of the Sisterhood with their arms outstretched in welcome.

"I'm here! I'm here!" she shouted as she ran forward.

One

The women laughed and hugged each other as Myra and Charles stood to the side, beaming with pleasure. Myra reached for Charles's hand and snuggled her own with his.

"Just in time for lunch," Charles said. "In honor of this cold, blustery day, we have vegetable soup and home-made bread. Unfortunately, Myra tells me it isn't quite as good as the bread she received as a tip in Kalorama during Nikki's mission. But she did say it was good. I regret to say I didn't churn the butter, but it is soft."

"I'll take it," Kathryn said. Everyone knew about Kathryn's ravenous appetite. It was said that she would eat anything that wasn't nailed down.

Charles added two more logs to the kitchen fireplace and Myra carried one of her heirloom soup tureens to the table.

"It smells heavenly, dear," she said, real happiness ringing in her voice. "Charles started the soup at five o'clock this morning. He made an apple pie, too, with apples from the root cellar. Remember when you girls picked them in the fall?"

They ate lunch and chattered like magpies, happy to be together again after their long hiatus. And then it was time to adjourn to the war room to begin business.

Myra Rutledge called the meeting to order and then Charles stepped down from his bank of computers that would have been the envy of the White House war room itself if they had ever known this particular room existed.

"Let's run through old business first. Before you can ask, Nikki, there is no news on the Barringtons, who were to be your original mission. I personally take responsibility for that fiasco. I'm not giving up on my attempts to locate them, nor do I want you to give up hope either. The main thing we can be grateful for is that all the horses are safe and the Barrington farm is deserted. Not only is it deserted, it is crumbling to the ground. Five days ago, the property went up for sale. From what I've been able to gather, it appears that the property was turned over as a quitclaim deed and the new owner immediately put it up for sale. Myra has placed a bid on the property, but we haven't yet heard if that bid has been accepted or not. The reason I'm telling you all of this is because it enters into Isabelle's mission. But before I get to that, do any of you have anything to say? Any questions?"

"Is there any news on Paula Woodley or her husband, the National Security Advisor?" Alexis asked.

Charles allowed himself a brief smile. "It's not beneficial to any of us to continue a dialogue with any of the parties after a mission is completed.

When we walk away, we walk away completely, never to return. However, I did pick up a few tidbits on the Internet. Mr. Drudge seems to have information that had not previously been released."

"And that would be . . . what?" Kathryn asked.

"That the NSA is back in the loving arms of his wife. He resigned his post with the administration—under pressure, according to Mr. Drudge. In addition, it seems the President has not seen fit to call or visit his NSA. Mr. Drudge speculates to the why of that, but has no concrete answers. It appears we will have to stay tuned for further *informative* gossip."

"What about the three special agents found in the NSA's backyard? The President's secret little force?" Nikki asked cautiously.

"'Hogwash,' says the President. The three men in question did not belong to a special presidential squad as was reported, since no such squad exists. The President said the three men were in fact FBI agents. The *Post*'s star reporter, Mr. Ted Robinson, says he has proof that what he reported is not hogwash. His proof is being held by the *Post*. It's over and done with and we're all moving forward now. It won't behoove any of us to dwell on the past. Having said that, I suggest we get down to business and decide how best to help Isabelle with her case."

Myra pointed to the orange folders that had been placed in front of each of the women. "We can follow along with Isabelle, but I think it will be better if she tells us in her own words what happened to her and what she wants done."

Isabelle took a deep breath as she looked around at the women. She cleared her throat. "As you all know, I'm an architect. I had my own business, which I worked at eighteen hours a day. I designed shopping malls, high-rises, churches . . . you name it and my name was on it. I moved three times to accommodate my business as well as my staff. At the time, I was also engaged to a man named Bobby Harcourt. I was supposed to get married on Valentine's Day. That was several years ago. . . .

"I hired a young woman called Rosemary Hershey. She had just passed her boards and I thought she was just right for our office. She was a real go-getter. Dedicated, beautiful, made a great impression. She was a sharp dresser and a hell of an architect, with great, innovative ideas." Isabelle looked over at Nikki. "Rosemary was my Allison Banks, the woman who almost ruined you. *Almost* is the key word in your case. In my case, Rosemary Hershey did ruin me.

"In less than six months, Rosemary became my right-hand woman. I started to depend on her more and more. In a way it was a godsend because it freed me up to spend more time with my fiancé." Isabelle's voice turned wistful. "I was so happy during that time. Then I came down with a vicious head cold that ended up settling in my chest. I started to doctor myself because I was stupid and didn't want to take the time to sit in a doctor's office. I was a hair's breath away from having to give a presentation to pitch for the contract for a new shopping mall in Pennsylvania. Everyone in the office worked together to help, including Rosemary.

"The day I had to make my presentation I was sick as a dog and was swigging cough medicine by the bottle. I was also running a fever, so Rosemary drove me to the presentation. On the way, there was . . . there was an accident." Isabelle licked at her dry lips as she struggled to continue. "I was knocked unconscious. When I woke up I was in the hospital and I couldn't remember a thing about the accident. Then I developed pneumonia. They told me the alcohol content in my blood was . . . was high, that I was drunk and had run a stop sign. A family . . . a mother, a father and a little two year-old girl were killed, and Rosemary was severely injured, too. Everyone sued me. I believed what they said, that I had been driving. Bobby made himself scarce and finally disappeared altogether. I lost everything trying to defend myself.

"When I didn't think it could possibly get any worse, it did. Rosemary said I'd stolen her design for the shopping mall. She said we were arguing in the car and that's how I ran the stop sign. I couldn't prove otherwise. Rosemary saw to that. In the end they believed her and I lost my license and my business.

"It took almost a year for my memory to return, and even then it was just in little bits and pieces. But by then all the damage had been done. Another year went by as I tried to earn a living. I went to see Rosemary, to plead with her. She laughed in my face. When I was leaving her big, plush office, I ran into Bobby and found out that he and Rosemary were engaged. He couldn't look me in the eye. A couple of months later, I saw in the paper that they'd gotten married. Of course, I wasn't invited to the wedding. Shortly after that, I went to see Nikki. Without any kind of proof, there was nothing her firm could do for me. She helped me get a job that paid the bills, but I couldn't work in my field again."

"And you didn't scratch that bitch's eyes out!" Kathryn barked, outraged.

"I knew if I touched her, I would have killed her.

The only thing I could do was walk away. Rosemary is at the top of her game now, clients standing in line to hire her. Bobby is her partner. Since Charles got my license reinstated I've started over and actually have several small clients. I have to supplement my income with odd jobs just to make my rent, but I'm surviving."

Myra tapped her pencil on the tabletop. "What would you like to see happen to this awful woman, Isabelle?"

"I'd like her to tell the truth. Then I want to see her stripped of everything she holds dear. Including that miserable husband of hers. I don't want to believe he was in on it with Rosemary, but common sense tells me she needed a cohort. By the way, the two of them took all my clients. Something also needs to be done for the family who were killed. My insurance didn't pay the family's heirs that much. Rosemary got there first with her lawsuit and got just about all of it. My umbrella policy was for three million dollars. She got two and a half million and the family got the other five hundred thousand. When I went to see Rosemary, I asked her if her conscience bothered her about that family. Do you know what she said to me? She said, 'Get real, Pollyanna.'"

"We'll just have to make Ms. Rosemary eat those words, now won't we, girls?" Alexis drawled. The others nodded.

Charles stepped down from his computers and said, "Myra and I have come up with a plan. We would like you to consider it when you think about Rosemary's punishment. Our plan depends on the sale going through on the Barrington property next door, so at the moment it is nothing more than an idea."

Nikki settled herself more comfortably in her padded swivel chair. "Let's hear it then, Charles."

Charles looked like a Cheshire cat as he smacked his hands together. "Since Myra has the where-withal," he said, referring to Myra's vast fortune, "to do pretty much as she wishes, we took the liberty of renting a very posh, high-end suite of offices on K Street in the District. It will be the new offices of Isabelle Flanders, architect. Anyone wanting to con-fer with Ms. Flanders can only do so by appoint-ment. Since you've had your license for a year now, Isabelle, we've managed to give you an impressive résumé to match your offices. Courtesy of some of my friends," he added, false modesty ringing in his voice.

If the women wondered about the why or the how of what Charles was saying, they didn't mention it out loud. They knew better. In their eyes, Charles, a former MI6 operative, could do anything, thanks to his network of spooks, spies and the covert world he'd worked in until his cover was blown. When Myra had told the girls that Charles was on first-name terms with the Queen, they never again questioned anything he did or asked of them.

"What that means is that Isabelle can take credit for designing a theme park owned by a friend in California. She can also take credit for a brand-new mall that's about to open in Chicago. Another friend. Anyone curious enough to make inquiries will run up against a brick wall.

"The new offices will have impressive plaques, citations, blow-your-mind pictures of Isabelle with dignitaries. There will also be an article in the papers today, courtesy of the AP wire service, announcing that my friend on the other side of the pond is requesting Isabelle's presence for a memorial she is considering. It doesn't matter if the event materializes or not."

"Whoa! Way to go, Charles!" the girls squealed in unison.

Charles preened and bowed low. In spite of himself, he burst out laughing. "Sometimes it pays to have friends in high places."

Myra was so excited she almost broke her pearls, which she was never without. "Can you imagine the look on this Rosemary's face when she hears about *that*? Whatever would we do without this dear man?"

Charles's cheeks turned pink as he cleared his throat so he could continue. "Now, if the sale goes through and Myra is able to purchase the adjacent property, she's going to contact several architects to bid on the project she's considering. There are several very large firms in the District, but the two we are going to be interested in are Rosemary's and Isabelle's. Rosemary will know she's being pitted against the woman she ruined. It should prove interesting."

"Charles, that is so devilishly clever," Nikki said in awe.

Charles twinkled. "Yes, I thought so. Since today is Valentine's Day, I'm taking my lady love to town. We're going to pick up Judge Easter and have a nice dinner out. You're all more than welcome to stay or leave. We'll reconvene tomorrow at the same time."

Nikki felt enormous relief. She'd been wondering for hours how she could possibly get away to join Jack on this all-important lovers' day. She did her best to feign indifference by saying, "I think I'll head for my office. I'll see all of you tomorrow."

Isabelle was the only one who opted to stay at the farm. The others said their goodbyes and drove away.

Left to her own devices, Isabelle sat down at the kitchen table and sipped at her cold cup of coffee. A mighty sigh escaped her lips. What would she do when her mission was over and she was vindicated? Neither Charles nor Myra had said anything about her continuing to work in the fancy new offices and she didn't have the nerve to ask if she could take it over. The rent alone scared her out of her wits. Maybe she could open a small office somewhere and just be a one-woman operation. The thought of being vindicated left her feeling light-headed. Maybe she needed to go outdoors and run till she dropped.

She wished then, as she often did, that she had family to call on, but there was no one but a great-aunt who was so distant she couldn't even remember her name. All her friends were gone and she hadn't bothered to make new ones. The Sisterhood was her family now, Myra and Charles her surrogate parents. Maybe someday she'd meet a man who would make her blood sing the way Bobby had. So many maybes.

Life was suddenly becoming interesting again.

Isabelle smiled, then grabbed her lightweight jacket and went for her run. Seven miles today.

* * *

In the car, Nikki called Jack on her cell phone. "I've been sprung. I'm all yours for the rest of the day and night."

Jack groaned. "Nik, I can't get away until at least four. I'll try for earlier but I can't promise."

"Do your best. I'll cook us a nice dinner and . . ."

"And?"

Nikki laughed. "And I'll leave it to you to fill in the blanks. Bye." She heard Jack groan again as she ended the call.

Jack gathered up his topcoat and briefcase and left his office. He had fifteen minutes to get to court. It was sleeting when he hit the street, the stinging spray hitting him smack in the face. He walked with his head down, hunkered into his topcoat.

"Hey, Jack, slow down!" a voice called to be heard over the driving wind. Jack turned to see Ted Robinson on his right.

"Can't. Gotta be in court. Walk along with me. I hope to hell you aren't here to ask me what to buy your lady love, the one with the bodacious ass, for Valentine's Day."

The reporter loped alongside Jack, his breathing heavy. Finally, he had to slow down. "Well, yeah, that too, but I need to talk to you about something else first. How long are you gonna be in court?"

"Thirty minutes if all goes well. Wanna grab some lunch? Listen, I have to sprint the rest of the way. I'll meet you in the lobby, OK? Forty minutes tops."

"Yeah, sure."

Jack felt bad for his friend as he sprinted off. Ted still wasn't up to snuff since he'd had his spleen removed following an almost-fatal beating by some very special federal agents. Jack had taken care of that little matter, but he still felt guilty over the beating Ted had suffered.

Jack barreled through security and raced down the hall to Judge Easter's courtroom. He blew in like a gust of wind, shrugging out of his topcoat as he raced to take his place just as Judge Easter stomped her way to the front of the room and saw Jack wiping at the sleet on his face.

"All stand. The Honorable Judge Cornelia Easter presiding," the bailiff shouted to be heard in the back of the courtroom.

"Nice to see you this morning, Mr. Emery," she barked.

"Happy Valentine's Day, Your Honor," Jack replied, grinning.

The judge settled in her chair.

Forty minutes later Jack was on his way to the ground floor where Ted Robinson was waiting for him.

"How about the Rusty Nail?" Jack asked, referring to a steak house a block away.

"Sure. I'm in the mood for a big thick steak with onions and mushrooms. I'm getting tired of eating tofu. Maggie is a vegetarian so I have to be carnivorous on my own time. So what do you think, Jack? Flowers, candy, jewelry, or all of the above? What? Are you seeing anyone? What are you getting her? Who is it?"

"Like I'm really going to tell you her name! Tomorrow I'll see it in that damn paper of yours. I'm going the flower route. Champagne-colored roses. I ordered them yesterday. You're only going to get leftovers now. Why'd you wait so long?"

"Because I didn't know what to get her. She does have a bodacious ass, doesn't she?"

Jack held the door to the Rusty Nail open for Ted to enter. "That she does, my friend. Now, if you really want to win some points with Maggie, get something for her dog. Women love it when you include their pets. I read that somewhere, so don't blame me if it doesn't work." He shrugged out of his wet topcoat and hung it up next to the booth. Then he plopped down and swiped at his wet head with a wad of napkins. "What a shitty day," he mumbled. "So, I know damn well you didn't come all the way to the office to ask me about Valentine's Day. What's up?"

Ted grimaced as he waited for the waitress in her skimpy, almost non-existent uniform to take their order. "I'll have a porterhouse steak, medium, twice-baked potato and a side of onion rings and I'll have a Miller Lite."

"I'll have the same," Jack said.

"She must be freezing," Ted said, jerking his head in the waitress's direction.

"Nah, those girls have to hustle. In case you don't know this, buddy, they wear those skimpy outfits so dumb schmucks like us tip big. So, what's up?"

"I don't know for sure. Maybe something, maybe nothing. I'd like your spin on it." Ted whipped up a folded section of the *Post*, a small column highlighted in yellow.

Jack reached for the paper, his eyebrows shooting upwards. *Shit, shit, shit!* The ladies of Pinewood were on the march again.

Two

The moment Nikki heard the ping of the alarm system going off, she ran to the foyer to throw herself into Jack's arms.

"Ohhh, I've missed you! It's been . . ."

"A whole week. I missed you more," Jack said, nuzzling her neck, loving the way she always smelled like wildflowers, even in the dead of winter. He held out the florist's box with its huge red ribbon.

Nikki accepted the box, *ooohing* and *aaahing* over the gorgeous champagne-colored roses—her favorite. She quickly put them in a vase and then carried them into the living room to the coffee table. That way they could both enjoy the flowers while they cuddled on the couch after dinner. She wiggled her finger to show Jack she was wearing her engagement ring. He smiled from ear to ear, knowing that in the morning it would go back on the chain around her neck and then under whatever she was wearing for the day. She could wear it on her toe for all he cared, as long as she wore it.

"How's the weather out there?" Nikki asked as she led Jack back to the little breakfast nook where they would have their romantic candlelit dinner.

"Rain, sleet, a little snow. The roads are freezing. By morning, if this keeps up, we'll be socked in." Jack wiggled his eyebrows to show what he thought about that. "What's for dinner?"

"Your favorite. Leg of lamb, Irish potatoes, mint jelly, baby carrots. I made yeast rolls. And I baked a blackberry cobbler. Just for you, Mr. District Attorney."

Jack looked down at the pretty table setting, the linen tablecloth, the matching napkins, the fine crystal, the gleaming silver and the decorative china. What he really liked were the blue candles that smelled like blueberries. His sister always used to chastise his mother for never using her fine things. "They're for company," his mother would always say. The only thing was, they never had company. Not even at Christmas. Nikki said she liked to use her things every day because they made her feel good. She even had a Baccarat crystal glass in the bathroom that she used to gargle with. Now he had one, too. His glass was on the left, Nikki's was on the right.

"Give me a minute to change my clothes and I'll be right back."

"Take your time. By the way, I have a present for you, too."

Jack took a swipe at her rump as he left the kitchen. He was back in ten minutes wearing jeans and a navy-blue sweatshirt that said Georgetown Lacrosse on the back. He was like a kid again. "Can I open my present now?"

"Well, sure," Nikki said as she settled platters on

the table and then opened a bottle of Jack's favorite Merlot. She sat down and waited for him to untie the ribbon and open the small flat box. Finally, when he had ripped at the paper and at the Scotch tape holding the box together, he stared down at the present.

"Oh, wow! Uh-huh. This . . . I can see you put a lot of thought into this. I don't know what to say. Honest to good God, Nik, I'm speechless."

Nikki leaned across the table, the light from the blue candles casting her in an almost iridescent glow. Her voice was soft, solemn. "The big question is, will you accept this gift from my heart?"

Jack stared at the woman he loved and replied just as solemnly. "I accept. The big problem is this: with such a tribute, where can I . . . put it? I'm assuming it's a secret?"

Nikki reached for the burled-walnut plaque with the bronze faceplate that proclaimed Jack Emery an honorary member of the Sisterhood. "This makes it official, Jack. You don't have to accept. You said you were committed to me, and committed to me means you're committed to the Sisterhood. It's not too late to back out."

Jack reached for her hand over the leg of lamb. "I'm in. I'll do whatever I can to help you. In secret, of course."

"Of course."

"Now, can we eat?"

"You betcha."

Hours later, after dinner, the pair cuddled on the comfortable sofa.

"Bring me up to date, Nik," Jack said.

When Nikki was finished outlining the plan they had for Isabelle's mission, Jack fished around in his briefcase to show her the article Ted Robinson had given him at lunch. "He's already on to you guys. I have to say, you're pretty clever. What are the chances of Myra getting the property?"

"Actually she has it, but she may not know it yet. Isabelle called from the farm around three and said that the Realtor had called to say her client had accepted Myra's offer. She said she tried calling both Myra and Charles but their cell phones must be off. So, yes, she's got the property and it's a go."

"Is that guy Charles so influential he got the Queen to go along with him on that news release that hit the paper?"

"Yep."

"Damn!"

"Jack, can you dig out the old files on Isabelle's case? I have them in the office but I don't want to pull them out now and draw unwanted attention. The firm has picked up a few more clients through word of mouth from some of our more loyal clients. I'm not going to replace Jenny. I learned my lesson when I hired Allison to take Barbara's place. Perhaps down the road, if our client base increases, I'll give it some thought. Right now, Jenny's death is still too raw with me—and all the partners at the firm. What's going on in the DA's office?"

Jack poured from a second bottle of wine. "Same old, same old. Crime never stops, you know that. I had to appear before Judge Easter late this morning. She's no fun anymore. She used to crack up the courtroom with her one-liners. She's all business these days, and I understand that. I did wish her a Happy Valentine's Day, but she gave me the evil eye so I shut up."

"Ted?"

"Yeah, well, Ted is something else. Ink runs in that guy's veins. He's got something going with Maggie Spritzer these days, so what he doesn't come up with, she does. He was pretty excited about the little article I showed you. He sees political intrigue and governments colliding, that kind of thing. He knew immediately who Isabelle Flanders was. Not because of the lawsuit way back when, but because she's a member of your . . . ah . . . little group. Now he's on the alert. Maggie, too. Don't worry, I have the inside track with Ted, and he owes me now."

Nikki twisted around in the corner of the sofa so she could see Jack better. "Does he know about *us*? That you're staying here?"

"Not to my knowledge. He fishes around from time to time, wanting to know if I'm seeing anyone. If push comes to shove, I'll call in Marcey, one of my assistants, to pose as my girlfriend. She's engaged to a really nice guy, so don't get worried. If it happens, it will all be playacting for Ted's benefit. Ted knows I'm staying here in Georgetown but I don't know if he knows it's your place or not. I tend to think he doesn't know or he would have needled me. In other words, so far so good."

Nikki yawned elaborately. "Are you really OK with being an honorary member of the Sisterhood?"

"Yes, I am, and I'm going to hang my plaque on my side of the bathroom. You should call it the Sisterhood Plus One Brother."

Nikki laughed. "You bank the fire and I'll lock up. First one in bed gets to . . ."

Jack was like a living, breathing streak of lightning as he beat Nikki to the bed with a minute to spare. "You were saying . . ." He grinned.

"Charles, I feel so guilty about fibbing to the girls."

"Myra, you didn't fib. Cornelia said she would have dinner with us and then she changed her mind. You didn't know she was going to cancel when you told the girls we were going to stay in town for the evening. It's too late now, we're almost to Sunstar Farms. It will be so nice to see Nealy again."

"Charles, isn't she the most fascinating woman? She's just this little bit of a thing and yet she rode to a Triple Crown for Blue Diamond Farms. She said she loves being back at her old homestead here in Virginia with Hatch. They're retired, the way you and I are supposed to be retired. I know she's going to jump at the chance to help us. My father took me to Blue Diamond Farms when I was about sixteen. It was just wonderful and beautiful but it wasn't the famous horse farm that Nealy turned it into in later years. Actually, Blue Diamond Farms has the distinction of being the most famous horse farm in the world, with so many Kentucky Derby winners that I've lost track. All thanks to Nealy. My father and my mother knew Maude and Jess, Nealy's adoptive parents, for years. Nealy had just come there to live when I first met her. We lost track of one another for a while, but when I got back from Europe, I made it my business to look her up again. We may not see much of each other, but we never lost touch."

Charles was almost giddy. "When news of Nealy Diamond Clay coming to our neck of the woods gets into the papers, Rosemary will pitch a fit. I have the whole script in my head, Myra. We'll have to get Isabelle to pose for pictures with her."

"I know, dear. Oh my, it's starting to sleet. That is sleet, isn't it?"

"Yes. We only have a mile or so to go. Everything looks so depressing in February. I think it's the worst month of the year. Nealy is expecting us, isn't she?"

Myra waved her hand under Charles's nose. "Earth to Charles! No, dear, she is not expecting us. Nellie only told us she couldn't do dinner on our drive into town. You and I decided on the spur of the moment to drive here. Not to worry, Nealy loves company just the way we do, as long as it's the *right* company. Oh look, there's the arch and the sign. We're here and not a minute too soon. Tap the horn, dear. I so love it when people are waiting in the doorway to welcome you. Ooh, I can't wait to see Nealy. I think it's been three years, maybe four. We spoke on the phone last week, though."

Charles smiled at the excitement in Myra's voice. He loved to see her so happy and excited. He was looking forward to spending time with Hatch, Nealy's husband. The ladies could gossip and he and Hatch would smoke good cigars, drink fine brandy and tell tall tales. He obligingly tapped the horn.

"Look, the door is opening. They're waiting for us! Oh, this is so wonderful!" Myra squealed. "Nealy!" she shouted as she ran toward the front porch before Charles could even bring the car to a complete stop.

"Myra!" Nealy said, running down the steps to embrace her old friend.

Charles went over to greet Hatch, who towered over Charles by at least eight inches. The men shook hands and manfully clapped one another on the back. Nealy offered up one of her famous Black and Decker handshakes before she loosened her grip to hug Charles.

"This is such a nice surprise! Come in, come in. Hatch and I are bored out of our minds. We were doing crossword puzzles to pass the time."

"I know I should have called ahead," Myra said, linking her arm with Nealy's, "but it was a spur of the moment decision. Charles and I need your help but we can talk about that later. Let's visit. Coffee would be nice. Do you have to do anything for the horses?"

"It's all taken care of. I have wonderful people these days. Hatch and I are just like two old fogies waiting around for someone to need us. When they don't call on us, we do crossword puzzles. You know the coffee is always on in my house. Hatch is a little worried as we're expecting an ice storm. It looks to me like it's under way. You and Charles may be marooned here for a few days. What could be nicer?"

Myra laughed. "There's nothing better than spending time with old friends over a good cup of coffee. Let's sit in the kitchen and catch up."

"Wonderful!" Nealy beamed.

* * *

Three days later, on a cold but bright and sunny February afternoon, the ladies of Pinewood sat around the kitchen table eating lunch while they waited for Myra and Charles to get back from their trip.

"Are you sure it's the same Nealy Diamond, the one who won the Triple Crown?" Alexis asked.

Nikki laughed. "The one and the same—and she's agreed to help us with Isabelle's mission. Only her name these days is Nealy Littletree. And yes, she rode her horses to the Triple Crown, not once but twice. The first woman to do it, too! The town will turn out the red carpet for her since this is horse country. She's a great lady. I only met her twice but she sure is a woman you never forget. Being in the horse business and all, I'm hoping she might know or maybe have heard something about the Barringtons."

"I don't understand, what can she possibly do for Isabelle?" Alexis asked.

"Window dressing. Photo ops for Isabelle. It's Myra's PR machine kicking in. To make Rosemary livid in the hopes she does something stupid. It will be obvious to everyone that Isabelle will have the inside track. That will make Rosemary green with envy. She's going to start poking around, trying to find out how Isabelle got back on her feet and how she got her license reinstated. Since she's the devil in the woodwork, wouldn't you be a little nervous as well as angry that the woman you ruined is back on top?" Nikki said. "Myra is hosting a dinner party at the Silver Swan to kick off this huge endeavor, and will invite every notable she can find. Even the governor. Photo opportunities out the kazoo. Rosemary's invitation will conveniently get lost in the mail only to arrive in her mailbox *after* the dinner party. How's that for devious?"

The women laughed for a long time.

Three

The sign outside the building was simple and stark with a single name on it: Rosemary Hershey. Anyone caring enough to wonder who Rosemary Hershey was had to enter the building and ask the skinny receptionist with the see-through hair and fake nails. If Rosemary was within earshot of the person doing the questioning, her reply was always succinct: "K.I.S.S." Keep It Simple, Stupid. Then she'd blow an airy kiss to the person who had asked the question and walk away.

Bobby Harcourt didn't like the sign and had had many heated conversations with his wife about his name not being on it even though he was a full partner. During each one of those conversations, Rosemary would remind her husband that she'd used her settlement money to buy the building and start up her own firm. Bobby had been in the picture at the time of the accident and she'd made him buy into her firm, but by that point the sign had already been commissioned and there was no room for his name on it.

Bobby had gone along with the whole thing because of the bedroom gymnastics. But, as in most cases, even that side of things had worn thin and he'd later married Rosemary and bought into her firm because it seemed reasonable at the time. Now, though, the whole thing was starting to get under his skin. He was a damn good architect and had made Architect of the Year two years in a row. Rosemary had won the award once. He was the workhorse of the firm and Rosemary was the show horse. Filly, if you will. All three plaques hung in the lobby of their office building.

Bobby no longer looked at the sign on the door or the plaques on the lobby wall. Today, just as on every other day, he entered the building, the morning paper tucked under his arm, and headed straight for his office with its spectacular view of the Washington Monument.

He stopped at the receptionist's desk for his messages, hating how sleazy the young woman looked. He'd spoken to Rosemary about the receptionist's appearance and all she'd done was cluck her tongue and ask him if he wanted a lawsuit on his hands. It wasn't just the way the young woman looked, it was her stupid name as well. Sasha. No one named their kid Sasha except maybe a Russian mother. This Sasha was from Mud Creek, Mississippi. White trash, all ninety pounds of her. He rather suspected that Rosemary kept her on because Sasha made her look beautiful, which she was, but she was also a cold, relentless, heartless bitch of a woman. He'd found that out as soon as the honeymoon was over, much to his regret.

Bobby looked at his watch. Ten-fifteen. Time to ruin his wife's day. He smiled as he crossed the hall to her suite of offices. He rapped on the door and opened it without waiting for a response.

"Got a minute, Rosemary?"

"Yeah, sure. How'd the Rotary breakfast go? Any gossip?"

Bobby looked at his beautiful wife. Spun sugar candy was what she always reminded him of. No matter what time of the day or night, she always looked like she just stepped out of a bandbox. Perfectly coiffed, expertly made up, exquisitely dressed, subtle perfume that never seemed to fade, and always with her twenty-four-carat smile that was as phony as the caps on her pearly white teeth.

"Actually, I did hear quite a bit of gossip," he said, feeling smug, "but you aren't going to like it. You know, Rosemary, it was your turn to do the Rotary breakfast this month."

"Oh, poo, you good old boys didn't need me there. All you do is tell risqué jokes and pretend to shock me. So, what's the gossip? And for heaven's sake, why won't I like it?"

Bobby shrugged inside his tweed jacket. "Because, my darling, it has to do with Isabelle Flanders and we both know how much you despise her."

If he was expecting a reaction, he wasn't disappointed. Rosemary stopped what she was doing and just glared at him. Bobby thought for a minute that she looked frozen! But she recovered quickly. "That crazy woman, What did she do now?"

"Evidently something good. The Queen of England commissioned her to design some kind of memorial. She did get her license reinstated a while back. I saw it in the newsletter, so you must have seen it too, even though we never discussed it. Roscoe Cummings, who heads up the realty board, said Isabelle signed a lease on some very impressive office space. She's got contractors working round the clock. Roscoe said, and this is a direct quote, 'Her offices will make yours look like a dump, Bobby.'"

"Really?"

Tongue in cheek, Bobby said, "*Really*. Terry McGovern said he spoke to Isabelle one day last week about some of the furnishings she's buying—which, by the way, according to Terry, are the high end of high. Lots of plush furniture, paintings, tons of marble and mahogany. He said it's probably costing her about three hundred grand just to outfit the place. Nine rooms in all, so you can imagine the kind of rent she'll be paying. Rumor has it she paid for a full year in advance. But it's just a rumor. Max Turgold said he heard Isabelle enticed two heavy-hitters from New York to join the firm and another guy from California who is hotter than hot. They're bringing along their own roster of clients. Guess Isabelle hit the mother lode. If all that's true, this outfit is peanuts compared to what she's starting out with. Guess we better look to our laurels."

Rosemary fingered a set of blueprints but Bobby could see she was upset. "Wait till they find out about her past," she snarled.

Bobby wagged one of his fingers. "Now it's funny you should say that. Roscoe said everyone knows about it; Isabelle didn't pull any punches. She's got *beaucoup* bucks so who cares? And the rumor is that now that she has all those *beaucoup* bucks, she's talking about reopening her case. She said she was shafted. I always thought the same thing myself," he added slyly. "You know why I always thought that, Rosemary?" Not bothering to wait for a response, he continued. "Because Isabelle never drank. She was a one glass of wine kind of person and she never even finished that. Sometimes she'd have a beer and she'd never finish that, either. Yet, they said she was drunk. They said it because you told them that."

Rosemary bared her teeth. "The next thing you'll be telling me is you made a mistake dumping Isabelle and marrying me. She was drunk that day. Go check the police report. They did blood alcohol tests on her."

Bobby ignored this. "See ya. Gotta get ready to go to that Pioneer luncheon, unless you want to take my place."

"For God's sake, you just had breakfast. All right, I'll go, you weasel," Rosemary snarled.

Bobby walked across the hall to his office, closed the door and flopped down on his ergonomic chair. He felt lower than a snake's belly at his sense of satisfaction. He should have walked out of his marriage and this partnership a long time ago. Bobby Harcourt, last one out of the gate. His claim to fame.

He thought about Isabelle then because he always thought about Isabelle when he was unhappy. They'd had a good thing going back then. Back then. Isabelle with the laughing eyes and ready smile. Workaholic Isabelle. Isabelle who never drank. He'd tried telling that to the police, but they wouldn't listen to him. He'd testified in court, but no one had believed him. They didn't believe him when he said Isabelle was a cautious driver and would never have run a stop sign. They didn't believe him when he said Isabelle would never steal someone else's work. Of course, he'd testified after Rosemary. Poor, poor Rosemary with her injuries, wearing all those different braces, crying into a lacy handkerchief. With nine men on the jury, Isabelle was dead in the water.

He'd tried to visit Isabelle in the hospital but he hadn't been permitted to see her because he wasn't family. He didn't know until much later that she'd almost died with pneumonia. After the trial, Isabelle went off somewhere to lick her wounds. He'd tried everything he could to find her but she seemed to have dropped off the face of the earth. Little did he know at the time that she had just moved across town.

Wounded to the quick over Isabelle's rejection, he'd allowed himself to wallow in Rosemary's attention. Before he knew what was happening, he was having a torrid affair with her that was more about lust than anything else.

Bobby looked at his day planner. Meetings out the kazoo. Screw the new clients. They now had so many they couldn't handle them all. He called through to the secretary he shared with Rosemary.

"Cancel all my appointments. I'll be back by three o'clock. If Rosemary wants to know where I am, tell her something came up. If she needs me for anything, tell her to call my cell phone." Bobby reached for his overcoat and left the office. Brad Olsen was an old friend. He'd see him even if he had to cancel someone else to fit him in. It was time to find out where he stood legally, both business-wise and marriage-wise. His gut told him it was time to bail out. Something was going on and he sure as hell didn't want to be around when it all went down.

Rosemary tugged at her short powder-blue skirt before she opened the door to the meeting room at the Holiday Inn. If there was one thing she hated it was these civic meetings where everyone had to make nice to each other and then, when the meeting was over, the little cliques tore each other to pieces. The meeting was nothing more than a gossip session under the guise of what's-new-in-our-field.

The Pioneer Club dated back to the 1930s when Cyrus Canfield, the town's leading architect, formed it after being forced into retirement at the age of seventy-three. It was a way for Cyrus to keep his hand in the business and to stay as up-to-date as he could with the young whippersnappers who were fighting tooth and nail for their share of the building boom. When the club first met, it boasted seven members. Today there were a good three hundred—not that they all showed up at these little monthly luncheons, where everyone had to pay for their own lunch and drinks. It was still a gossip session and most of today's members were young in comparison to Cyrus Canfield and his original band of retired architects.

These days the Pioneers allowed women, but only because Sadie Longberry had filed a discrimination suit against them. Sadie had said in her lawsuit that even on her worst day she could out-think, outrun, outwork and outdrink any member

of the Pioneers and that just because she was a
woman they had no right to exclude her. Judge
Cornelia Easter had heard the case. She had
agreed with Sadie and had ordered each member
of the club to pay Sadie two hundred dollars. Sadie
walked away with a little over twenty-four grand.
Then she did what any red-blooded fifty-year-old
woman would do. She got a facelift and perky
breast implants and managed to find a toy boy hot
enough to melt her brand-new acrylic nails, and
all within three weeks. Then she took the rest of
the money and ran full-page ads in the local paper
denouncing the Pioneer Club until the money ran
out. And she never once set foot in a Pioneer Club
meeting. Sadie then proceeded to form her own
organization that boasted four hundred active members. Isabelle Flanders had been president four
years running. Bobby was the treasurer. Rosemary
had never joined.

Rosemary gave her mini skirt another tug and
plastered a smile on her face before she entered
the room. She was aware instantly of two things.
One, the tension was high. Two, Maggie Spritzer
from the *Post* was sitting at the table munching on
a chunk of cheese right next to the *Post*'s star reporter, Ted Robinson. Because the meetings were
always as boring as the lunch itself, the reporters
usually opted to call the president after the meeting to find out if anything new or noteworthy had
gone on. She looked a little farther down the long
table and was stunned to see the *Chronicle*'s leading
reporter, Zack Elderman. Her belly did a flip-flop.

Her smile intact, her expensive perfume waft-
ing about, Rosemary greeted everyone at the table

as she took her seat. This was not going to be an ordinary meeting of the Pioneer Club.

Toby Wiseman brought the meeting to order. He whittled away at the dry, boring business on his agenda before he finally said, "And now, ladies and gentlemen, there's a new game in town with a whole new bunch of players. We're all going to have to watch our p's and q's from here on in."

"What are you talking about, Toby?" Rosemary asked, as if she didn't know the identity of this new player in town.

"I'm talking about Isabelle Flanders. Surely you heard. It's all over town. My God, woman, the Queen herself has commissioned Isabelle to do some sort of memorial for Buckingham Palace. It doesn't get any better than that."

Rosemary feigned indifference. "Oh, that," she drawled. "I'm not impressed. I wonder whose work she'll steal this time to pass off as her own. I'd like someone to tell me how she got her license back."

"Oh, I can tell you that, Miss Hershey," Maggie Spritzer chirped. "The board only suspended her license for five years and gave her a two-hundred-thousand-dollar fine. The board said they wouldn't give back the license until she paid the fine. Miss Flanders paid the fine, and then donated another fifty thousand dollars to the board to disperse to ailing and retired architects housed in the nursing home you all had built years ago. The board lifted the suspension five months ahead of schedule and Miss Flanders is back in business. I'm surprised you didn't know that. It was in the paper last week."

Ted Robinson flipped open a dog-eared notebook and said, with relish, "Miss Flanders issued a statement through her office manager. While I don't want to quote her verbatim, what she said in essence is this: 'I'm back and I remember all the people, my colleagues, who turned away from me when the case against me was circumstantial at best. I'm reopening my old case because the statute of limitations has not run out.' In the meantime, she plans to aggressively seek new business for her new firm. She also said that all those people who testified against her had better hire some damn fine attorneys because she's going to war."

The smile on Rosemary's face finally slipped away. "Why are you all looking at me like that? If Isabelle wants to go after everyone involved in that ugly mess, let her. I certainly have nothing to hide. A jury found her guilty and saw fit to award me compensation for my injuries. The board revoked her license, not me. The woman is just another architect like the rest of us. She's no Frank Lloyd Wright, for God's sake."

Ted Robinson looked down at his notebook. "According to Miss Flanders's spokesperson, Miss Flanders used the word 'perjury' quite a few times when preparing her statement. However, she didn't name names. Is there anyone here who would like to make a comment?"

"Don't insult me," Rosemary said. She looked around the table, mentally counting all the men she'd slept with over the past five years. She noticed they had a hard time meeting her gaze.

Tamara Wheatley, a mousy woman with thin hair and oversized glasses, leaned toward the two reporters. "Do either of you know if it's true that Myra Rutledge bought the Barrington farm and is going to turn it into something like that famous racing farm in Kentucky? I think it's called Blue Diamond. Owned by the woman who won the Triple Crown. I heard that she's a personal friend of Mrs. Rutledge and she's called on her for help. Supposedly she's going to be asking for bids from all of us. If what I've heard is true, that's a hundred-million-dollar project. Possibly more. That's going to be fodder for the newspapers for months to come."

Rosemary felt sick to her stomach. She reached for a piece of cheese she didn't want. She could feel the heat of the moment start to creep up her neck into her face.

"It's true," Maggie Spritzer said. "Mrs. Rutledge is going to close on the Barrington property sometime this week. I called her myself yesterday and she confirmed it. She said she's going to host a dinner party at the Silver Swan and will be inviting all the dignitaries, the governor, and all you architects so she can tell you what she wants in person. She said Nealy Diamond Clay will be in attendance to further elaborate on what is needed." Maggie looked around at the shocked and awed expressions on everyone's face. "I'm surprised none of you knew this. Would anyone care to give me a quote, make a comment?"

Rosemary nibbled on the cheese in her hand. She wondered what her voice would sound like if she made a comment. She decided silence was her best friend.

Carla Peabody said, "Aside from the dinner at the Silver Swan with some dignitaries, what makes this deal so spectacular? Of course, my firm will submit a bid, but why this huge interest? Myra

Rutledge is a wealthy woman and does stuff like this all the time. A racing stable is not new to the state of Virginia."

Ted Robinson closed his notebook and stuck it back in his pocket. "This is just my opinion, ladies and gentlemen, so hear me out. I think it's news because it's rumored that your outcast, Isabelle Flanders, has the inside track. What say you now?"

The group was saved from replying as the huge double doors opened to admit waiters and waitresses ready to serve lunch.

"OK, I'll just report that you were all dumbfounded," Ted said, getting up and then holding Maggie's chair for her. "Enjoy your lunch, ladies and gentlemen. It looks . . . ah . . . interesting."

Rosemary Hershey jabbed her fork into her fillet of sole, wishing it was Isabelle Flanders's neck.

Four

Outside in the blustery February wind, Ted Robinson walked Maggie Spritzer to her car. They eyed each other warily, their reporting instincts kicking into high gear. Both their noses had picked up something in the Pioneer meeting and neither of them was willing to confide in the other. They might share a bed these days, a bottle of wine, hold hands and whisper sweet nothings in each other's ears, but they would never consider sharing thoughts, notes, nuances on a possible story. When it came to a byline, it was every man for himself and no hard feelings.

"See ya tonight?" Ted said. It was more of a question than a statement.

"Not tonight, baby, I have things to do." Maggie's eyes twinkled. "I'll call you."

Ted frowned. His eyes didn't twinkle. "That's supposed to be my line." Damn, being a woman, Maggie had probably picked up on some hot tidbit he'd failed to notice because he was a miserable shit-kicking man. The twinkle in her eyes was all the proof he needed that she had an edge. Well, he'd never groveled in his life and he sure as hell wasn't going to start now. "Dinner, breakfast?" he asked, groveling.

"Sorry, can't. I'll call you."

Well, once a groveler, always a groveler. "When?"

"When you hear your phone ring, it might be me. Answer it. If it isn't me, wait for the next ring."

"Bitch!"

"Bastard!" Maggie said, driving away.

Ted walked back to his car. He should follow her. He really should. Instead, he shrugged and started his engine. Another visit to Jack Emery was called for.

Ted drove across town to the courthouse, parked, worked his way through security and finally made it to Jack's office, where the District Attorney immediately threw his pencil across the room at the sight of him.

"Jesus, Ted, what now? I'm up to my eyeballs in a high-profile capital murder case. It's looking like I'm going to have to try this one myself, which means I will have to move in to this place as I'll be here twenty-four-seven." Jack could feel his stomach muscles crunch into a knot. He hoped his feigned indifference to whatever Ted was going to tell him was working.

"You get a break morning and afternoon. It's the law, so take it now and then I'll get out of your hair. We can go to the cafeteria."

"Are you nuts? If you step foot in that place you get sick. OK, OK, we can go to Mo's for coffee. Fifteen minutes and that's it, Ted."

"I'll take it. I want to run something by you."

"I thought you had a reference desk at the paper. When did I become your primary source?" Jack said, holding the door of the elevator.

"When you got lily-livered and told me about the ladies of Pinewood. Suck that up, Mr. DA."

"Yeah, well, that was then and this is now. I'm outta that mess. I thought when I squared it for you that you were going to let things lie."

Ted walked through the revolving door, the wind driving him backward. "It's supposed to get warmer tomorrow."

"Oh yeah, how warm?" Jack asked, struggling to walk against the wind.

"Maybe forty."

"Shut the hell up, Ted. Forty is for Eskimos. Tell me it will be eighty degrees tomorrow and you will have my undivided attention," Jack said as he opened the door to the greasy spoon called Mo's Place. It was so hot and steamy indoors that Ted's glasses fogged up straightaway. Jack started to sweat as he shouldered his way to a spindly table at the back of the diner where he bellowed for two coffees. Everybody bellowed for coffee at Mo's.

"Christ, this is even worse than the last time I was here," Jack griped. "It tastes like licorice and someone's sweaty sneakers. Spit out whatever you brought me here for before this shit kills me."

"One of the ladies of Pinewood is flying high, Jack. She's throwing money around like she's printing it herself. From low income and qualifying for food stamps, all of a sudden she's spending like she won the lottery. Since she belongs to that little group out there in McLean, my gut tells me Myra Rutledge has got to be backing her."

Jack tried another sip of coffee. It wasn't any better than the first. He slid the heavy mug to the center of the table. "Myra Rutledge is a philanthropist. So what? What's that bloodhound nose of yours telling you? Who are you talking about, anyway?"

Ted gulped at his own coffee. "I can't believe you don't like this coffee. Isabelle Flanders, that's who. It tells me the ladies of Pinewood are getting ready to pull another . . . event. It's been about four months since they hit the National Security Advisor, and don't even pretend they weren't responsible for that stunt. We both know they were."

Jack sighed. "What do you want from me? Did I tell you I'm involved in a high-profile capital crime? I am. I don't have time for this crap."

Ted settled his glasses more firmly on his nose. "You're good, Jack, I'll give you that. You know what I think, old buddy? I think you're involved up to your eyeballs with those women. I hate to admit, that never occurred to me before. Maggie also pointed it out to me. That would make you a pimp or a shill, Jack. Maggie's got a lot on the ball. She also blew my mind when she asked me what you were doing living in Nikki Quinn's house in Georgetown. I didn't know that, Jack. I felt like a fool when she told me."

Shit, shit, shit! "And you're bent out of shape because you think I should have told you that, right? Well, old buddy, I hate to prick your bubble, but there's a logical explanation. Nikki is living out at the farm. I asked her if I could rent the house until I found a place of my own. We don't have a hate on for each other, Ted. We were engaged at one time. We're still friends. At least I hope we are. We share a lot of good memories. I traded on those memories when I asked for the lease. She obliged. Here, take a look," Jack said, flipping open his wallet. He withdrew a single sheet of paper folded over enough times to fit in his wallet. He unfolded it and handed it over. "All properly notarized and everything. I pay her eleven hundred bucks on the first of every month. I have to change the light-bulbs, take out the trash, water the plants, shovel snow, rake the leaves, etcetera. Satisfied?"

"Do you always carry your lease around with you? I don't even know where mine is."

Jack grimaced as he drummed his fingers on the tabletop. "I don't have to explain how and why I do what I do, but because I'm a nice guy, I will. I didn't have my briefcase with me the day I signed the lease. I just folded it up and put it in my wallet. To tell you the truth, I forgot about it till just this minute. If you want, I'll fax Maggie a copy of it for her perusal." Jack was relieved to see Ted shrug. The lease had been Nikki's idea to cover his ass.

"Anything else?"

"Do you know Bobby Harcourt?"

"Can't say that I do. Should I?"

"At one time Bobby Harcourt was Isabelle Flanders's fiancé. I did a story on him a while back. I thought he was a stand-up guy. He used to fly Tom-cats in the Navy. Any guy who can pull nine and a half Gs in a Tomcat has got to be a good guy. He married the chick that ruined Isabelle Flanders. See where I'm headed with this?"

"No, Ted, I don't see where you're headed with

this. Flying airplanes makes someone a good guy? A grown man going by the name Bobby? Is he a pretty boy?"

Ted favored his friend with a sour look. "Maggie seems to think he's good-looking. Tall, works out, dresses well, good architect. Gets manicures, blow-dries his hair. Why is it that women notice stuff like that? Harcourt made Architect of the Year twice in a row and his wife made it once. That Flanders woman made it twice, too. Now, *she's* a looker. The Hershey broad, not Flanders."

"And this means . . . what?"

"I don't know. I was hoping you could tell me something."

"You're on your own. Did I tell you I'm working on a high-profile capital murder case?"

"Shit, yes, three times, Jack. Give it a rest. You're in charge of that office, so don't pull that garbage with me. Help me out here. Those ladies at Pine-wood are going to go after Bobby's wife, aren't they? Myra is shilling for Flanders and the others are helping. It makes sense."

Jack rummaged in his pocket for money to pay for the coffee. He slapped some bills on the table. "Is that your assessment or Maggie's?"

"Contrary to what you might believe, Jack, just because I'm sleeping with Maggie doesn't mean I share my sources or my info. I also have a mind of my own that I use on a regular basis. Maggie and I are independents—and adversaries to a certain point."

"I bet Maggie is just using you for sex. Think about this, Mr. Reporter, you gotta sleep sometime. Women are sneaky. They go through your things when you're asleep. Especially after you just had sex and you're down for the count. They have all these little tools—hairpins, nail files, hat pins that can pick a lock. Chew on that one for a while and just remember, you heard it from me. I really have to get back to the office. What's your next move, you intrepid reporter, you?" Jack guffawed.

"Like I'm really going to tell you," Ted said huffily as he shouldered his way through the crowd that was waiting in line for their table.

"Tsk, tsk, then don't come sniffing around my office, and when that lady you're sleeping with screws you over, don't come crawling back to me for help."

Outside in the driving wind, Ted pulled a watch cap out of his pocket and settled it on his head. Jack's hair started blowing in all directions. He pulled his coat collar up as high as it would go and stared at his friend.

"Let's cut the shit, Jack, and get serious. You said you wanted those women caught. If you don't feel like that any longer, I'll fade into the night and not bother you again. Wherever the chips fall, they fall. I just feel that I'm closing the gap between me and them. Reporter's instincts."

Jack pretended to think. "I still feel like that," he lied. "I just don't see how I can be of any help. Sometimes, you're like a bull in a china shop. You need to cover your ass, Ted. Those women are smarter than both of us put together—and remember, there are seven of them, plus that English guy, not to mention the English guy's buddies. Those guys are still out for your blood—and mine, too. Just because we took out the first string doesn't mean the second string isn't warming up in the bull pen. Be careful, Ted, OK? Did I tell you—"

"You have a high-profile criminal case to prepare for. Yeah, three times. I get it, Jack. See ya."

Jack watched his friend trudge off into the wind. He pushed his way through the revolving door, smoothed down his hair and then walked over to a quiet corner where he called Nikki to tell her what just happened.

Was he a snitch? Hell, yes, he was a snitch, but he was also a bona fide honorary member of the Sisterhood. He didn't want his ass to get kicked out of the organization by a bunch of savvy women who wouldn't think twice about slicing off his dick and pickling it just for fun.

Nikki stared across the table at Isabelle's empty seat. She raised her eyebrows at Myra, expecting an explanation for Isabelle's absence.

"Isabelle is in town hard at work on the public relations plans we laid out for her. Has anyone heard anything, gossip, speculation, anything at all during the last few days?"

Nikki waggled her index finger. "I heard something a short while ago, but I will only tell you if you can accept it for what I say it is and don't ask for my source. Otherwise I can't say anything."

"You got it. Tell us what you know," Kathryn said.

Nikki fought the tickle in her throat. She chose her words carefully and hated that she couldn't tell the others that Jack was her confidant.

"If you all recall, Isabelle told us about the Pioneer

Club that meets once a month for a luncheon to discuss whatever it is that architects discuss. Mostly, I'm told, it's a gossip session. This time there were three reporters there, two we have to worry about as they're from the *Post* and are personal friends of Jack Emery. The other reporter, Zack Elderman from the *Chronicle*, as far as I can tell, poses no threat. He was probably there simply to get the scoop on Isabelle.

"From what I've been able to gather, these little luncheons or get-togethers are not usually attended by reporters because one has to pay for one's own lunch and drinks. The reporters usually call the acting president after the meeting for the highlights."

Isabelle chose that moment to slip quietly into the war room and take her seat. The others smiled at her.

"Every day there is a new tidbit in the local papers, so we have to believe that Myra's PR blitz is starting to work. Rosemary Hershey, the lady who did our Isabelle in, is usually the life of the party, so to speak. Today she wasn't her usual self. Normally she wears provocative clothing, lots of cleavage, shows a lot of leg and flirts with all the old geezers— and the young ones, too. When one of the members made the announcement that Isabelle was reopening her old case, it seems Rosemary turned green. I think it's safe to say that Operation Rosemary is under way. She won't be sleeping well from here on in."

Nikki allowed herself a small smile. "There's more. Bobby Harcourt, Isabelle's ex-fiancé, who is now married to Rosemary Hershey and who is also a partner in the firm that she started up with her ill-gotten gains, went to see a lawyer today to ask what his rights were in regard to his marriage and the business. His lawyer called Donna Frankel with whom he is having a relationship. Donna is a partner in my firm. Donna called me and now I'm telling all of you. It looks like Bobby might be trying to bail out on Rosemary."

Alexis played with the medallion she was wearing around her throat. "Well, that's a lot of news. What do we do now?"

"We wait," Myra said. "Charles is checking into Miss Hershey's finances. And a few other things, too. Charles drove into town to pick up our invitations. We'll meet after dinner to address them. You girls can do that while I plan the dinner party at the Silver Swan. I have to make a decision as to delivery of the invitations. What do you think, girls? Should we messenger them, overnight them, or just send them first-class mail?"

It was unanimous that Myra should send all the invitations by special messenger.

"All right, special messenger it is. Are we out of line by making it black tie? The governor is going to be there. He loves black-tie affairs, as do I."

"Definitely black tie," the women agreed.

"Very well. We're done here, girls. Please, continue with whatever you were doing before I joined you. Would you all care for some coffee?"

"Not if you're going to make it, Myra," Kathryn said.

"Your loss," Myra quipped as she left the war room.

"Girls, I have a question," Isabelle said. "What do you all think it would take to drive Rosemary

Hershey over the edge? I don't think me coming out on top is enough punishment for that bitch. She killed three people. Shouldn't we make her pay for that? Look," Isabelle added vehemently, "that bitch has to pay for all the panic attacks I had over the years. Those damn things rendered me useless. I almost killed myself trying to work through them. By God, I want to see her pay and pay and pay for that!"

"How did you escape going to jail for vehicular homicide?" Alexis asked.

"Two of the jurors weren't convinced; the judge ended up giving me ten years' probation, five years' community service, a hefty fine and I lost my license. I guess they thought that was punishment enough. In fact it was way too much since I didn't do what they charged me with, but the jury spoke. That was the end of it," Isabelle said.

"Then our goal should be to make sure Rosemary gets the real punishment, whatever it would be without the jury's charitable decision. Ten to twenty years or so in the slammer without parole sounds about right to me. She took three lives. We can make this happen, can't we, girls?" Kathryn said.

"Oh, yeah," Alexis drawled.

"I do like the way that sounds," Yoko smiled.

Nikki laughed. "What do you have in mind, Kathryn?"

The women shivered at Kathryn's evil laughter. Isabelle simply smiled.

Isabelle sat alone in the war room after the others left. Sometimes she just needed a bit of what she called "me time." This was one of those times. She looked around, marveling at the high-tech room that would play such a big part in her mission. She leaned back in her chair and let her thoughts run wild.

She was so close, so very close to vindication. It almost seemed surreal. She gave silent thanks for her sisters who were going to make it happen. She thought about the crippling attacks she'd gone through over the years. The first time she had one, she'd gone to a free clinic to find out what was wrong with her. A kindly nurse helped her, gave her a hotline number to call, and a mentor had helped her through the worst of it. She shivered when she thought back to how she'd gasp for breath, certain she was going to die. The shaking, the lightheaded feeling, the spike in her blood pressure. She was worthless for hours after one of her attacks. Until her mentor told her she could talk herself out of it, work her way through the attacks with physical exercise. God, how she'd suffered in the aftermath of Rosemary's betrayal.

She was fit now, "hale and hearty" as her mentor said. The last attack had been eighteen months ago. These days, in her free time, she counseled others who were in the same position she had been in. She loved talking to the women at the crisis center, telling them her story, promising them they could and would conquer their panic attacks. She realized now that she would never walk away from the crisis center no matter how busy or famous she became. She owed the center her wellbeing and she would never forget it.

Isabelle got up from her chair, pushed it back under the table and prepared to leave the war room. Her gaze drifted to the corner where Julia's chair was turned to face the wall. She offered up a snappy salute to her fallen sister.

"It's my turn, Julia," she whispered. "I wish you were here to help. I miss you. We all miss you. I'll never forget you, either."

Five

Rosemary Hershey slammed on the brakes of her champagne-colored Mercedes, made an illegal U-turn, and headed for the elegant town house she shared with her husband. *Shared* was the key word here. The town house was hers, this car was hers. For the last ten months she'd tried to figure out a way to buy out Bobby's share of the business without bankrupting herself. They both knew the marriage was over; all they did was squabble at the office and at home, too. When something was over, it was over. But the marriage was tied to the business in more ways than one. The big question was, did she seek a divorce first or make the buy-out offer first?

She had an excellent line of credit at the bank she dealt with. Maybe she should apply for a loan so that when they checked her finances, Bobby's end of the business would show up on the P&L sheet. The bank didn't need to know she planned to divorce him. She could use the loan monies to buy him out and keep her own funds intact. It was a given that Bobby would take his clients with him, unless her lawyer turned out to be smarter than his, which she didn't think would be the case. For months now, she'd been toying with the idea of hiring a new lawyer. A female attorney. She could concoct some kind of story that would make the lawyer sympathize with her.

Rosemary brushed at her hair in frustration. She'd thought her scrambling days were over. Now she could feel her world starting to teeter right under her feet and it was all Isabelle Flanders's fault. She wouldn't be one bit surprised if Bobby still had feelings for Isabelle. The thought made her furious. So furious that she almost ran a stop sign. She slammed on the brakes a second time and was rewarded with blaring horns.

"Screw you!" Rosemary shouted. She drove another block before she barreled into her parking space opposite the town house. She sat for a moment staring at her house. It looked like a narrow, skinny building—and it was—but she'd purchased the building next to it, leaving the door intact. Inside, she'd knocked out walls and ended up with a 4,200-square-foot abode. She had four bathrooms, three fireplaces, a state-of-the-art kitchen, a huge family room and a huge home office that she shared with Bobby. She'd lucked out when she bought the building and had had the renovations done while the building was still under construction. Today, the house was worth almost two million dollars. She refused to even think about all the times she'd had to sleep with the contractor so he would whittle the price to what she wanted for both units.

Rosemary locked the car and looked around. It

was a lovely neighborhood, with huge trees, manicured lawns and colorful flower beds during spring and summer. A fitting place for someone like her. No children running and romping and no mangy dogs pooping and peeing on the pricey landscaping. Bobby didn't like it; he said it reminded him of some sort of Stepford community. In the beginning, Bobby had wanted a house with a backyard so he could putter. Bobby also wanted a dog. He'd gotten over that notion in a hurry. Bobby was a stupid man. She'd only married him to get back at Isabelle Flanders. It was time to get rid of him once and for all.

In her bedroom, which she didn't share with Bobby, Rosemary took off her designer suit and hung it up. She wasn't going back to the office so she pulled on a warm jogging suit. It was a beautiful room, a perfect backdrop for her delicate, beautiful persona, she told herself. She'd had it decorated in yellow and pale green with a white carpet. Bobby said it hurt his eyes and he always felt like he was sucking on a lemon when he entered the room. Bobby was a hunter-green, deep-burgundy, dark-brown kind of guy. She always felt like she was on a hunting trip when she condescended to even enter his room. Once Bobby had suggested that when they got around to having sex they should do it in the hallway and then neither of them would have to enter the other's room.

Rosemary tried to remember the last time she'd had sex with her husband. When no date came to mind, she gave up because she simply didn't care.

In other words, Bobby *who?*

In her office, Rosemary went straight to her custom-made desk. The safe she'd built into the floor right under the bottom drawer beckoned her. She hadn't trusted the contractor to install it so she'd done it herself by going to a class on home repairs at Home Depot. While it was a sloppy job, the safe was intact and secured with bolts. When the desk drawer was in place, you couldn't tell the floor had been cut up and a safe installed. Even Bobby didn't know about it. Telling Bobby about the safe would have meant sharing herself with him. She wasn't a sharing person. It took some people a long time to figure that out. When they finally did, it was too late.

Rosemary ignored the urge to open the safe, opting instead to flick through the Rolodex. For some reason the name of the law firm she wanted eluded her but she knew she'd copied it down at one point and had added it to the Rolodex. It was one of those things you do with no rhyme or reason to it. Halfway through the Rolodex, Rosemary threw her hands in the air, unable to come up with the card for the law firm she had in mind. Then she started from the back and found the little card almost immediately. NBJ Legal Offices. She wondered why she'd put it in the back. She read her scribbled notes. A twelve-woman law firm. Women helping women. Sharks. Barracudas. Just what she needed, a female lawyer that was either a shark or a barracuda. She smiled as she dialed the number listed on the card. She hung up before the call could be completed. What did the NBJ stand for? Probably something to do with the original founders of the firm. Vaguely she remembered reading something at one time about the firm in the Lifetime section of the local paper.

Rosemary was about to redial the number but

she withdrew her hand a second time. Something niggled at the back of her mind. She'd never been one to ignore her instincts or her hunches. Maybe she needed to rethink this particular move. Or possibly do a little research on the firm. She got up from the desk and started to pace. She touched this and that, looked out the window, paced some more and then made her way to her state-of-the-art stainless steel kitchen.

She didn't want to lose any of this. Not one little thing. Not after what she'd gone through. Well, that wasn't going to happen. Still, she felt uneasy, the conversations at the Pioneer luncheon still fresh in her mind.

Isabelle Flanders! She had thought she was done with her. For all intents and purposes, Isabelle Flanders was dead to her. But now Isabelle was rising from the dead with a big club in her hand aimed straight at her head.

"Well, dearie, that isn't going to happen!" Rosemary snarled.

While the coffee dripped, she walked back to the office, calmly picked up the phone and called the NBJ law firm. She spoke quickly and confidently.

"This is Rosemary Hershey. I'd like to schedule an appointment with one of your senior partners."

The chirpy voice on the other end of the phone said, "Miss Hershey, we only have one senior partner, Nicole Quinn. She's booked through to the end of March. Would you care to schedule an appointment with one of our other fine attorneys?"

The end of March! Isabelle Flanders could club her to death by then. "No, no, I need an attorney now. Where are the other senior partners? I was under the impression there were three partners."

"Yes, Miss Hershey, there were three partners when the firm was founded but two of our partners passed away. Miss Quinn is . . . is the surviving partner."

Rosemary didn't know why, but the news stunned her. "I have to think about this. I'll get back to you if that's all right."

Rosemary walked back to the kitchen to pour herself a cup of coffee she didn't want. Normally, she allowed herself one cup of coffee in the morning. If she drank more, her nerves would twang for the rest of the day. But she wasn't going anywhere now, so what difference did it make if she twanged all over the place?

She almost jumped out of her skin when the phone rang a few minutes later. She backtracked into the kitchen to look at the number on the caller ID. Bobby.

"What?" she barked down the phone.

There were no pleasantries. "You have three clients sitting in the lobby. Is this any way to run a business, Rosemary? Are you coming in or what?"

"No, I'm not going back to the office. I have a blinding headache, one of my migraines. I can't see straight. I called in and left a message that those appointments were to be cancelled. Fire that woman, Bobby, and do it as soon as you hang up. Then call the employment agency and get a temp until we can hire someone permanently."

"What brought on the headache, Rosie? Was it the Pioneer luncheon? Guess you heard more than you wanted to, eh?" Bobby needled.

"Shut up, Bobby, and stop calling me Rosie. You know I hate it. Stop slobbering all over yourself because I did not—I repeat, I did not—hear anything at that luncheon that I didn't already know. This is what I get for doing you a favor." Rosemary cut her husband off in mid-sentence by hanging up the phone.

Maybe she didn't need a lawyer after all; maybe what she needed was a private detective with lock-jaw. Then again, the minute you took someone else into your confidence, things started to go wrong. She'd handle this herself. She'd done OK, going it alone, so there was no reason to think she couldn't do it this time, too. For starters, she had to find out where Isabelle lived and where all this sudden new money was coming from. Isabelle had to bank somewhere and there were a lot of bankers listed in her private Rolodex. Right now, she had to go on the assumption that Isabelle Flanders was her archenemy. Rosemary knew a thing or two about damage control.

She flipped through the Rolodex, pulling out card after card. What good was it knowing influential people if those influential people didn't come to your aid when they were needed?

The war room was silent, the only sound coming from the whirring fans overhead. Lady Justice stared down at the women from the three large monitors. In the center of the table were two glossy white boxes filled with invitations.

"This box," Myra said, "holds the invitations we're going to send to every architect in the area, asking if they would like to be included in our project. There is an RSVP card with an envelope that will be included. The second box contains the invitations for our dinner at the Silver Swan. We will be addressing the envelopes for both boxes but will not messenger the dinner invitations until it is time. Did we make a decision in regard to Rosemary Hershey's husband, Bobby Harcourt? Since Miss Hershey goes by her own name, they appear to work independently of one another, and I think we should send separate invitations. Mr. Harcourt will receive both. Miss Hershey will get the first one but her dinner invitation to the Silver Swan will arrive a day too late. Each person attending will have to show their invitation at the door. Rosemary will be turned away if she shows up without one."

"Sounds like a working plan," Alexis said as she reached for an envelope.

"How are you doing, Isabelle?" Kathryn asked.

"Happier than I've been in a long time. I jumped in with both feet. Tomorrow Nealy Diamond Clay arrives, but she's only going to be here for one day for the photo call. I'm really looking forward to meeting her and having our picture taken together. Rosemary will turn green when it hits the paper. I understand Nealy can't stay long but will come back any time we need her. I am beyond excited," Isabelle said.

Nikki turned around to get Charles's attention. "Any other news, Charles?"

"Actually, there is a little news. I've managed, and don't ask me how, to create a small problem with Miss Hershey's credit cards."

"What exactly does a small problem mean, dear?" Myra asked.

Charles allowed himself a small smile. "It means she no longer has them. I'm working on her driver's license at the moment. I expect it to disappear from the system any second now."

Nikki turned all the way around in her chair, her expression full of awe. "Do you mean as in *poof* and it's gone with no record of there ever being a license issued to her?"

"Exactly," Charles said proudly. "I'm toying with the idea of erasing her business license, too."

"Why?" Yoko asked.

Charles laughed out loud. "Because I can. I'm quite confident I can erase the woman's identity completely. She won't be able to prove she was born. But only if we need to do that. Time will tell if such drastic measures are called for."

All the women could do was stare at the former MI6 operative in awe, simply grateful that he was working on their side.

Isabelle blew Charles a kiss of gratitude.

Six

Maggie Spritzer's nose twitched as she let her gaze sweep across the newsroom to where Ted Robinson was poring over a stack of photocopied material. She knew what he was looking at because she had the same material on her own desk. Page after page of the *Post*'s coverage of Isabelle Flanders's trial years ago. Maggie covered the high-powered gossip that went on in the nation's capital, and she had to wonder why Ted was interested since he was the in-house expert on political intrigue. He hated gossip, especially political gossip. She wondered if she could force herself to sink low enough to indulge in some pillow talk with him. She decided she could.

Maggie meandered her way around desks and cubicles before she found a straight path that would take her to Ted's desk, which just happened to be on the way to the bathroom.

"Hey, sweet cheeks, whatcha up to this morning? Looks like a slow day today. Want to get together this evening? I was thinking I'd split early and make a nice meat loaf with mashed potatoes, gravy, biscuits and some fresh string beans. I might even whip up a peach pie if I can find some fresh peaches at the market. You can bring the wine."

Ted looked up, his eyes suspicious. "Is this in lieu of the phone call you never made? Just because we sleep together from time to time doesn't mean I'm easy. OK, I love meat loaf. But if you have any ideas about picking my brains, give them up."

"Baby, baby, baby, I wouldn't dream of poaching on you. If you want my opinion, the system shafted Flanders. Sounds to me like someone is giving her a second chance and I'm all for it. I heard she was a kick-ass architect until that Barbie doll, Rosemary Hershey, took her to the cleaners. I'm going to try and get an interview with her today."

Ted leaned back in his chair and then propped his feet up on the desk, Jack Emery's words ringing in his ears about how women went through a guy's things after sex when the guy was sleeping. He made a mental note to buy some No-Doz on his way home. He wondered if he talked in his sleep. "I'm just feeling guilty with no news to work on. She's all yours," he said, pointing to the clippings on Isabelle Flanders. "Good luck on the interview. What time tonight?"

Maggie pretended to think, crunching up her face, her freckles forming a tight bridge across her nose. "Seven-thirty should do it. If you can't make it, call me."

Ted waved airily, his thoughts on where he was going to stash his backpack when he arrived at Maggie's. There was no way in hell he was going to ignore his buddy's sage advice when it came to women. No sireee.

He went back to Isabelle Flanders. Out of the corner of his eye he saw Maggie go out of her way to avoid walking past his desk again. Devious. She was definitely up to something. He preened at his sharp instinct. Jack Emery 101 on women.

He started to make notes. He scribbled furiously. *IF says falsely accused, lost everything, including fiancé, BH. One of seven women. Pinewood.* Ted made a long line of question marks. *LOP. Ladies of Pinewood.* More question marks followed. Next to the question marks he made a second row of dollar signs. *Myra Rutledge buys horse farm next to her own.* More question marks. Even a rookie reporter would come up with the obvious: that Myra was funding whatever Isabelle Flanders was up to. But what was she up to? *Vengeance.* Of course! Ted reached for a red pencil and circled the word. Then he made a crude red star next to the circle.

But she couldn't extract vengeance on her own. Oh no, she needed help. Who better to help her than the ladies of Pinewood? LOP. Aha!

Ted leaned back, gave his chair a solid push, and whirled around three times before his feet could hit the floor. The ladies of Pinewood were going to go after Rosemary Hershey. That's where he had to start. Never start with the result, start with the cause. Hershey was the cause of Isabelle's demise and she would ultimately . . . what?

He gathered up his papers, stuffed them in his bedraggled backpack, shrugged into his jacket and left the newsroom. He could feel Maggie's eyes on his back. He made one stop in the paper's library, where he spent an hour printing out everything he could find on Rosemary Hershey. When he was finished, his stack of papers was a half-inch thick. They also went into the backpack.

Ted hit the lobby at full throttle and then sailed through the revolving door to wind, rain and cold air. Christ, how he hated February. He should be on some warm island sunning his ass off. Preferably with Maggie Spritzer. For one wild moment he envisioned himself rubbing coconut oil all over her freckled body. The thought, while titillating, and giving him a hard-on, had to go. He was on the hunt for a story and there was no room for suntan oil, freckles or lustful reactions.

Twenty minutes later, Ted breezed through the security and made his way to Jack Emery's office. What he didn't see was Maggie Spritzer trailing behind him in a dark-colored poncho.

Jack groaned when he saw Ted standing in his office doorway. "You're starting to give this place a bad name. What the hell do you want now? Listen, pal, you cannot keep coming here like this. People are starting to talk. I mean it, Ted. Call me but stop coming here. What's with you anyway?"

"I got it. I know what's going on. I just need to pick your brains a little before I forge ahead. Mind if I sit down?"

"Hell, yes, I mind. You need to get your ass outta here. Oh, fuck," he muttered under his breath.

Ted looked up and immediately turned pale. "Is that who I think it is?"

"Damn straight it is. The second string. Can't you smell him? Those jerks all smell the same. It must be written in the spook manual that they're to wear cologne capable of overpowering whomever they're trying to beat to death. See where he's going? My boss's office! If you leave now, it will look more suspicious. Make it quick, Ted, what do you want?"

"A rundown on the Flanders woman. Those ladies of Pinewood are gearing up for . . . *something*. I can smell it. Maybe a sting. Look, if they ream your ass out, just say I'm here on that high-profile capital case you're working on. They gave the assignment to someone else but no one here has to know that. OK, OK, I'm leaving," Ted said, stuffing his notebook back into his backpack. "I'll call you later."

"Can't you forget you know me and my phone number?" Jack said, his eyes on his boss's office door.

Ted grinned. "Yeah, I could, but I'm not going to. You're precious to me, Jackie," he said, blowing Jack a kiss as he left the office. It took every ounce of Ted's willpower not to turn and look at Jack's boss's door. His breathing was shallow and harsh as he made his way down to the lobby of the building.

It was still rainy and windy. Ted let his thoughts run wild. What the hell was the second string doing in Jack's office building? Like he didn't know. The power of wealth and pure, raw power. In other words, Myra Rutledge and Charles Martin. He felt a degree of satisfaction as he made his way down the windy street. He was glad no one could see how badly he was trembling. Under his breath, he muttered over and over, *there's nothing to fear but fear itself*. Jack Emery 101 on fear. What a crock.

Jack busied himself doing nothing but scrolling down Amazon.com on his computer. He tried to keep his eyes off Seymour Ridley's office door. He didn't think Ridley could be intimidated, but what the hell did he know? If the second string of gold shields was as powerful as the first, he was going to be standing in the dark brown stuff within minutes. Jack clicked off Amazon and turned around to see a shadow cross his well-lit desk. He sucked in his breath when he looked up. Six feet two. Two hundred and ten pounds. Full head of hair. Gleaming white teeth. Light suntan. In *February*? Jack's ribs started to ache at the sight of the man.

"Yeah?" he said calmly.

"Chuck Nevins. Just wanted to say hello. How's it going, Mr. District Attorney?"

"Smooth as silk, Mr. Nevins. Boring but smooth."

"Thought you might like to know my colleagues are still undergoing physical therapy."

"And you think I want to know this . . . why? Obviously you have me mixed up with someone who gives a shit. Do those friends have names?"

"Nah, they're anonymous, just three guys without spleens."

"Ah, those guys. Wanna go for four?" Jack said, standing up. "Listen up, you overgrown gorilla, don't fuck with me. Stop with the theatrics already. They only make you look stupid. By the way, real men don't blow-dry their hair. Now, take your fucking ass out of my office; you're smelling it up. And another thing, no one wears Polo anymore. It's passé."

Nevins narrowed his eyes. "You're a wiseass, Emery. That's going to be your undoing."

"You can't shut me up. I'm a taxpayer. I have rights. Didn't you learn anything from Watergate?"

The door closed softly behind Chuck Nevins.

Jack watched until the man was out of sight before he turned his gaze to Seymour Ridley's office. His stomach started to crunch up when Ridley beckoned him. He pretended to scribble a few notes on a blank piece of paper before he made his way through.

Seymour Ridley could have worked as a Donald Trump lookalike, right down to the strawlike, blow-dried hair. "Sit down, Jack, and tell me what that bird said to you when he stopped by your desk."

"He introduced himself, reported on the medical conditions of some of his buddies. I made a few snide comments. He called me a wiseass when I said he couldn't shut me up because I was a citizen and a taxpayer. I don't think he believed me. I didn't lie, did I, Seymour?"

"Are you still working on all that crap you told me about a while back? I thought I told you to lay off unless you had concrete proof—two sources outlined in blood and willing to testify in court."

"I dropped it after they beat the crap out of me. I did what you said, Seymour."

"Is there any truth to the rumor that you took out three of his guys with a bunch of . . . ah . . . ninjas?"

Jack snorted. "I wish. The short answer is no," he lied with a straight face. "What did he want?"

Ridley laughed. "He wants me to fire you."

Jack gaped at his boss. "Did he say why?"

"Said you get in his way. He showed me a lot of impressive credentials. I showed him your court record and told him you were the best of the best. He did some more blustering but stopped short of threatening me when I asked him how he'd like to see his name above the fold in the *Post*. What's going on, Jack? Why has Robinson been here so much? We should be charging him rent."

Jack debated for all of five seconds before he responded. He couldn't find one good reason to lie. "He picked up where I left off, Seymour. He's on to something and comes by to pick my brain. That's as much as I'm involved. Ted has an axe to grind now; he's minus a spleen these days. He says he's OK, but he's not. It's going to take a while for him to totally get back in the groove—and you know reporters; they're like elephants, they never forget."

Ridley peered over the top of his glasses. Jack thought he looked like he was trying to make up his mind about something. It wasn't the look in his eyes; it was the way his fingers were drumming on the desk. "So, in fact, you signed off on something you can no longer pursue."

Jack eye-balled his superior. "More or less. If Ted needs me, I won't let him down. It's the best I can do right now, Seymour. I swore to uphold the law. What else do you want me to say?"

"Not a thing, Jack. I just like to know where my people stand. You're a hell of a prosecutor, almost as good as myself," Ridley said, without a trace of modesty. "All I ask is that you try to keep this office out of your extra-curricular activities. If you find yourself up to your knees in shit, call me. Your *knees*, Jack, not your ankles."

Jack nodded. "About those credentials . . ."

"Jesus, Jack, this is the nation's capital. Every dude walking down the street has credentials, some more impressive than others. If you're referring to those eye-catching presidential gold shields, let's just say I wasn't impressed. I know some influential people on both sides up on the Hill. Don't go off half-cocked, is all I'm asking."

Jack nodded again as he walked out of the office, his shoulders straighter than when he'd walked in. He knew he had to call Nikki quickly and alert her to what Ted was about to do.

Cell phone in hand, Jack walked over to the window and looked down at the traffic below. All he could see was pelting rain, umbrellas and people running to and fro. There was a traffic jam at the corner. Even though he was on the eleventh floor, he could hear the blaring horns.

"Can you talk?" Jack asked when Nikki answered her phone.

"No, not really, but I have good ears. Whatcha got?"

Jack told her. Nikki thanked him and then clicked off.

In the lobby of the building that was going to be Isabelle Flanders's new home, Ted sauntered over to the newsstand to pick up a copy of the *Chronicle*, his competition. He whistled when he snapped the paper open to see a picture of a smiling Nealy Diamond Clay astride her Triple Crown horse. It was an old picture, but that wasn't what made him whistle. It was the picture of Isabelle Flanders standing next to Nealy Clay. "The plot thickens," he muttered as he folded up the paper into a cylinder. He walked over to the sign-in area, signed his name, showed his credentials and was allowed to advance to the elevator. Reporters' privilege.

He saw her at the same moment she saw him. She quirked an eyebrow just the way he did. Ted unrolled the *Chronicle*. "I was wondering, Miss Flanders, if you'd care to give the *Post* a comment?"

Isabelle pushed the yellow hard hat she was wearing farther back on her head. "What would you like me to comment on?"

"A few things. What was it like to meet Nealy Diamond Clay?"

Isabelle relaxed a little. She knew who Ted Robinson was. Jack Emery's buddy. "It was very interesting. I was in awe. She's quite a lady. Actually, I met her by accident. I was out at the farm site looking around and there she was. I didn't know there was a reporter there until he stepped forward to identify himself."

"Would you care to comment on Rosemary Hershey and your past baggage?"

"No, I wouldn't care to comment. That's a personal matter."

"Fair enough," Ted drawled. He waved his arms about. "Pretty impressive. Care to comment on the high rent in this building?"

"No, I wouldn't care to comment," Isabelle said, her eyes narrowing.

"Would you care to comment on the ladies of Pinewood?" Not bothering to wait for a response, Ted continued. "Are you ladies preparing to take on Rosemary Hershey to make her pay for what she did to you? That's what you do, isn't it? Like that National Security Advisor. I lost my spleen over that little deal. I just thought I'd throw that in as a tidbit of interest."

Isabelle's heart pounded inside her chest. For one split second she thought she was going to faint. "What in the world are you talking about? By the way, how did you get up here? This is a secure building."

Ted flashed his credentials. "You didn't answer my question, Miss Flanders."

"No, and I'm not going to either. It might be a good idea for you to leave now before I call security."

"Is that your comment? If it is, I want to report it verbatim." Ted thought the architect looked like a startled deer caught in headlights.

and the red shoes. He said he had to go home because his sitter ... Seven o'clock.

Seven

Charles listened with amusement as the ladies
of Pinewood clustered around Alexis to hear
about her most recent date. He stacked and sta-
pled his papers as he tried to concentrate on what
he was doing but had to admit what he was hearing was more interesting than what he was doing.
At times he found himself saddened at the women's
jaundiced, jaded view of men, even though he understood how and why they had the attitudes they
had. He waited for the finale to Alexis's story.

"Yeah, yeah, and then what?" Isabelle demanded.

"Did he kiss you, try to swallow your tongue . . .
what?" Kathryn asked.

Alexis sighed. "None of the above. He shook my
hand, said good night and went home. He said he
had a pleasant evening."

"Get out of here!" Nikki said, disbelief ringing in
her voice. "Did you wear that red dress we picked out
for you, the one that screams Come to Mama, Baby?"

Alexis sighed again. "Yes, I wore the red dress

and the red shoes. He said he had to go home because his sitter couldn't stay past eleven o'clock because she had school the next day. He has a five-year-old boy."

Myra chirped up. "But that's wonderful, dear! It shows he's a family man. And conscientious. Did he make another date with you?"

"No. He said he'd call. We all know what *that* means. Maybe the red dress was too much for him to handle. Maybe I shouldn't have worn the red shoes, too. Grady did like him, though. His name is Braden Gunderson. He's a partner in some computer company in the District."

Isabelle groaned. "Just tell me he doesn't drive a pickup truck."

"Actually, he drives a burgundy Jaguar convertible. The whole back seat, even though it's quite small, was full of his son's stuff. He talked about his son all night, and I talked about my dog. It wasn't very romantic but it was nice and comfortable. First dates are usually horrific."

"When do you think he'll call?" Kathryn asked. "You must have a feel for what he's about."

Alexis rolled her eyes. "He's *not* going to call. I'm too much woman for him. The truth is, I think I scared him. I suspect he's looking for a mama for his son. The kind who will cook, clean and run the boy to and fro. Right now that is not on my agenda."

Charles silently cheered her on as he stepped down from the bank of computers he constantly monitored. "Are we now up to date on Alexis's social life, ladies? Can we proceed with the business at hand?"

Kathryn flipped him the bird. "Any time you're ready, Charles."

Charles settled into a chair next to Myra. "First things first. From this minute on, Isabelle must be able to account for her time with a witness. Around the clock. I've arranged for everything. Now, this is what we're going to do."

The women watched as Charles separated his files. "We're going to do a mail campaign where Rosemary Hershey is concerned. Pictures of the family killed in the accident. Copies of the different articles that appeared in the newspapers. Different pages of the transcript of the trial. Each day she will receive a new piece of mail. We're going to play with her mind. We'll be sending the mail from different towns—Arlington, Alexandria, Vienna, Springfield, and so on. Nothing will be sent from McLean or the District. Of course, Miss Hershey will immediately blame Isabelle, but she won't be able to come up with any proof. Isabelle will be beyond such shenanigans."

Charles handed a folder to Alexis. "This is the family that was killed in the accident. Their names were Thomas and Patty Myers. They were taking their little girl, Diane, to the ear doctor in town. Diane was two years old. They left behind a little boy named Tommy who is now seven years old. His grandmother is caring for him. After the lawyers were paid—and let me say here, the grandmother didn't have a very good lawyer—she walked away with very little. The lawyers took the lion's share of the jury award. What was left, she put in a trust for the little boy's college fund. They're managing, but just barely. The grandmother's name is Irma Myers. Thomas Senior was her only son. Patty was the daughter she never had but always wanted. A wonderful little family.

"Alexis, I want you to go to their home and make contact. I have a cover story all made up for you. You'll take this Game Boy for Tommy," Charles said, handing over a boxed gift. "Tommy wants one desperately but it is not in their budget. I want current pictures. I want confidences shared by Irma about her family. Then I want you to promise her that Tommy's life will be made as whole as we can make it. You're going to be a new insurance investigator who decided to reopen their file. When the insurance company paid out, they left a pending sticker on the file. It's your job to finish off the report and put it to bed. Do you have any problems with this, Alexis?"

"No."

"Ladies?"

The others shook their heads.

"That's it? We're going to send things in the mail? When do we get to the good stuff?" Kathryn asked, a stupefied expression on her face.

Charles allowed himself a brief smile. "How do you feel about breaking and entering, Kathryn?"

Kathryn leaned forward. "Now you have my attention! What are we looking for?"

"Money! Aside from Miss Hershey's business account—a joint checking account with very little money in it—I haven't been able to find where she keeps her money, which tells me she's got it in the house. She's one smart lady, I can tell you that. Everything she did, she did on paper. That means she borrowed money from the bank and used their money to build and buy her house, start up the business, buy her cars. By the way, she has an excellent credit rating and pays her bills on time. It's my opinion that she has a crackerjack accountant. Now, Mr. Harcourt is a different story. His finances check out one hundred percent. He has a robust brokerage account. He has a healthy 401 (k) plan, certificates of deposit, and a personal checking account with quite a few zeros in it. His share of the profits from the business are all accounted for. But then he is a top-notch architect so it is to be expected. With the exception of being married to Rosemary, the man has a sterling reputation. Miss Hershey's share of the business profits do not show up anywhere, nor does her settlement money. I suppose it's possible that it's offshore somewhere and I just haven't found it yet. What I really think is she's got it in her house somewhere. The woman is paranoid, that much we know. She lied, cheated, betrayed Isabelle, caused an accident that killed three people and showed absolutely no remorse. That alone convinces me that if she went to those lengths out of greed, she isn't going to trust her money anywhere but with herself.

"What I want you to do is go to her home, find where she keeps it, but don't touch it. For now we just want to know she actually has it. The woman is an architect. She's more than capable of building a safe into her home that no one knows about, not even her husband, but I may be premature in my thinking where Mr. Harcourt is concerned. Kathryn and Yoko will do the breaking and entering. Isabelle will be overseeing the remodeling of her offices. Myra will be up to her ears with the farm next door. Nikki, you will start to figure out a way to get Miss Hershey's money to the Myers family so that no suspicion is aroused. Assuming we find it, of course."

Isabelle's voice became a whisper. "What about

Bobby? I feel like I'm not contributing to my own mission here. All I do is sit at the new office and watch the renovations. Isn't there something I can do?"

"But you're needed at the office site, Isabelle. And as for Bobby, I guess it will depend on whether he was involved in the ugly things that Rosemary did. We'll deal with that when the time comes," Charles said.

"What about the reporter who came to see me the other day?"

"At the moment, Mr. Robinson is just sniffing around. We have him in our sights."

We have him in our sights. Nikki felt a chill race up her arms. That had to mean Jack was in their sights, too.

"When do we start?" Yoko asked.

"Right now. Isabelle is heading for her office. Nikki is going to *her* office. Myra is going to the farm next door. Alexis, here are the directions to the Myers home in Arlington. You can mail the first letter on your way. Kathryn and Yoko, here is the address to the Hershey home. I took the liberty of placing a few necessary objects on the kitchen counter for you. You all know how to disarm a security system so that will be the first thing you do. There are two rather small state-of-the-art metal detectors that will indicate a metal safe. Check all the walls, the floors, the garage, the bathrooms. Go through the place with a fine-tooth comb."

"How sure are you that neither of the Hersheys will return home?"

"Reasonably sure. I will be outside the Hersheys' office. If either party leaves, I'll call you on your cell. I'm assuming they will both be busy getting ready to design the new horse farm since the invitations went out last week. We gave everyone a rather short deadline for just this reason. I think it's safe to say you have a good two hours. Be quick but be thorough. Good luck, ladies."

Bobby Harcourt, tie off, shirtsleeves rolled up, turned around at the sound of his office door opening. The stool he was sitting on at his drafting table squeaked as he made a full swing in his wife's direction.

"What do you think you're doing, Bobby?"

Bobby's eyebrows shot upward. "Say again?"

"I said, what do you think you're doing?"

Bobby looked at his wife and wondered what he'd ever seen in her. "I'm getting ready to start designing a top-of-the-line horse farm, Bobby Harcourt style. Why are you asking? Did you run out of ideas? Or is this where the rubber meets the road? Meaning there are no designs for you to steal?"

Rosemary stomped her foot. "Oh, no. No, no, no. Only one design comes out of this office. *Mine.* Be very careful what you say, Bobby, because it could come back to bite you in the ass. Do not—I repeat, do not—say anything like that to me ever again."

The squeaking stool swiveled back around. Bobby reached for his personal invitation. He waved it. "This invitation, personally addressed to me at this office, reads: 'Dear Mr. Harcourt, you are being asked to submit your designs for my new horse farm.' Then it gives the specs they want and it is signed by Myra Rutledge. Every architect in town got one. You got one, Rosemary. I saw it in the incoming mailbox."

"*One* design goes out of this office. Cease and desist, Bobby, or you're out of here," Rosemary snarled.

Bobby laughed. "I'd like to see how that threat holds up in court. You better keep your voice down unless you want everyone in this office to hear you. It doesn't work that way. I own half of this business. Before you can ask—*demand*—I already checked with my attorney. I'm prepared to buy you out. If you want, you can make me an offer and I'll consider it. And, Rosemary, I'll be filing for divorce before the week is out. I'm going to charge you with all kinds of good stuff."

"What?" Rosemary screeched. "Buy *me* out! You're crazy, Bobby. What do you mean, you're divorcing me?" Not bothering to wait for a reply, Rosemary's voice rose shrilly. "Oh, I get it. You sleaze! Now that Isabelle is a front-runner with what appears to be money to burn, you're going to go after her. Well, it isn't going to work."

"Oh, yes, it is going to work. I've had it with you sleeping around, your backstabbing and all that other shit you pull in the guise of being a top-notch architect. We never had a real marriage. You've never been a wife. I wanted kids. You said you did, too. I don't see any kids, do you? Maybe you think I've been asleep at the switch but I haven't been. My decisions have nothing to do with Isabelle Flanders. I want out because I think you're finally going to get your comeuppance and I don't want to be around to see it. And I want to be able to testify if it goes to court. If I'm married to you, I can't testify. Same principle as hanging with a dog; you're bound to get fleas. Close the door on your way out, Rosemary."

Rosemary glared at her husband. Her heart was beating so fast and hard she thought Bobby could hear it. She needed to have the last word. "*One* design goes out of this office. Mine."

"Fine. I'll rent office space somewhere else until we settle things with the business." To prove that he meant what he said, Bobby started to pack up his things.

Speechless, Rosemary could only sputter as she stomped her way back to her own office. Blind with rage, she slammed the door so hard she thought she'd broken the stained-glass panel she'd personally installed. She started to pace and then a knock sounded on the door. Was it Bobby, wanting to apologize? Not in this lifetime.

Rosemary jerked on the doorknob, a vicious comment on her lips, and saw a tall gangly man staring at her. She knew him from somewhere. Whoever he was, he probably wasn't important, otherwise she would remember him. "What is it?" she asked.

Ted Robinson flipped out his press card. "I'm doing a human interest story on Patty and Thomas Myers. I wonder if you would care to comment?"

Rosemary looked genuinely puzzled. "Who?"

Bobby took that moment to open his office door. "The people you killed a few years back, darling. Tell your lawyer to call my lawyer if you need to reach me."

Whoa! What had he just stepped into? Ted looked at the couple. The pair of them looked like

two spitting alley cats. He tried to blend into the
woodwork, hoping the couple would throw cau-
tion to the wind and give him something juicy.
Instead, Bobby hoisted the box he was carrying up
to his shoulder and walked down the hallway.
Rosemary then slammed the door in Ted's face.

"Hey!" He turned the knob and opened the
door a crack, not sure if the angry architect would
slam it on his nose. "You didn't give me a comment. Should I print your response?"

"What response, you jackass? I didn't give you a
response."

"You sure did, ma'am." Ted flipped the button
on his mini recorder. Rosemary's puzzled, "Who?"
was loud and clear, followed by her husband's explanation. "I can go with that," Ted said, smiling.

"Do that, you vulture, and I'll drag your ass
through every court in the land. Now get out of
this building before I call the police. From this
moment on, you're trespassing."

The door slammed in Ted's face again. Satisfied
that he'd stirred up a hornet's nest, he grinned as
he made his way to the tastefully decorated lobby,
the walls of which were lined with built-in fish
tanks. If he remembered correctly, Bobby Harcourt
was the one who designed those fish tanks. Maggie
had done a feature story for the Sunday edition.
She'd even named the colorful fish. Impressive article as he recalled. And Bobby had won an award
of some kind for the design.

Outside, in the frosty February air, Ted was reminded again of how much he hated this particular month. The raw gray day grated on his nerves.
It must be true what they said about sunshine ver-

sus gray, cloudy days and the effect they have on one's emotions. He felt like picking a fight with someone.

Across the street and out of sight, Charles Martin debated for all of five seconds. Should he follow the reporter or Bobby Harcourt? Bobby Harcourt, of course. He'd promised the ladies of Pinewood that he would keep Rosemary and Bobby in his sights. Just to be on the safe side, he called Kathryn on her cell phone to tell her he was following Bobby but didn't know what Rosemary's agenda was. "Stay alert," was the best advice he could give under the circumstances. They were pros now, and would do whatever they had to in order to get away unscathed in the event that Rosemary Hershey decided to go home in the middle of the day.

Eight

Alexis steered the Mini Cooper up the narrow driveway and parked. It was a neat-as-a-pin piece of property. She knew in the spring the flower beds would be a rainbow of color and the old trees with the gnarled trunks would create beautiful shade for the little Cape Cod house. Now, though, it looked barren and lonely. She climbed out of the car and made her way to the front porch. There wasn't a doorbell that she could see. She knocked on the door and waited. When it opened, Alexis stared at a tall, gangly woman with steel-gray hair and wire-rimmed glasses who was wearing a flannel robe.

"Yes," she said.

"Mrs. Myers?"

"Yes, honey, that's me. What can I do for you?"

"My name is Pamela Nolan. I'm with the insurance company that covered your son when the accident happened. I need to talk to you. We've decided to reopen the case."

Mrs. Myers bit down on her lower lip. "I thought that was all over and done with. What good is it going to do to reopen the case? But, yes, come in. I'm just getting over a bad bout of bronchitis. That's why I'm home today. I really don't see how I can help you, Miss Nolan."

Alexis seated herself in a deep, comfortable, tweed chair. She looked around. The inside of the house was just as neat as the outside. The mantel was covered with photographs of little Tommy and, she assumed, Big Tommy, his dad. She cleared her throat. "I think it will be easier on both of us if you just tell me what you know, from the time you were notified until the end of the court case. I don't take notes but prefer to use a recorder. That way nothing gets lost. If you object, I can take notes."

"The recorder is fine, miss. The police came to the door. I was playing checkers with Tommy. I was babysitting. They told me what happened. It took the police three hours to get here. The accident happened ten miles away. My son and his little family had been dead for three hours and I didn't even know it. I was . . . I was playing checkers. To this day I don't understand how I didn't feel something, sense something.

"It was a lady officer who came to the door. She was so young and I could tell she didn't want to have to tell me the bad news. She said my son ran a stop sign and hit the lady architect. I said that had to be wrong. My son was a very cautious driver, especially when he had the baby in the car with him. My son was a wonderful father and husband and he always treated me with love and respect. A mother knows her son, Miss Nolan. But no one would listen to me. I had to get a lawyer. He sided with the police. He billed me an astronomical amount of money. In the end, the car insurance did not pay. We sued the lady architect. There were two of them in the car. That lawyer wasn't any better than the first one. In the end, when it got to court, I had to sit there and listen to one lady say all kinds of terrible things about my son and the other lady in the car. The jury gave her a lot of money. They awarded little Tommy half a million dollars. But by the time the second lawyer took his fee and I paid off the first lawyer there was only forty thousand dollars left. I was able to put thirty-one thousand into a college fund for Tommy. The reason I kept the remaining nine thousand was to pay for . . . for the funerals. Are you here to tell me you want to take the money back?" Tears gathered in the eyes behind the wire-rimmed glasses.

"No, ma'am. I'm here to tell you we think there was something wrong. We aren't going to close out the case. We keep pending files for six years. We . . . I agree with you that something was . . . wrong. What that means to you and Tommy is that we are going to reopen the case and do another investigation. Tell me something. Is this where you lived when the accident happened?"

"Why, yes it is. Oh, I see, you think because the address on all the legal papers was my son's address it might make a difference? I told you, my lawyer wasn't very good—or thorough. He didn't even have a secretary. This address never appeared on any of the legal papers. By the time the case came to trial, my son's house had gone into default. I just didn't have the money to pay the mortgage and the utilities. It's all I can do to keep up with this house. I was hoping to retire this year but my meager pension won't support both Tommy and myself. I have to take him to a free medical clinic for poor people because I can't afford the insurance. And before you can ask, I can't bring myself to touch the money in the bank. My son wanted his children to go to college and Tommy is going to go, no matter what. Oh, there's the school bus. Excuse me, I have to get his cookies and milk ready."

Alexis felt like crying. She wished Rosemary Hershey was standing in front of her so she could jam her foot down her throat.

The door opened and a little boy with blond hair and eyes the color of cobalt bounded into the room. "I'm home!" he bellowed before he noticed Alexis. "Hello, ma'am. I'm Tommy Myers."

"Hi, Tommy. I'm Pam Nolan and I have a present for you. Here," she said, holding out the gift box.

The boy made no move to accept the gift. "I'm not allowed to take gifts from strangers."

"That's a good thing, but I'm not a stranger. I think your grandmother will let you accept it. Why don't you go in the kitchen and ask her?"

"OK. What is it?" he asked curiously.

"A surprise!" Alexis laughed. "I think it's something all little boys want."

The boy scampered off and returned within minutes. "She said yes."

"There you go," Alexis said, handing over the gift box.

"Oh, wow! A Game Boy! Grandma, the lady gave me a Game Boy!"

"Did you say thank you, Tommy?"

"No, Grandma, I didn't. Thank you, ma'am."

"Then run along to the kitchen for your cookies and milk. I need to talk some more to this lady." The boy disappeared in seconds. "That was very nice of you, Miss Nolan. Tommy wanted one for Christmas but it just wasn't in my budget."

Alexis hated lying to this nice lady. Still, she had a job to do, and she hoped the woman would forgive her when things were made right. "I need to take some pictures of you and Tommy. Do you mind?"

"If it will help you, not at all. Do you really think there's a chance you can clear my son's name? I don't care about the money."

"Mrs. Myers, I think there's more than a good chance I can do that. I need to ask you to do something for me. If anyone comes around asking questions, I don't want you talking to them. Even though what you say might seem harmless, it could ruin our investigation. We need to be very clear on that. Tommy, too. Children tend to chatter."

"I can do that. Tommy is very good about obeying the rules, just like his daddy was when he was little. We'll do whatever is necessary. Goodness gracious, if you're planning on taking my picture, I better get dressed."

"The robe is fine, Mrs. Myers."

Thirty minutes later Alexis, armed with a stack of Polaroid shots, climbed into the Mini Cooper and was on her way back to Pinewood.

Meanwhile, Kathryn picked the lock on the Hershey house and immediately went to the alarm panel on the wall. Charles had said she had exactly one minute to disarm the system. A blizzard of numbers raced across the high-tech gizmo that spit out the code in twenty-seven seconds.

"Done! How stupid is a code of zero-seven-one-one? She must have gambling instincts." She looked around. "Looks like no one lives here. A little too stark for my taste. How about you, Yoko?"

"It's an architect's dream, I guess. Sharp lines, lots of chrome. I don't personally care for stark black and white. I like color. Which floor do you want?"

"I'll take the second floor; you cover this one. There's no garage so that makes it easier." The women separated, each carrying a metal detector.

Kathryn made her way down the upstairs hallway looking in one room after the other. Four rooms and two full baths. Well, what have we here, his and hers bedrooms? First she tackled Bobby Harcourt's bedroom, liking the coziness of it. The bed was neatly made and nothing was out of place. His closet was just as neat, his suits and casual wear carefully aligned. Shoes, polished and shined, sat on shoe trees. The drawers were just as neat. No hiding places here. Everything was so tidy it was suspect. And yet, there was no sign that a maid worked here. Maybe the couple had a once-a-week cleaning lady. Kathryn hoped today wasn't the day a domestic showed up with a bucket and mop.

Bobby Harcourt's bathroom was as neat as his bedroom. There was no water on the sink, no toothpaste specks on the mirror over the vanity. Shaving gear neatly stowed in a zippered leather bag. Today's wet towel was hung up neatly. No water on the floor. The toilet seat was down. His mother must have trained him well early on. The linen closet held burgundy towels, bedsheets and bathroom supplies, extra aftershave, soap and shampoo. All were neatly arranged. The medicine cabinet was almost empty. A bottle of Advil, a prescription bottle of penicillin with two tablets left in it, a bottle of mouthwash and some breath mints were the only things it contained. No hiding places here.

The couple's joint home office was next door. Kathryn walked around, opening drawers and closets. The closets held supplies. The drawers held more supplies. Bobby's desk and drafting table were tidy whereas Rosemary's looked like a work in progress. Kathryn waved the metal detector over the walls. She listened intently for a beep to signal that there was metal somewhere. Nothing so far.

Yoko appeared in the doorway. "The downstairs is clean. Nothing in the freezer. They must eat out a lot; there are a lot of takeout containers in the refrigerator. Nothing in the washer, the dryer or the microwave—the places where people tend to hide things. The foyer closet has nothing but winter wear. There are no boxes anywhere. There's nothing in the kitchen cabinets other than dishes and pots and pans. I checked the fireplace and there are no loose bricks, nothing hidden. No pictures on the walls. This place is cold and stark. Did you find anything?"

"No, not yet. Take Rosemary's bedroom. I'll finish in here."

Yoko trotted off as Kathryn started waving the metal detector. She blinked when she heard the beep, at first faint and then stronger as she moved closer to Rosemary's desk.

"Yoko! I think I found something. Quick! Wave your detector, see if it beeps. It must be the floor."

"This desk is custom-made," Yoko said. "It's mahogany and heavy. It would take four men to move it. The other desk looks like they got it at Staples."

The metal detectors continued to beep as the two women struggled to move the desk. It wouldn't budge. Kathryn looked at Yoko. "This is stupid. If the two of us can't get this thing to budge, that woman wouldn't be able to move this desk on her own. All we're going to get for our efforts is a hernia. I'm thinking if she is hiding something she would want to be able to get to it and not have to call in a moving company to shift the desk every time she wants to check whatever it is she's hiding."

Yoko was on her knees. "The drawers? A false bottom?" Before Kathryn could blink, Yoko had the bottom drawer out. Kathryn peered into the depths of it but there was nothing there but sticky pads, a ruler and a few drafting pencils with fine lead points. Yoko reached for the metal detector and waved it around.

"Whatever it is, it's here, under the desk drawer. If you notice, Kathryn, the drawers are oversized, as is the entire desk. You can see where someone cut out the bottom of the desk. When the drawer is in place, you would never know something is under it."

"Should we pry up the boards?" Kathryn looked at her watch. "We still have time and Charles hasn't called back. I think we need to know what's under the floorboards."

Yoko's tiny hands worked quickly. The boards

came up easily to reveal a square gunmetal-gray safe with a dial. From what they could see of the safe it looked to be about as big as a microwave oven. Two flanges were bolted to the studs underneath the floor, securing the safe in place.

Kathryn sat back on her haunches. "This is one very clever lady. I never would have thought of this. Safes usually go in a wall behind a picture or in a closet somewhere. I'd say this lady is hiding something that she probably doesn't even want her husband to know about."

Yoko's eyes popped when Kathryn's cell phone rang. Kathryn flipped it open. She listened and then snapped the phone shut. "Charles thinks Mr. Harcourt is on his way home. Charles is following him. I don't know how much time we have. Quick, Yoko, put everything back. I'm going to run out and move the car down the street. Hurry!"

Her hands trembling, Yoko slipped the floorboards back into place and then struggled to put the drawer back on its track. She broke into a sweat when the drawer wouldn't fit. She sucked in her breath and tried to calm herself before she tried a second time. This time the drawer slid neatly into place. At the door, she realized she didn't have the metal detector. She ran back for it, her breathing ragged, and then she bolted down the steps. She heard the key in the lock, realizing the alarm was in daytime mode, which meant it wasn't armed. Well, there was nothing she could do about that now. Besides, Kathryn had the electronic device that would reactivate it. She raced toward the kitchen and let herself out the back door. She forced herself to walk toward the parking area as if she belonged there. She crossed over the barrier and then walked out to the street and down to Kathryn's car. Charles was parked directly behind Kathryn.

Kathryn floored the gas pedal and roared down the street as Yoko gasped out what had happened. "He's going to know someone was in the house. The alarm wasn't armed and there was no way to relock the back door. Do you think he'll call the police?"

Kathryn's face was grim. "I doubt it. He'll probably think his wife forgot to lock up if—and this is a big if—she was the last one to leave. If he was the last one to leave this morning, then, yes, he might suspect someone was prowling around inside the house. Will he call the police? Maybe, maybe not. Nothing was taken, so that rules out robbery.

"Charles said when Mr. Harcourt left his office he was carrying a huge cardboard box on his shoulders like he was moving out. That's a guess on Charles's part. He drove to a lawyer's office, still carrying the box. When he came out forty minutes later, he didn't have the box. He drove straight here. Charles is going to monitor the house. We're to go back to the farm." She turned to look at her friend. "Are you OK now, Yoko?"

"Yes. I thought he was going to catch me."

"All's well that ends well. At least we now know that Miss Hershey has a safe. We know where it is if we have to make a second visit."

"Did Charles say if he had heard from Alexis or Nikki?"

"No, he didn't. Hey, want to get a burger? An adrenaline rush always makes me hungry."

"I could eat an egg roll but not a burger. You

shouldn't eat so much red meat, Kathryn, it is not good for you."

"Yeah, yeah, yeah. Like a deep-fried egg roll isn't going to clog your arteries! We'll get you an egg roll and I'll get a burger. Howzat?"

Yoko giggled. "Fine."

Nine

His reporter's nose quivering, Ted Robinson stopped midstride, whipped around, and walked back to Rosemary Hershey's office. He crossed the street and pretended to look at a display of American Tourister luggage. The plate-glass window afforded him a clear view of the architect's office. He looked down at his watch. If his reporter's instinct was working at top speed, the lady should be exiting about . . . now. He waited to see if his quarry would hail a cab or drive. He made a quarter bet with himself that she was too agitated to drive. Two minutes later, he congratulated himself just as a second cab slid to the curb.

"Follow that cab!" Damn, he'd always wanted to say that to a cabbie. "There aren't any cops around. C'mon, c'mon, make a U-turn and let's go. Twenty bucks plus tip if you keep up with the lady's cab."

"She do you dirty or something?" the cabbie said, getting into the swing of things.

"Hell, yes, she cleaned me out. Stashed the family car somewhere, closed out the bank account and is selling off the furniture."

"Damn! You just can't trust dames these days. You think she's got something on the side?"

"Yeah, yeah, that too. I gotta catch her, though. Look, her cab is stopping. What's that building?"

"A bunch of law offices, insurance companies and a couple of dentists. Oh, yeah, a couple of accounting firms, too. I bring fares here all the time. Looks like she's going after your skin, buddy. Maybe your teeth, too." The cabbie laughed at his wit. "You got a lawyer?"

"Damn straight, a real shark," Ted said as he dug in his pockets for the fare, the tip, plus the twenty-dollar incentive he had promised. "Thanks, cabbie." He hopped out, head down in case Rosemary turned around and saw him. She didn't. Even from where he was standing he could see the anger in her face, the veins bulging in her neck.

Ted followed the architect into the lobby and watched her go over to the directory. She signed in, waited to be issued a badge, and then walked to the elevator. He waited until she stepped in and the door closed, saw where the elevator stopped before he walked over to the sign-in desk. He picked up the pen and looked like he was about to sign his name when he suddenly slapped at his forehead.

"Damn, I forgot the envelope! I'll be back in ten minutes." The security guard just looked bored.

Outside, Ted took a deep breath. Son of a bitch! What was Rosemary Hershey doing at Nikki Quinn's law firm? He knew that's where she was going because she'd pressed the right floor button. The Quinn law firm had the entire floor. Hiring an attorney, you jackass, he told himself. Why else would she go to a lawyer's office? So, something had gone awry between her and Bobby earlier at the office. Divorce? Business squabbles? Maybe both.

Ted walked around the corner to the parking lot to see if Nikki Quinn's BMW was there. That's when he saw Maggie Spritzer's Honda.

Shit!

Nikki stood at the window of her office sipping a cup of tea. As she stared out at the sea of cars in the parking lot she wondered, and not for the first time, if she was really meant to practice law. She was so far off track these days with her activities in the Sisterhood, she doubted she could ever get back into the swing of things.

It simply wasn't the same anymore. Her two best friends—Barbara and Jenny, the two friends she'd started the firm with—were gone now, both victims of tragic accidents. Both had been pregnant at the time, and now neither Judge Easter nor Myra would ever have grandchildren. Why, she wondered, do I feel so guilty because I'm still alive, going on with my daily life?

Nikki felt her eyes start to puddle up. She missed her friends. Truly, truly missed them. Barbara's fiancé was long gone, living in New York and married with two children. She never saw him or heard from him anymore except for a Christmas card. She wondered if Jenny's husband would send a card next Christmas. He also had a new life, with no place for old, sad memories. Jenny's husband had moved to New York, too. They would connect for a few more months until the legal end of Jenny's share of the business was settled and then he'd fade out of her life as well. That left only Jack and herself out of the group of six old friends.

"I want out," she said under her breath. "I don't want to practice law anymore. I can't keep breaking the law with the Sisterhood and come back here and pretend I'm on the side of law and order."

Easier said than done, she thought as she heard a knock on her door. Maddie poked her head in.

"I need to talk to you a minute."

"Come in, Maddie. Close the door. Don't tell me Allison Banks is out there." Nikki shuddered, remembering the temporary attorney she'd hired and fired. "If it's bad news, I really don't want to hear it."

"No, that bitch is history. There's a new client in the waiting room. She looks like she's about to explode any minute now. Who do you want me to assign her to? Or do you want to take it on?"

"What's her problem?" Nikki asked.

"She's an architect. I've actually heard of her—I've seen write-ups on her in the Sunday paper. She says her husband is trying to . . . ah . . . to screw her. Not in the literal sense," Maddie said, blushing. "He wants a divorce and to dissolve their business. She said she thinks there's another woman involved. Sounds juicy to me. In case you're interested, she's wearing a fortune in clothes and jewelry."

Nikki walked over to the desk and set her cup down. She was amazed to see that her hand wasn't trembling. Lordy, lordy, someone must be sprinkling fairy dust around and she was fortunate enough to be standing under it. What were the odds of something like this happening? A million to one? Two million to one?

"Assign her to Opal Quintera. Did you tell the client what our standard retainer is?"

"Twenty-five big ones. She didn't blink. In fact, she was searching for her checkbook but I told her that would come later. Opal it is, then."

Nikki kicked off her shoes, plopped down on her chair, swung her long legs up onto the desk and let her breath out in a loud *swoosh*. She clicked on her cell phone and pressed her speed dial. She didn't wait for a greeting. "It's me, Charles. You are never going to believe who is sitting in one of our offices!"

"Rosemary Hershey."

"Charles! How *do* you do that?"

"It just stands to reason that she's going to want to hire an attorney about now, and what better attorney than a woman in your office? She certainly wouldn't want to go back to the attorney she had when she duped the insurance company and Isabelle. Like I said, it stands to reason. Is there anything else?"

Deflated, Nikki said, "No, that's it. Bye, Charles."

Nikki sat quietly for long moments staring out her window, contemplating her future as a lawyer. She jumped when her phone buzzed. She pressed the button in time to hear Maddie's voice.

"Boss, you have forty minutes to get to the courthouse. Traffic's a bitch out there."

"OK, thanks, Maddie. I'm on my way."

Nikki slipped on her shoes, checked her makeup, straightened her skirt and suit jacket. She fluffed her hair with her fingers before she grabbed her coat and briefcase. Having no desire to run into Rosemary Hershey, she took the stairs for three floors and then the elevator to the lobby. She debated whether to take her car or walk to the courthouse. Her heels weren't that high. She could use the exercise. But she decided to drive.

If she hadn't been in such a hurry, and if she wasn't thinking about seeing Jack Emery after she filed her brief, she might have seen Ted Robinson hugging the buildings behind her, and Maggie Spritzer window-shopping on the other side of the street.

Jack Emery hoped the sparkle in Nikki's eyes and the rosy glow on her cheeks was because of him and not from the sharp winds outside. He smiled from ear to ear as he left the courtroom, Nikki at his side.

"What brings you down here at this time of day?"

"I had to file a brief before court closed for the day. I wanted to see you. Can you leave now or do you have to go back to the office?"

"I can leave. Do you want to go to dinner or straight home?" He leered at her, making his wishes clear.

"Let's go home. You can pick up some Italian. I'll meet you there if you're sure."

"I need an hour at the most. Damn, I hate this weather. Do you think spring will ever get here?"

Jack leaned forward. "I feel like I should kiss you. I want to." He turned when someone clapped him on the back. He waved a colleague off and stepped backward. "I'll see you at home. Hey, anything going on I should know about?"

Nikki crunched her face into one of dismay. "You aren't going to believe it when I tell you. I'll have the manicotti. Is there any wine at home?"

Home. Jack smiled. "I bought some over the weekend. Make a fire."

Nikki looked around before she blew a kiss that Jack returned before she headed for her car in the parking lot.

In the doorway of Squire's Pub across the street, Ted Robinson watched the couple. He felt like he'd just been socked in the gut. "Well, you suspected it, Mr. Ace Reporter, so don't be so surprised," he muttered under his breath as he walked off. His next stop: the house in Georgetown to see if the couple were all set to canoodle for the evening.

Nikki inched her way into traffic and headed for Georgetown. She looked forward to spending a nice relaxing evening, sharing her thoughts with Jack. Her eye on the traffic, she reached down for her cell phone and hit the number two on her speed dial. Maddie's voice came over the wire.

"Maddie, it's Nikki. I'm on my way home. How did it go with our new client?"

"She's a strange one, Nikki. She doesn't do or say anything until she consults the stars. Opal said she consulted some book she carries with her before she would even talk. She left a retainer and said she would call us back to see what day the stars say will work to her benefit for her next appointment. According to Opal, Miss Hershey's affairs are on the complicated side. She's interested in a divorce. That's how she put it, *interested.* She doesn't want to give anything up. And she wants to find a way to keep all of her company and not pay her husband a cent. She said her husband hooked himself to her red wagon. Look, she's strange, I'll grant you that, but we've had a lot of strange people walk through our doors."

"So she didn't schedule a second appointment but she did pay the retainer?"

"Yes, boss, that sums it up."

Nikki's mind raced. "OK, thanks, Maddie. By the way, I won't be in tomorrow. Call me on my cell if Miss Hershey gets clearance from the stars." She forced a laugh she didn't feel.

It was five-thirty when Nikki found a parking spot on the street, four doors down from her house. It was already dark out so she didn't pay attention to any of the other parked cars. As she walked against the wind she didn't see Ted Robinson across the street from her, or Maggie Spritzer on her side of the street. Nor did she notice the nondescript dark car two doors from her house or its single occupant.

Inside, as she changed into more comfortable clothes, Nikki called Pinewood to speak to Charles. She repeated the conversation she'd had with Maddie. "Maybe we can bring in her obsession with that hocus-pocus stuff."

"Good thinking, Nikki. Are you staying in town this evening? Did you remember to mail the letter?"

"Yes, Charles, I mailed it from Alexandria. I'm going to stay in this evening and have some scrumptious Italian food, listen to some good music and build a fire. It's quite cold here and exceptionally blustery. I'll see you tomorrow."

It wasn't *really* a lie, Nikki told herself. She *was*

going to stay in this evening. She *was* going to have Italian food and she *was* going to build a fire. She just didn't say she would have company.

She hung up the phone and ran downstairs where she swept the fireplace clean before laying a stack of logs. She turned on the gas starter and was rewarded with a burst of shooting flame. She looked around, expecting to see a mass of clutter because Jack was not a neat person. She smiled at how neat and tidy her living room was. Good old Jack. He was trying, doing all the right things. She couldn't wait to snuggle in his arms.

Outside in the dark, windy evening, Ted Robinson hunched inside his flannel-lined jacket, completely unaware that Maggie Spritzer was on the other side of the street with easy access to the alley behind Nikki Quinn's house. It looked like Nikki Quinn was in for the night. He felt like smashing the windshield of the car he was hiding behind when he saw Jack Emery loping down the street.

"You fuck, you lied to me to my face!" Ted swore under his breath. He was a sharp enough reporter to recognize the bright red and green striped shopping bags that held takeout Italian food. So there was going to be a *tête à tête* inside tonight.

"I have your number now, Mr. DA," Ted whispered.

Ten

Rosemary Hershey dialed her husband's cell phone for the fiftieth time since returning to the office. When there was no answer, she tossed the phone across the room. She blinked when she saw the cover break off and rattle across the hard-wood floor.

She was alone, everyone from the office long gone. It was almost nine o'clock and she was still here, doing nothing but stewing and fretting. She looked around her office; it was a mess. She should tidy it up but if she did that she would never be able to find anything.

Her intention, after returning from the law firm, had been to start her design for the McLean horse farm. So far she hadn't made a mark on the clean paper tacked to her drafting table. She knew squat about farms, especially horse farms. She had planned to fly to Kentucky to take a look at Blue Diamond Farms but she hadn't had time. Then she tried to figure out a way to have a design come out of her office and take the credit for it. Bobby had chopped her off at the knees on that one. Now he was gone. She rather thought he'd come slinking back at some point. Then again, if he was seeing Isabelle Flanders again, that wasn't going to happen.

White-hot rage ripped through Rosemary at the thought of Isabelle Flanders. How had things gotten off track so quickly? She yanked at the middle drawer of her desk to pull out the three books that she consulted daily. She flipped through the pages till she found what she wanted: today's date, her sign, which was Virgo, the worst sign of the zodiac according to some people, and today's message for her.

The first message read: *Tread carefully today. All is not what it seems.* Rosemary snorted. The second message was: *There are unseen forces working behind the scenes against you.* The third message sent a chill up Rosemary's arms. *Everything today is colored gray. Be careful all the color doesn't leave your life.*

She shoved the books back into her desk drawer. She slammed it so hard that a container of pencils toppled over. She booted up her computer and waited, then moved her mouse to the icon she wanted. Her horoscope for the day appeared immediately. Why was she doing this? Why was she torturing herself? She'd read the computer-generated message earlier, just as she'd checked the three books the moment she set foot in the office this morning. Her gaze lowered to the screen. *An ill wind has swept into your life. Prepare for a storm.*

She clicked the mouse to read the forecast for tomorrow, even though she knew what it said. She then checked the three books in the drawer again for tomorrow's forecast. Her face drained of all color when she reread the forecasts. She slumped back in her chair. That's when she noticed the pile of mail sitting in her in-basket. How could she have forgotten to check the mail? Bobby's announcement, that's how. She rifled through it. Bills, advertisements, announcements, a thank-you card from a client and a white legal-looking envelope with no return address. She ripped at it and pulled out a picture of a toddler with a nimbus of gold hair. A beautiful chubby little girl sucking her thumb.

Rosemary's hands started to shake. The picture fell to her desk. Her lips pulled back into a snarl as she recoiled into the depths of her chair. It was *the* child. Well, she wasn't touching that.

She reached for the phone with a shaking hand. She dialed a number she knew by heart. "James, this is Rosemary. I need an emergency tarot card reading. I know it's late but you have to do this for me. Please, I'll pay you double—triple if necessary. I can be there in thirty minutes. You will? Oh, thank you. Thank you, James. Yes, yes, I said triple. I know you prefer cash. It's not a problem. Bye, James."

Rosemary grappled in her purse for her sunglasses. She put them on and then fumbled around inside her desk drawer for a pair of tweezers. She picked up the Polaroid snapshot with the tweezers and carried it to the bathroom sink where she burned it. She rinsed the curled black ash down the drain. Then she removed her sunglasses, washed her hands and tossed the tweezers in the wastebasket.

This never happened.

Ninety minutes later, Rosemary slumped back in the chair across from James, the tarot expert. In the dim yellow light, her face was pasty white, her blonde hair straggly, in need of a brush. She struggled to find her voice.

"How . . . ? I don't understand. How could things turn so . . . black, so quick? Two weeks ago you told me my cards said I was on the high road with things falling into place just like I wanted them to."

"Things change, Rosemary. Good winds, ill winds. New people entering your life, old people exiting your life. Change is constant. What does the baby mean to you? There's never been a baby in your cards before. Do you want to talk about it?"

"I don't know," Rosemary lied. "What is there to talk about? You just painted everything black." Her voice turned desperate. "Can't you read the cards again?"

James looked at the clock on his desk. "It's late, Rosemary. Why don't you go home, think about this and come back tomorrow?"

"I won't be able to sleep. Please, read them again. I'll pay you the same, triple, to read them again."

"Rosemary, that's six hundred dollars. Are you sure you want me to do this again? You're very upset. Are you sure you can handle this?"

Rosemary shrugged out of her suit jacket. She ran her fingers through her messy hair, making it worse. "You just rocked my nice beautiful world from under me. Of course I'm sure. I'm tougher than I look. Now do it!"

Forty minutes later, James gathered up his cards as Rosemary burst into tears. "What the hell does all this mean?"

James struggled for a soothing tone. "It means this is a time of transition for you. It's up to you to make sense of it all, Rosemary. I can only tell you what the cards say. Do you want me to drive you home?"

Rosemary gathered herself together. "No. I don't live that far away. I just can't believe that there wasn't one positive in the whole reading. I'm beginning to think this is all a bunch of claptrap. Mercury is in retrograde. That might account for some of the negative aspects."

She counted out six hundred-dollar bills. "I can't believe I'm paying you six hundred dollars for you to tell me my life as I know it is about to be ruined."

James pocketed the money. "Sometimes the readings are temporary, Rosemary. Sometimes they are meant as a warning to give the person time to . . . to . . . rectify certain situations."

"Well, that would be peachy-keen if I knew what the hell you were talking about, James. Rectify what? I don't know what any of this is all about," Rosemary lied again as she fished around in her bag for her car keys. "I feel like evil forces are out to get me."

James debated for a few seconds before he responded. "Rosemary, that's not what the cards said. Weren't you listening? The cards indicate that there is an evil force whirling about you. You have to find a way to purge it or succumb to it."

"That's garbage. Do I look evil to you? Well, I'm not. I never heard such rubbish in my life. I guess I should thank you for doing this so late at night."

James shrugged. He couldn't wait for tomorrow when he would go back to work at his nice normal job in the deli department of the Publix supermarket where he didn't have to deal with people like Rosemary. Tarot card reading was just a side-

line for him, something he really enjoyed doing
for friends. It was an easy way to supplement his income. He had to admit that the two readings he'd
conducted tonight were the two worst he'd ever
done. Rosemary wasn't the only one who was upset.
Who *was* this strange woman who wanted to have
her cards read every ten days or so? When he had
finally bolted the door behind her, he slumped
against it. He hoped she would never come back.
He sprinted toward his bedroom, shed his clothes
and hit the shower.

A while later, a towel wrapped around his middle, James gathered up the cards, tossed them into
a trash bag and carried it out to the hall and the
laundry chute. Now, he was rid of her. First thing
tomorrow morning he was going to call the phone
company and request an unlisted number.

Rosemary let herself into the house. She walked
over to the alarm pad and was stunned to see that
it wasn't armed.

"Bobby! Are you here!" she shouted, not caring
if she woke him up. When there was no response,
she ran through the house calling her husband's
name over and over. She blinked when she saw his
empty bedroom. She ran to the office, turning on
lights as she went. His side of the home office was
even neater than before because everything was
gone.

Bobby was gone! And he hadn't bothered to set
the alarm. He knew how paranoid she was about the
security system. He never forgot to set the alarm,
nor did she. This was Bobby's way of thumbing his
nose at her.

Rosemary sat down, still wearing her coat, still holding her purse. Her gaze dropped to the bottom drawer of her desk. She opened it with her foot, looked inside. It didn't look like anything was disturbed. Or was it? Weren't the sticky pads stacked up the last time she'd opened it?

She slid off the chair, removed the drawer and stared down at the floorboards. They didn't look like they'd been touched. Unwilling to take any chances, she lifted them up and stared down at the safe. Her cold fingers turned the dial. When she saw that everything was as she'd left it, her sigh was so loud, it startled her. Satisfied, she closed the safe and returned the drawer to the desk. She ran down the stairs and out to the foyer to set the alarm. Bobby had stacked the mail on the foyer table. She shrugged out of her coat, gathered up the mail and walked back upstairs. It was past midnight; time to go to bed. If she took a couple of Xanax she *might* be able to relax enough to fall asleep.

Her nerves twanging all over the place, she ran a bath. While the water was running, she poured in almost a full bottle of avocado bath salts, which were guaranteed to eliminate stress completely. She didn't believe it for a minute. While the bath foamed and bubbled, she went back downstairs for a bottle of wine and a fine crystal glass. She rummaged around in one of the kitchen drawers where Bobby kept his cigarettes. She stuck them in her pocket as she headed back up the stairs. She didn't smoke but tonight she needed *something*.

Diane. That was the toddler's name. The name that wasn't on the aged Polaroid. The name she'd deliberately blocked from her memory. A name she never ever said aloud. And now she couldn't get the name out of her mind.

Rosemary was about to step into the deep tub when she remembered the mail. Naked, she walked back to the office to pick up the slim bundle. It was probably all bills. Still, opening bills was normal. It was something she did most nights when she took the time to run a bath instead of taking a quick shower.

Sinking down into the silky wetness, Rosemary sighed. Now, if she could just shift her tortured emotions into the neutral zone, maybe the Xanax, the wine and a cigarette would help. She flipped through the mail, seeing nothing that needed her immediate attention, until she saw the plain white legal-looking envelope. The same kind of envelope that had come to the office. She sat bolt upright, bubbles all about her as she ripped at the envelope.

It was a newspaper clipping this time. A picture of her walking up the courthouse steps with a cane and a brace wrapped around her neck, a brave smile on her face. Someone had scrawled the words *liar* and *thief* across the article in red ink. She felt the same white-hot rage that she had experienced at the office. In the blink of an eye, Rosemary was out of the tub. Dripping water and bubbles all over the floor, she ran to the toilet, ripping the article to shreds. She flushed it, her eyes murderous. Then, when the water ran clear, she flushed it again and again before she crumpled to her feet, beating at the tile floor, crying hysterically.

Who was doing this to her? Isabelle Flanders,

that must be who. But maybe it wasn't Isabelle. Maybe it was Bobby. Or maybe that crazy grandmother who had cursed her out in court that day . . . No, it was Isabelle Flanders trying to make a comeback at her expense.

She reached for a wad of toilet tissue and blew her nose. "Well, we'll just see about that, Isabelle! I'm one person you don't want to mess around with. You should have learned your lesson the first time."

The wine, the Xanax, and the cigarettes forgotten, Rosemary went into her bedroom to get a nightgown. She cursed when she realized she hadn't dried off. Bubbles were still stuck to her body. She stomped back to the bathroom and rinsed off in the shower. She dried off, powdered herself and then pulled on a fresh nightgown. She was finally about to crawl into bed when the phone rang. Her eyes narrowed, her hands shaking, she picked up the receiver. She didn't offer a greeting.

"Whoever this is, it had better be good; it's after midnight."

"I'm returning your calls, Rosemary, all fifty of them. What is it you want?"

"Oh, it's you!" Rosemary screeched. "Where are you, Bobby? Do you know what time it is? Why are you sending me that garbage in the mail? I want an answer and I want it right now!"

Bobby's voice was soft, almost gentle. "Why is it always about what you want, Rosemary? It's none of your business where I am. You never cared before. Of course I know what time it is. You said you wanted me to call you as soon as I got your message. I just checked my messages. My cell was off, being charged, so I didn't have it with me—not that that's any of your business. I haven't sent you anything in the mail. Why would I send you something in the mail? So, there's your answer. Now, if there's nothing else, I'm going to bed. You should go to bed yourself. Don't you need your beauty sleep?"

"You're with *her*, aren't you? You sneak! You sleaze! How dare you humiliate me like this? How dare you, Bobby! Another thing, why didn't you turn on the alarm when you left today? This is my house and you know how I feel about keeping the alarm on."

Bobby never lost his patience, knowing his calm voice would only irritate his wife further. "I'm not going to dignify that ridiculous question about Isabelle with a response. I didn't turn the alarm on because it was turned off when I went into the house. I thought you didn't want it on. You were the last one to leave this morning, so I assumed you left it off for a reason."

"You liar! I distinctly remember setting the alarm. Do you know how I remember? I remember because I nicked my new manicure and I got angry over it. What do you have to say to that, Bobby Harcourt?"

"Not much. The alarm was off, that's all I can tell you. I'm going to hang up now. From here on in, it's not a good idea to call me. Have your lawyer talk to my lawyer. Good night, Rosemary."

Rosemary hung up the phone. Damn, now she had a full-blown headache. She sat on the edge of the bed, her head clasped on her hands. If there was one thing she could say about Bobby, it was that he wasn't a liar. If it wasn't Bobby who sent the picture and the article, then it had to be Isabelle.

"You bitch!" Rosemary seethed as she struggled with the covers and her pillow. "You just don't know who you're messing with, Isabelle Flanders."

Eleven

Ted Robinson, his eyes on the weather outside his apartment, slurped at his morning coffee, his two cats cuddled in his lap. He could stay home today and work—if there was anything to work on. Life and news in the city had been so boring for the entire month, it was as though Washington had taken a break from life. Even Maggie complained about the lack of political gossip—unless you counted the newsworthy item that made the front page of the *Post* when Senator Candice Mitchell's button gave way on her slacks, revealing that she wore zebra-striped thong underwear. Another two lines explained that Senator Mitchell was fifty-eight and if she kept a secret like thong underwear, what else did she keep secret from the Hill and her constituents? Maggie Spritzer said she was almost embarrassed to report the tripe but hey, she said, the world has a right to know what the senator from Delaware wears under her clothes.

They should have had a good laugh over that

but they didn't. Maggie was following him, sneaking around, trying to get the goods on him. He'd always been vigilant when covering or investigating a story, but with Maggie in the picture, creating his sexual epiphany, things were not going smoothly.

Then there was Jack Emery. Ted sneezed and scowled deeply. He knew he was catching a cold and it was all Jack's fault. Everything he was going through was Jack's fault, and that included his sexual epiphany.

His coffee finished, Ted dumped Minnie and Mickey on the floor. They hissed their disapproval before they leaped back onto the couch. Ted shuffled to the kitchen to refill his cup. He added three sugar doughnuts to his plate and two cat treats laced with catnip. The cats were still hissing when he plopped back down on the sofa. Everyone knew the sofa belonged to Mickey and Minnie; the chair belonged to Ted. Both cats refused the treats as they eyed the doughnuts.

"All right, all right, I'll move. You can have the couch. All these cat hairs are making me sneeze anyway." He tossed the two cat treats onto the sofa and then moved over to the chair that for some reason the cats didn't like. He ate and drank, his thoughts on what had happened the night before, his eyes on the stormy weather outside.

The phone rang just as Ted stuffed one of the mini sugar doughnuts into his mouth. He grabbed for the receiver and made a noise that sounded like some kind of alien greeting.

"It's Maggie, Ted. I was wondering if you'd like to catch some breakfast?"

Jack Emery's words of advice of—*play hard to get*

once in a while—sounded in his brain. Not that he ever paid attention to what Jack said. Ted swallowed the doughnut and said, "Can't. Sorry." Never, Jack said, ask for a rain check.

"Oh. Aren't you going in today?"

"Nope. I'm hanging out with Mickey and Minnie. It's Friday," Ted said as if that explained everything. "Besides, it's raining like hell out there and I think I'm catching a cold." According to Jack, this was where she would volunteer to bring him some aspirin and chicken soup.

"Are you afraid you'll melt in the rain? Do you want me to bring you some chicken soup?"

Ted grinned and snorted to himself. Old Jack was only half right. "Nah, I got it covered. There's a deli on the corner and they deliver."

"I could bring you some aspirin," Maggie said. "Guys never remember to buy aspirin. You'll probably need some cough medicine, too."

OK, so Jack was *always* right. Well not quite. He hadn't mentioned the cough medicine. "Got that covered, too. Bought a bottle of both last week, but thanks for the offer." Ted felt so smug with his quick-witted response that he tilted the recliner back too far and spilled coffee all over himself. Minnie was on him like a shot, licking it up.

"Are you blowing me off, Robinson?"

The recliner shot bolt upright as he tried to think of a response. Now *that* hadn't come up in any conversations he'd had with Jack. Clearly, he was on his own. He needed to be cool here, play her like a violin—another one of Jack's tidbits of advice. He thought he would try being cagey.

"Now, why would you ask me something like that?"

"I hope you get pneumonia!" Maggie screeched in his ear before she ended the call. Ted looked at the phone, heard the dial tone. He was forced to admit to himself that Maggie Spritzer was first and foremost a reporter. Like she gave a shit about whether he had chicken soup, aspirin or cough medicine. He might be dumb about women but he was smart enough to know that Maggie only wanted to get into his backpack while all he wanted was to get into her pants. He guffawed at his astute insight. Good old Jack would clap him on the back and say something stupid like "Way to go, big guy!" Oh, yeah, good old Jack could say that; his dick wasn't hanging out to dry. "I hate you, Jack!" Ted muttered.

He cleaned up the sticky mess on his recliner before he changed his clothes. Just for the hell of it he checked his medicine cabinet. No cough syrup. No aspirin, either. He called the deli on the corner and asked for the soup of the day. Broccoli cheese. Ted groaned as he poured the last of the coffee into a clean cup. "I really do hate you, Jack."

Ted walked into his bedroom, which doubled as a home office. He looked around, making a mental note to tidy up one of these days. He sat down, turned on his computer, and went to work. He knew he was on to something but before he could really make sense of anything, he would have to have a little talk with Jack. Maybe a big talk.

With court dark on Friday, Jack Emery felt surrounded with paperwork as he growled and cursed at his underlings.

"This isn't summer camp, people. This is the

goddamn District Attorney's office. Now get your asses in gear and let's play catch-up here. No one goes home today until this," he said, pointing to the pile of folders on his desk, "gets squared away. That does not mean we transfer it to someone else's desk, it means we complete it and file it appropriately. No one goes out to lunch, either. Now move, before I really get mad."

When in authority, delegate. He just loved Fridays. He was already looking forward to a long, leisurely lunch all by himself so he could sit and daydream about Nikki and the night they'd spent together. He was shrugging into his already-drenched raincoat that hadn't had a chance to dry after this morning's race from the parking lot when he saw Ted Robinson lurking out in the hallway. His mood immediately turned sour.

"I guess we're doing lunch, huh? Your turn to buy, Mr. DA," Ted called from his position in the open doorway.

Jack reached for his umbrella. There was no sense fighting it. He'd have to do his daydreaming about Nikki later. "People are going to start talking about us if we keep meeting up and eating together all the time." At Ted's dumb look he hastened to clarify what he meant. "You know, like we're gay or something."

"What's the *something*?"

"Oh, shit, I don't know. I was just . . . Never mind. What do you want this time?" Jack said, trying to hold the umbrella over both their heads.

A strong gust of wind slammed into them, saving Ted from a reply. Jack's umbrella sailed upward to join three others as they whipped across the lumbering gray sky.

The District Attorney and the reporter soldiered on, valiantly fighting the driving wind and rain. When they finally reached Squire's Pub, both men were soaked to the skin. Inside it was wall to wall with wet people grousing and cursing at the weather. Jack heard someone say this was the worst February in forty years as he made his way to the back of the pub to find a lone booth with a reserved sign on the table.

"I called ahead. The owner tries to accommodate the DA's office," Jack said by way of explanation. Both men slipped into the booth. A waitress appeared almost immediately.

Jack didn't bother with the menu. "I'll have a bowl of chili, a cheeseburger and a double order of fries. Bring a draft with that." When Ted started to sneeze, Jack ordered for him, too. He sat back and waited until Ted was comfortable. He knew something was wrong; he could sense it, feel it, smell it. Whatever was about to come out of Ted's mouth, he knew he wasn't going to like it. "Well?"

"I thought we were friends, Jack."

"We are. You feeling insecure or something? Where are you going with this, Ted?"

"You know what, Jack? You need to stop blowing that phony sunshine up my ass or else I'm going to charge you for a sun umbrella."

"Huh? What *are* you talking about?"

Ted snorted, a hateful sound. "Like you don't know. You're just renting the house from Nikki Quinn. Yeah, right. I saw you, Jack. I saw Nikki. You were together last night. You've been trying to snooker me and I fell for it. I believed you because I thought you were my friend. My mistake, I admit. You've been running back to those women, telling them everything I've been telling you, right? Don't make me even madder by denying it. You joined forces with that crew, didn't you? Didn't you, Jack?"

Jack felt so light-headed he thought he was going to pass out right in the booth. Man, that would look super on the evening news. "So I was right, you've been following me. Well, Mr. Ace Reporter, ask yourself this. If I was doing what you said I was doing, do you think I'd be stupid enough to lead you to the house? I'm a District Attorney, for Christ's sake. I would have dumped you and met Nikki somewhere else. You need to get real here, Ted.

"Yeah, Nikki came to the house to collect the rent. She called me at work and asked me to pick up some dinner. What's wrong with that? I paid her the rent, she paid for half the dinner, we ate together. She cleaned up. I went to bed and she went to bed. Separate rooms, Ted. She made coffee this morning, offered me a cup, which I declined. End of story."

"Bull*shit*!" Ted said.

"Sounds like you're calling me a liar, buddy."

"Sounds like you're blowing that phoney sunshine up my ass again. If the shoe fits, wear it, buddy!" Ted snarled. "You're in bed with that pack of jackals out at Pinewood."

Jack felt his blood run cold. "Hey, I'm good but I'm not *that* good. I hope you aren't planning on telling any of this to my main squeeze, Marcey Watts. She's jealous as hell. By the way, just for the record, Nikki has been seeing some guy named Adam Jester. You might want to check that out, too."

Ted leaned back when the waitress placed his

food in front of him. He wondered if he'd be able to eat it. His throat felt scratchy. The spicy chili might burn his throat. He dipped the spoon into the bowl. He looked over at Jack, who was already wolfing down his food. "You're lying," he said coldly. "This is where the rubber meets the road, Jack. Either you tell me the truth right now or I'm gonna hang you and those women out to dry. Your call." He was right, the chili *was* burning his throat.

Jack raised his head. They were eyeball to eyeball. "I did tell you the truth."

Ted slapped some bills on the table as he fought to put on his wet jacket. He didn't say a word.

Jack continued to eat the spicy-hot chilli. His eyes burned and then started to water. He couldn't ever remember feeling as bad as he did at this moment.

Rosemary Hershey tried to avoid the flooded areas of the parking lot. She should have had more sense than to wear designer shoes with open toes and high heels. And she didn't have a spare pair of shoes at the office, either. She was halfway across the lot when she remembered the golf shoes that she had in the trunk of her car. She grimaced at the thought of wearing golf shoes with her Donna Karan outfit. If she didn't get out of this rain, the pricey suit would be as wet as her shoes and she'd be hiding out in her office in her underwear.

It was hard going walking into the driving wind and holding an umbrella at the same time. Eventually her problem was solved when the umbrella was wrenched from her hand. She watched in horror as it bounced across the parking lot and landed

on top of a green SUV. Now she really was drenched.
A howl of outrage escaped her lips as she ran the
rest of the way to the front door where she met the
mailman dressed in rain garb from head to toe.
He held the door for her and Rosemary rushed
through, gasping with the effort, rain dripping
down her face, her makeup smeared, her hair
clinging to her head and the sides of her face in
wet strands.

"Do you want to take the mail, Miss Hershey?
It's light today."

"Do I look like I want to take the mail? No, I
don't want the mail. Give it to the receptionist,"
she said coldly. She was halfway across the lobby
when she remembered the type of things she was
getting in the mail. "Never mind, give it to me!"

As she squished and dripped her way down the
hall to her office, Rosemary pawed through the
mail. She sucked in her breath when she saw another plain white envelope. This one had been
sent from Springfield.

In the office, Rosemary slammed the door shut
and kicked off her ruined shoes. She dumped the
light load of mail and her purse on Bobby's clean
desk before she wiggled out of her wet coat. Then
she proceeded to dry her face and hair with wads
of paper towels. She felt cold, wet and clammy. She
hissed to the emptiness around her, "I'm pissed to
the teeth and I didn't even open the goddamn envelope yet!"

She sucked in her breath as she ripped at the
white envelope. Another picture. A recent Polaroid.
Tommy. For one wild second, she felt like her eyeballs were on fire. Where did that name come
from? Yesterday she hadn't known the boy's name.

Diane and Tommy. She sat down, the Polaroid shot clasped in her hand. She reached for her glasses to see the picture better. It showed a sturdy little boy holding some sort of toy. He looked well nourished, well dressed. She peered closely at the background to see if she could tell where the picture was taken. There was nothing to see except a kitchen table with a pile of school books and a window over the sink.

Trembling all over, Rosemary chewed on her lower lip. Had this picture come from the grandmother? Or had it come from someone else who had a close association with Isabelle Flanders? Not Bobby, she was sure of that. Who did that leave besides Isabelle? That stupid reporter! Where did the grandmother and the boy live? If she'd ever known, she couldn't remember now. Her eyes burned with hatred as she slid the picture into one of Bobby's desk drawers. She wasn't about to cave in to someone's blackmail scheme, because that's what this was all about. She was sure of it.

Rosemary started to pace her office. If she went on the prowl for information now, how was she going to design a horse farm? She had to decide what her priorities were.

She opened the door to her office and called over to the secretary she'd shared with Bobby.

"Call a staff meeting right now."

She would have her two associates and the promising intern start on the design. If it came out of her office, she reasoned, it was hers.

Twelve

The room was dark, the new day beyond the window darker still. Two hours to go till dawn. Myra squinted at the red numerals on the digital clock on the nightstand.

"Oh, Charles, don't tell me you're getting up already." Myra struggled from her warm cocoon to prop herself up on one elbow. Alarm was in her voice. "Is anything wrong, dear?"

"No, no, go back to sleep, Myra. Today is a very busy day. I want to get an early start and you know we don't want the girls asking questions about my activities today."

Myra rubbed at her eyes, trying to fully wake up. "Yes, of course. I'll join you downstairs. Tea this morning, Charles. Later, when the girls get up, I'll make coffee. Do you still think you'll be home this evening?"

"That's my plan. We have it all under control, Myra. I'm on a tight schedule so I can't dilly-dally. The Prime Minister has carved ten minutes out of his busy schedule to speak with me and I must be on time." His eyes twinkled when he turned on the lamp on his side of the big sleigh bed. "His aide told me he has brought along a personal message from my dear friend."

"Oh, Charles, how exciting! A personal message from the Queen! That has to be akin to being invited to the President's personal quarters for a sit-down." Myra swung her legs over the side of the bed and reached for her robe. She quickly adjusted the thermostat before heading for the bathroom. Charles was already in the shower and he was *singing*. She smiled but couldn't make out the words. Probably some cowboy ditty. Charles had always loved the American cowboys of the Wild West and had watched every movie ever made, some more than once. One year she'd given him a pearl-handled six gun and holster for Christmas. He'd worn it for weeks, practicing his draw until the novelty had worn off. She knew the gun and the holster were still two of his favorite possessions. Dear, sweet Charles. She loved him so much she ached at times with the feeling. Sir Charles, knighted by the Queen herself. Myra smiled. Imagine taking a shower next to royalty. She laughed then, a sound of pure mirth as she stepped into her own shower, remembering the time she'd bought him a faux crown studded with paste jewels and told him he had to wear it in the shower. They had laughed for hours over that scene. Charles was such a good sport.

Twenty minutes later, Myra was dressed, her pearls around her neck but without makeup, joined Charles in the kitchen for her first cup of tea of the day. She eyed the stack of papers on the kitchen table that Charles was busily stuffing into his briefcase. He noticed the worry in Myra's eyes.

"We have to do this, dear. It's called planning for the future in case things go awry. After today, we can forget all about it until such time. We may never need to act on today's activities, but things will be in place. It's as foolproof as it can be, Myra."

"I know that. But what if . . ."

"If the other players don't do their part? That's a chance we have to take. Right now, that simply is not on my radar screen. I don't want it to be on yours either. How do you like this breakfast blend of tea?"

"It's fine. I think lemon spoils it, though. You're just making conversation, Charles, so I won't worry."

"How astute of you, dear. I really must go. I'm catching the first shuttle to New York. I'll be back in Washington before noon. You can call me on the cell if it's an emergency. Otherwise, I'll see you this evening. Come on now, stiff upper lip."

Myra held up her face for Charles's kiss. "I miss you already. Go!"

She looked down at the tea in her cup after the door closed behind Charles. When she was certain he couldn't see what she was doing, she dumped the tea in the sink and got out a good old American Lipton tea bag.

With nothing to do until the girls woke up, Myra treated herself to a cigarette. She coughed and sputtered but she kept puffing away until a blue haze filled the kitchen. She'd long ago given up the ugly habit, but once in a while she smoked a cigarette to remind her of why she'd given them up in the first place. Charles called it self-torture.

The other reason was that she was nervous, wondering if the plans she and Charles were putting into place would come back to bite her on the rear end, as Kathryn would put it. Only Kathryn hadn't said *rear end*; she'd been a lot more graphic. And as Charles said, if nothing ever came of their plans, so much the better.

Everything always came down to Charles. Without him, the Sisterhood couldn't function. It was his expertise, his worldwide connections, his reputation, that had gotten them this far. Without a doubt, Charles was the marvel in marvelous. The really wonderful part was that he loved doing what he was doing for her and the girls. He was, as he put it, back in the game. The game of espionage and covert operations that he'd had to retire from when his cover was blown years ago. He had been spirited away to the States with a little help from MI6 and the Queen. Charles had told her it was done all the time, on both sides of the pond.

Myra got up to fix herself a second cup of tea, wondering what time the girls would be getting up. The girls, meaning Alexis and Kathryn. Isabelle was staying in the District and Nikki had gone home late the previous afternoon. She hadn't seen Yoko in three days. She made a mental note to call her and then remembered that Yoko had called them last night just as she and Charles were getting ready for bed. She'd said she would be here in time for breakfast, which would be shortly. She should give some thought to breakfast. She hated cooking and somehow managed to either overcook, undercook or burn whatever she tried to make. Charles, however, was a gourmet chef, among his many other accomplishments. Maybe, if she waited long enough, Kathryn or Alexis would come downstairs and volunteer.

Myra sensed movement out of the corner of her eye. Then she felt a wet nose on her arm. Murphy. Another wet nose. Grady. She smiled as she petted both dogs and then let them out just as Yoko drove through the gate. Shivering, with her arms crossed over her chest, Myra waited in the doorway for Yoko to get out of her car and do a little dance for the dogs. They thought she wanted to play. She ran after them, zigzagging this way and that to the dogs' delight. Once, she'd been afraid of them, but that was a long time ago.

Winded, Yoko ran to the door, hugged Myra and then slipped out of her coat. She found two dog biscuits in one of the pockets and held them out to the dogs, who took them daintily and then ran back upstairs.

"Can I make you some tea, Yoko?"

"No, thank you. Where is everyone?"

"We're here!" Kathryn said, bounding down the steps, closely followed by Alexis. Both women were still in their flannel pajamas. "I'm starved!" she said.

"Me too," Alexis said, looking around for some sign of food.

"Charles had to leave early this morning. We must fend for ourselves. How does fresh fruit and a bagel sound?"

"Terrible. I was thinking more along the lines of a breakfast of champions," Kathryn said as she headed for the refrigerator. "Bacon, sausage, pancakes, scrambled eggs. Toast with soft butter and jam. I'll make it. Alexis, you do the coffee and the toast."

"I have good news," Yoko said.

The three women turned in her direction. Yoko rarely volunteered anything. They were all eyes and ears.

"My husband left me!"

"That's *good* news?" Alexis said.

"I don't understand," Myra said. "Are you saying you are happy that your husband . . . ah . . . left you?"

Yoko's almond-shaped eyes sparkled. "I am delirious with joy over his leaving. Actually, he is gone already. That is why I wasn't able to be here these past few days."

Kathryn slapped bacon onto the griddle. "Did he leave because of us? Because you spend so much time out here at the farm?"

"No, not at all. He was always glad when I wasn't around. It was an arranged marriage. My aunts negotiated with my husband's father. Money changed hands. It is our way. The old way. My husband and I had no say. He was unhappy. I was unhappy. He went to St. Louis where he has friends. He shook my hand when he left. It is so wonderful not to share a bathroom with him. I cleaned and scrubbed for three days. There is no sign now that he ever lived in the house."

"I'll be damned! Why didn't you ever tell us you weren't happy?" Kathryn asked.

"You never asked," Yoko said smartly. "I am telling you now."

"What about the nursery, the flower shop? Do you get to keep it?"

"Of course. My husband does not like working with manure. He doesn't like to smell the earth, the scent of the flowers. He said he got sick every time he had to go into the greenhouses. He's going to be a dancer on the stage. He's very graceful. And he doesn't like women."

"Uh-huh," was all Kathryn could say.

"I am now free as a bird. I love the feeling. I plan to ask Nikki to handle our divorce. How long do you think it will be before I can seriously start to look for a boyfriend? The kind who will shower me with love, appreciate my new . . . ah . . . boobs and hold my hand when we walk in the rain. It is not necessary for him to bring me flowers. I do like chocolates, though." Yoko rolled her eyes and started to giggle.

Kathryn eyed her sister. Tongue in cheek, she said, "Any day now, kiddo. If he's gone, you can start looking today. Who's going to run the business?"

"Lu Chow, Myra's gardener. Don't you remember? Myra loaned him to me back in the beginning when I first joined the Sisterhood. When it comes to the earth and plants, Mr. Chow has magic in his hands. And he has a very handsome nephew, as well as many uncles and cousins. My business is in good hands. It frees me up so that I can be more active with the Sisterhood."

"You little devil," Alexis said, clapping Yoko on the back.

"That is a compliment, no?"

Alexis laughed out loud as she hitched up the bottom of her pajamas. "The best kind, girlie."

"My goodness," Myra managed to say.

"I was hoping we could celebrate later today

when I return from town. I have been looking forward to this day since the day I got married. I want to celebrate with my friends."

The women hooted with laughter, Myra's laughter the loudest.

It was five minutes shy of ten o'clock when Yoko, dressed to the nines, walked down the stairs of the farmhouse to seek Myra's approval.

"Allow me to introduce Mrs. Kim Yee, who is wealthy beyond wealthy and who has an appointment with one Bobby Harcourt at eleven o'clock. There, she will be asking him to design a western-style house that she wants to have built in Yokohama, Japan, as well as a beach house on the Chesapeake for when she and her husband are in the States. Mrs. Kim Yee is also a not-too-distant relative of the Yee royal family in Japan," Alexis said.

Myra gaped as she fiddled with the pearls around her neck. "You look the part, dear. My diamonds look so well on you. It is my understanding that Miss Hershey is a designer's dream and it has been said that jewelry stores call her on her private number when a new piece comes in. The woman has very expensive tastes. But she can't hold a candle to you, my dear, and she will know that the minute she sees you."

Yoko giggled. "Thank you, Myra. My chauffeur-driven limousine will be here within minutes to pick me up. What if Miss Hershey isn't there?"

Kathryn clucked her tongue. "You only do business with the owner, meaning Miss Hershey. Mr. Harcourt is a partner and that's all well and good, but before you make a decision, you want to talk to *both* partners. You want her to think you have money to burn so you can be as demanding as hell. Play it up. Also, don't forget to wave that little Post-it with Isabelle Flanders's name and phone number on it. You will not be making a decision until you speak with a second architect. You tell them both you've lived here long enough to know that's how it is done in America. Two bids; two estimates. Neither one of them can fault you for that. Rosemary might, however, bad-mouth Isabelle," Kathryn said.

"You'll be getting to her office just about the time the mail is delivered. Keep your eyes and ears open. Today she will be getting the newspaper clipping of the picture the *Post* ran of the Myers family funeral. We think that picture is really going to spook her. Especially since she didn't attend the funeral. She was out of the hospital by the time the coroner released the bodies for burial and there was no reason for her not to attend, since her claim was that Isabelle caused the accident. The newspapers made more than a few snide comments. The grandmother just said she was disappointed."

"I can do this," Yoko said, slipping into a pure-white cashmere coat that shrieked dollar signs. The diamonds that Myra had loaned to Yoko sparkled under the overhead lighting. Yoko picked up the ostrich-skin briefcase that shrieked just as many dollar signs as the cashmere coat.

"Go get 'em, girl," Alexis said and grinned as she pointed to the overhead security monitor. "Your chariot awaits. In other words, your limo is here. Call us the minute you leave the office."

"I will do that," Yoko said as she sashayed out the door to the waiting limousine.

When the car had driven back through the gates, the women looked at one another. Kathryn and Alexis burst out laughing at the same time.

"I had no clue that Yoko . . . I thought she was happily married. And she's in the market for a boyfriend. Who knew?" Alexis quipped, laughing heartily.

"There is more to that little lady than meets the eye. She's got that martial arts stuff down to a science. I sure as hell wouldn't want to meet up with her in a dark alley even if Murphy was with me. Did you ever see how she can freeze Murphy just by staring him down? When she does that, he whines."

"It's the inner peace that is instilled in those who study martial arts," Myra said. "I saw a documentary on it a while back. The mindset of the student was incredible."

"How's it going with Isabelle?" Alexis asked.

"Very well. She called yesterday to say they're doing the pretty stuff today—installing the carpeting, polishing the marble, hanging the drapes and delivering the furniture. She thinks everything will be completed by the end of the day. Tomorrow morning, if things go well, she's open for business."

"Let the games begin!" Kathryn said.

Thirteen

Yoko garnered more than one appraising look as she walked through the lobby to the receptionist in the architects' office.

"I have an appointment with Mr. Harcourt. My name is Kim Yee."

"Ah . . . yes . . . well, Mr. Harcourt isn't . . ."

The lobby door swooped open. Footsteps could be heard on the tiled floor. "Ah, Mrs. Yee. I'm Bobby Harcourt. If you'll follow me, please."

The receptionist reared up and was half out of her seat when she said, "But Miss Hershey said . . ."

Bobby waved airily, his woodsy cologne trailing behind him as he ushered Yoko down a carpeted hallway. He knew that Rosemary already knew he was in the building with a client. He had no doubt there would be a blowup any second now. Within moments of seating Yoko in the conference room the phone on the wall rang.

"Excuse me, Mrs. Yee."

Yoko nodded as she opened the ostrich brief-case. She strained to hear Bobby's end of the conversation, but the words were indistinguishable. Bobby excused himself again and walked out of the office, closing the door behind him.

Yoko was off the chair in the blink of an eye and ran to the door. She cracked it open a mere inch as she strained to hear what was going on outside. A shrill, ugly-sounding voice ricocheted down the hall. Rosemary. Then she heard Bobby's voice, deep and even, explaining that Mrs. Yee was his client.

"Before you stomped out of this office, Mrs. Yee would have been *our* client. You left, Bobby. That means Mrs. Yee is *my* client now. She's sitting in *my* building, in *my* conference room. Your half is half of the business, not half of the building. It was your decision to leave. You said you were filing for divorce. You can't just walk back in here and act like you belong. Get out! I mean it. I want you out of here."

"Fine, but Mrs. Yee goes with me."

"Oh, no. She stays. I'll deal with Mrs. Yee."

"Why don't we ask Mrs. Yee what she wants to do? It is, after all, her decision. By the way, Rosemary, before you meet my client, I suggest you do something about your appearance. I would hate to have her frightened to death. What's wrong with you? Are you sick?"

"You wish I was sick, you bastard. And don't tell me what to do."

"Whatever you want. I hate to keep new clients waiting. Either you join us or I will take Mrs. Yee with me when I leave. I didn't have a number to call her, otherwise I wouldn't have met her here. It's your call, Rosemary."

Yoko scurried back to her seat at the conference table, her hands folded demurely in her lap as she waited. She hoped she could remember everything she'd just heard. She turned when the door opened, a small smile on her lips. She made a production of pulling back the sleeve of the cashmere coat to reveal a diamond-studded Presidential watch. She allowed a frown to build on her face. Both architects correctly interpreted the frown. The prospective client was rapidly getting pissed off.

Bobby took the initiative. "Mrs. Yee, I'd like to introduce my partner, Rosemary Hershey."

Yoko turned to stare up at the tall woman standing next to Bobby Harcourt. She looked nothing like the pictures Charles had shown her. In those pictures Rosemary Hershey looked glamorous, well dressed and bejeweled. What she saw now was hair whose roots needed touching up, makeup that looked like it had been put on with a trowel, dark half-moons under both eyes, a manicure that was chipped at the tips, and a sloppy outfit that looked like it had come out of a thrift store.

"I am most pleased to make your acquaintance, Miss Hershey." Yoko made no move to offer her hand. Instead, she inclined her head slightly to acknowledge the woman's presence. She waited to see what would happen next. She let her gaze drop to the diamond-studded watch again. When nothing happened, Yoko asked if there was a problem.

"In a manner of speaking, Mrs. Yee, the short answer is yes," Bobby explained. "Technically, I am still a partner in this business and will remain so until the partnership is dissolved legally. You contacted this office and specifically asked to make an appointment with me. You had no way of knowing I would be leaving the firm when you made the appointment. That's the reason I came back this morning to meet with you. Miss Hershey feels and believes you should stay here. I am willing to work with you at my new quarters. The decision must be yours," Bobby said.

"My husband, unfortunately, does not like dealing with women. He is . . . how do you say . . . stuck with me. He allows me to do these little things from time to time because I have become a little Americanized whereas he has not. Let me show you what I want. Perhaps when you see the pictures I brought with me it will allow you both to decide who is best to represent me and do what my husband and I wish."

Yoko opened the ostrich briefcase and withdrew several pictures that Charles had gotten from somewhere. He'd told her the minute the architects saw the pictures they would immediately translate them to square feet so they could compute their fee. She wasn't sure but she thought Rosemary Hershey sucked in her breath at what she now saw. Bobby Harcourt, on the other hand, was staring at the pictures with questions in his eyes. He was seeing a challenge. His wife was seeing dollar signs.

"How big is the lot in Japan, Mrs. Yee?" Bobby asked.

"What you here in America would call fifteen acres. My husband and I were thinking twenty-five thousand square feet for the house. A suite for my husband and me. Another for our two children, a boy and a girl. One for my husband's parents. We would like a tennis court and a swimming pool for the children. A pool house and all of the things the resorts have here in America. With an outside kitchen. In addition to the main house, we will need separate structures on the property for our servants. A six-car garage. Privacy is our primary concern. We would want security fencing, but it must be decorative. While my husband has not adopted American ways, he does like American architecture. My husband would like a home theater and a large library. My own personal wish is for a magnificent bathroom. I love to indulge myself." Yoko tittered behind her hands, holding them at an angle so that Rosemary couldn't miss the diamond rings on her fingers.

"It's all doable, Mrs. Yee. What about the beach house?" Bobby asked as he continued to scrutinize the pictures on the table.

"Ah, yes, the beach house. Something comfortable. Not too large, perhaps ten thousand square feet. Some Japanese flavor to the interior but not overdone. We won't spend all that much time there, with the children in school. We are prepared to give you free rein on the building but we do want to see the design before we sign off on it."

Bobby straightened up and met Yoko's gaze. "That's also doable."

Yoko nodded as she gathered up her pictures to return them to the ostrich briefcase. "Then what is our next step? Oh dear, I forgot to tell you, I have another appointment at one o'clock. I would like an estimate by the end of the week if that's possible. Our decision will depend on the price you give me and the price the other architect gives me. Now, where is that slip of paper? Oh yes, here it is. Miss Isabelle Flanders will be your competition."

Bobby didn't miss a beat. "She's an excellent ar-

chitect, Mrs. Yee. I believe I can have what you
want by the end of the week. Let's say Friday morning around this time. We can meet for a late breakfast or an early lunch. You'll have to give me your
phone number, though."

Yoko felt a twinge of fear when she noticed the
hatred spewing from Rosemary Hershey's eyes.
She nervously rattled off the number of the cell
phone that Charles had given her. Bobby copied it
down. Yoko stood up and gathered the cashmere
coat closer about her person. Suddenly she whirled
around, her eyes narrowed, her voice colder than
steel.

"I have no desire to get caught in the middle of
whatever machinations are going on between the
two of you. I want it understood that I will be dealing with Mr. Harcourt and not you, Miss Hershey.
If that is clear, we can go ahead. I have no desire to
return to this place. There is no serenity here, no
harmony. If you'll excuse me now. It was very nice
meeting you, Mr. Harcourt." Yoko inclined her
head slightly as she made her way out of the office.
She totally ignored Rosemary Hershey.

When the door closed behind Yoko, Bobby sat
down and propped his feet on the conference
table. "Guess she told you, huh?"

Rosemary's arm swept Bobby's feet off the table.
"You're a weasel, Bobby. Legal is legal. I get half
and you get to do all the work. Assuming she picks
you over that . . . that other architect."

"Say her name, Rosemary. Say 'Isabelle Flanders.'
If I have to give you half, I'll take a pass and let
Isabelle have it. Unless, of course, my lawyer tells
me I have a shot at it. You look like you've been
rode hard and hung up wet, dear. You might want

to do something about your appearance. I think you scared off Mrs. Yee. Oh well, gotta run; I have things to do and places to go. Don't even think about pitching one of your fits because I'm not interested in your theatrics."

"You snot! You slimy snot! You don't care if Isabelle Flanders gets the job! Just to spite me, you'd give it up to her!" Rosemary screeched, her voice ringing throughout the offices. "You're seeing her again! I knew it! I knew it! I'll get you for this! Count on it!"

Bobby blinked, shrugged, and left the office. His wife was becoming unhinged. He passed the secretary in the hall. She was carrying the mail. "Anything for me?"

"No, Bobby, just stuff for Rosemary. I'll forward your mail as it comes in."

"I put a change of address in at the post office, but a few pieces might slip through from time to time. I'd appreciate it."

Inside her office, Rosemary was staring at her reflection in the mirror. Bobby was right, she looked haggard. With no sleep in four days, what did she expect? She whirled around when she heard the knock on the door, and then the sound of the door opening.

"Mail!" her secretary shouted cheerfully.

"OK, put it on the desk," Rosemary called from the bathroom. The minute the door closed, Rosemary sprinted to the desk. Her breathing was ragged as she flipped through the mail. She knew there would be another white envelope, another article or picture referring to that awful time in her life. She tossed bills, flyers and announcements on the floor as she sought the plain white envelope. When she saw it, she dropped it straightaway. What was in it today? What would she find when she got home to still another envelope? Deal with this one first, she told herself. She started to shake as she bent down to pick up the letter. In the end she had to sit down because her legs wouldn't hold her upright. She ripped and gouged at the envelope and was rewarded with a photocopy of a newspaper article along with a picture. She stared at it, her eyes rolling back in her head. She dropped the article so she could grasp the arms of the chair.

"Oh, God. Oh, God!" she whimpered as she stared down at the paper on the floor. Three yawning square holes in the ground: two large ones, one very small one. People—mourners, she supposed. Off to the side, the media. She recognized the small boy and the grandmother who had unsuccessfully fought her in court.

Rosemary dropped to the floor and grabbed the piece of paper. She shredded it and the envelope and then scrambled her way to the bathroom where she flushed both.

She looked around for her coat, slipped into it, then grabbed her purse and car keys. Her mail at home came around eleven o'clock. If there was a letter at home she would go to the police and then to Isabelle Flanders's office.

"You aren't going to get away with this, you bitch! I'll sic the police on you!"

Rosemary was still mumbling to herself as she walked down the hall, across the lobby and out to the parking lot. The receptionist shook her head from side to side as she watched her employer race out of the building. She wondered where the fire was. Then again, maybe someone died. Not that her boss would care.

By the time Rosemary reached her home she was light-headed. She fumbled in the metal box for the mail. There was nothing there apart from a Nordstrom catalog and a flyer offering ten percent off for a first visit to the Paradise Spa. No white envelope. She felt giddy and relieved.

Her key in the lock, she turned it, opened the door and almost tripped over the long, slender mailing tube that lay across the threshold. She recognized what it was immediately. She mailed blueprints in the same kind of container all the time.

Inside she disarmed the alarm system as she made her way to the kitchen she never used. She ripped at the hard plastic end cap and withdrew a set of blueprints that made her clench her jaw so hard that she chipped one of her pricey porcelain caps. She spit out the piece of enamel as she looked down at the worn, tattered, dirty set of blueprints to the name of the architect at the bottom: Isabelle Flanders. The same set of blueprints on which she'd substituted her own name. Where in the damn hell had these prints come from? She'd destroyed them all, every last set of them. Yet here she was, looking at what appeared to be the original set of working blueprints.

"This is impossible!" she screamed to the emptiness around her. "It's impossible! Do you hear me?"

Rosemary ran to the fireplace, threw the blueprints inside and struck a match. Too late, she realized it was a gas fire, not a real one. How could she have forgotten that? She'd never used it, that's

how. The small flame curled and then went out.
How was she supposed to burn these now? Her
thoughts desperate, she reached for the blueprints
and carried them up to Bobby's bathroom where
she dumped them in the bathtub. No sense in
dirtying her tub. She lit a second match, then a
third and a fourth until all four corners were flam-
ing. It took a long time for all six pages to burn.
She wondered if it was the ink that took so long to
burn.

Finally, she was left with a large square mass of
black charred paper, which meant that the middle
layers hadn't burned through. Her eyes frantic,
Rosemary looked around for something to poke at
the mess with. She settled on a toilet brush. Bits of
black ash floated upward to settle everywhere in
the immaculate bathroom. "Oh, God! Oh, God!"
she cried as she struck another match and again
watched as the blueprints burned and smoked.

Tears streaking down her cheeks, Rosemary
tried stuffing the charred mess down the bathtub
drain. The water backed up almost immediately.
Hard sobs rocked her shoulders as she then tried
to scoop up the black mess to flush it. The first
glob went down easily enough, although it turned
the white toilet black. She started to sneeze with
the smoke that was circling all around the second
floor. She should have turned on the exhaust fan.

She turned on the fan before she reached for a
second huge glob of the sodden burned blueprints. She tossed them in the toilet and flushed.
To her horror, the water swirled to the top and over-
flowed. Before she knew it, she was ankle-deep in
gushing water. She dropped to her knees and

crawled to the back of the toilet where she turned off the water. She backed out of the cramped spot and looked around at the mess she'd created.

The reflection she saw in the mirror frightened her.

Fourteen

Ted Robinson looked around the newsroom to see if there was any sign of Maggie Spritzer. But she wasn't at her computer and her desk was tidy. His gaze swept the room for a sign of the striped doughnut box. He shrugged. She was probably out chasing some gossip that would titillate her readers for days to come.

Ted hooked his foot on his chair, pulled it forward and then sat down. He slid a floppy into the hard drive and proceeded to view the contents on his monitor. It was time to stop futzing around and get down and dirty. Screw Jack Emery and their friendship. He reviewed all the notes he'd taken over the past few months before he punched up the profiles of each one of the ladies of Pinewood. When he was satisfied he knew the contents by heart, he moved on to the *Post*'s archives. He typed in the name Dr. Julia Webster. Article after article appeared, most of them dealing with the doctor's husband, Senator Webster, who, according to one

article, had dropped off the face of the earth. Dr.
Webster herself had also disappeared.

Ted scrawled a note on a yellow legal pad. *Two
missing people.* He typed in dates of the Websters'
disappearance to see what else was going on at
that time. The big HMO scandal. Now defunct.
Senator Webster's name for the Vice Presidential
nomination and the ensuing scandal about his
womanizing. Two separate scandals and yet his instincts told him they were somehow tied together.
All the parties involved had dropped out of circu-
lation, never to be seen or heard from again. Ted
made more notes on the legal pad.

He worked steadily for two hours. At one point,
when his eyes started to ache, he reached for his
glasses. He hated wearing them. Maggie said they
made him look like a retarded owl. She could have
said *a wise old owl,* but no, a retarded owl. He hunkered down and continued with his timeline of
events.

At four o'clock, Ted closed up shop and prepared to leave the office. He took a last look around
to see if there was any sign of Maggie. There wasn't.
She'd been gone all day. His gut instinct told him
she was chasing down Myra Rutledge. He, on the
other hand, was going to chase down Nikki Quinn,
Alexis Thorne and the Japanese lady. First stop:
Nikki Quinn's law offices.

Ted parked his car next to a Mercedes 500 SEL.
His little scoot-about Honda looked shabby in
comparison, but he got almost thirty miles to the
gallon so he wasn't complaining. It got him where
he had to go and it was so nondescript that no one
paid attention to it. Perfect for tailing someone.
The sleek car looked familiar for some reason. He'd

seen it recently somewhere. This was Washington, where Mercedes cars were almost like mass transit. He walked around to look at the license plate. He grinned from ear to ear when he saw the registration: # 1 AOTY. Architect of the Year. Rosemary Hershey's car. Son of a bitch! Sometimes he just managed to step into the clover over the dark-brown stuff. Talk about pure dumb luck.

Ted's mind raced. Rosemary Hershey. Isabelle Flanders. Nikki Quinn. He tried to grasp what it all meant. If Isabelle, Nikki and the others really were vigilantes and Hershey did Flanders wrong, what was she doing here with one of the vigilantes? Unless . . . unless . . . Hershey didn't know that Isabelle Flanders belonged to that particular little group.

Ted retraced his steps to his car, got in and moved three spaces away on the other side of the aisle. He had a perfect view of the Mercedes through his rearview mirror. Hell, he could just hop out and conduct his interviews right here in the parking lot.

He waited.

The clock on the dashboard said it was five-thirty-five when he saw Rosemary Hershey walk across the parking lot. He blinked twice. This haggard-looking woman dressed in baggy slacks and a denim jacket bore absolutely no resemblance to the spit-and-polish architect he'd seen at the Pioneer Club luncheon. He was out of the car in a flash. He reached the Mercedes before his quarry.

"Miss Hershey, Ted Robinson from the *Post*. I'd like to ask you a few questions about Isabelle Flanders." He leaned against the door, preventing the architect from opening it.

Rosemary clutched her purse. Ted wondered if

she'd try using it as a weapon. He prepared to duck if necessary.

"I thought I told you to stay away from me. I don't have anything to say to you. I have no comment about that woman. All of that was a long time ago and it's been settled. We've all gone on with our lives."

"Maybe so, but I have questions. I'm doing a follow-up, human interest story about how a little boy and his grandmother got screwed by the system."

"You miserable cretin! Get away from my car or I'll call the police!"

As if she was really going to call the police. Ted gambled, his reporter's instincts kicking into high gear. "And open up *that* can of worms! They'll start asking questions that will eventually lead back to that tragic accident. The police aren't stupid. They'll put two and two together and they're going to come up with four. This law firm is not on your roster of legal eagles. I checked the old records." At the look of panic in the woman's eyes, Ted threw out a wild card. "Is someone threatening you? If they are, maybe I can help."

Rosemary's voice was shaky. "Don't be ridiculous. Why would someone threaten me?"

Ted threw out a second wild card. "Maybe the person doing the threatening has some proof that the accident didn't happen the way you said it did. I heard through the grapevine that Bobby Harcourt is no longer with your firm. Is that true?"

"I don't think that's any of your business, Mr. Robinson. Nothing either one of us does is any of your business. Now, if you will excuse me . . ."

Ted stepped away from the car. "Miss Hershey, I

can be a good friend or I can be a bad enemy. Let me help you in return for an exclusive when this is over, whatever *this* is."

"No one in their right mind trusts reporters," Rosemary said as she clicked her remote and opened the door.

"The reporters were more than kind to you during the trial. They gave you so much press it was almost laughable. Here," Ted said, pulling a business card from his pocket, "take this in case you change your mind. You can call me day or night."

Rosemary turned round, her face a mask of hatred. "I'll call you when they start handing out ice water in hell. Don't hold your breath!"

"Can I quote you on everything you just said?" Ted said, flourishing a mini tape recorder he had removed from his jacket pocket.

"Go to hell, you . . . you ink blob! You print one word of that and I will sue your ass off—and that rag paper you work for."

Ink blob. That was a new one. Ted jumped out of the way just in time, otherwise Rosemary would have ploughed him over. He grinned. The architect hadn't discarded his business card. It was still in her hand when she got into her car. As he walked toward the front of the building, he told himself that patience was definitely a virtue.

Ted found a seat in the lobby and prepared to wait for Nikki Quinn. After a while he jumped up, remembering that there was a rear exit that was closer to the parking lot. He made a beeline for the door and the parking lot where Nikki's BMW was parked.

He looked at his watch. Six-twenty-six. Maybe Nikki was going to work through the evening. He was trying to decide if he should leave or not when he saw her crossing the parking lot.

"Hey, there, Nikki! Got a minute?"

"Ah, the *Post*'s star reporter lurking in the parking lot. Is something big going down that I should know about?" Nikki quipped as she tried to get her wits together. Damn, what was *he* doing here? More importantly, had he seen Rosemary Hershey?

"Was in the area. Wanted to ask you a few questions. So you and Jack are back together again, eh? Does that mean he's joined up with your vigilante group?"

"What are you talking about, Ted? Jack and I aren't . . . we're not together anymore. What vigilante group are you talking about?"

"C'mon, c'mon, you two spent the night together at your house in Georgetown. I saw both of you. I certainly don't care if the two of you are canoodling. What I care about is my old buddy, who is known for *upholding* law and order, suddenly joining forces with you ladies out there at ye olde farm who are *breaking* the law. Care to give me a comment?"

Nikki forced a laugh. "What have you been smoking, Ted? Of course I mind giving you a comment. I make a point of never doing that. But because you are Jack's friend, I will tell you this: I've been renting the house to Jack because I'm staying out at the farm. I stopped by to pick up the rent. The weather was bad so I stayed over."

"Yeah, yeah, that's what Jack said. That Jack, he's a laugh a minute."

"Yes, Jack can be funny at times. I hate to cut you short but I have to get out to the farm."

"Well, sure. Before you go, how about a comment on Rosemary Hershey's visit to your offices?"

So he *had* seen the architect. He was probably stalking her. "Can't do it, Ted. Attorney-client privilege. You know how that goes."

"Absolutely. I sure wouldn't want to do anything unethical. Just the thought of breaking the law makes me come out in a cold sweat. How do you gals out at the farm do it? Do you just turn it on and turn it off? Oh, stupid me. Of course, it's not a problem for you because your bodacious asses are covered by those guys who stole my spleen and almost killed me. Those same guys who beat up that guy you rent your house to. Yeah, yeah, I understand." Ted turned on his heel and walked away, but stopped in mid-stride. "Sometimes what a person *doesn't* say is more eloquent than anything he or she could ever put into words. Drive carefully now. There are a lot of cowboys on the highway these days."

"I'll keep it in mind," Nikki mumbled, knowing Ted couldn't hear her.

Ted parked his car, gathered up his briefcase and his sub sandwich that was to be his dinner and got out of the Honda he'd parked behind a huge black SUV. Even so, he was almost at the end of the long block. Suddenly, he felt himself being jerked backward and shoved against the SUV.

"What the hell!"

"Shut up, Ted. They're up there in your apartment. I saw them go in. There's three of them. I got a really good look at their faces. These guys are new and they look mean and ugly."

"What the hell are you doing here, Maggie? Have you been following me? I only bought one sub."

"Will you shut up and get in the SUV? No, I wasn't following you. I'm horny. The back seat, you jerk, there's more room. We have to talk. You can have half and I'll eat the other half."

"I thought you said you were horny. Half? I'll give you a quarter, not a smidgen more. You can have the chips and the pickle."

"I lied about being horny. Half, Ted. You can have the chips. I'll take the pickle. What do they want with you now?"

"Who the hell knows? You're right, we do need to talk. I hope Mickey and Minnie hide under the bed. Maybe I should call the cops and tell them someone just broke into my apartment."

"Will you get real, Ted? This isn't a game. What did you do today to get them so riled up?" Maggie unwrapped the sub sandwich, relieved that it had already been cut in two. The smell of vinegar and oil immediately permeated the SUV.

Ted bit down on his half of the sandwich. "Whose rig is this?"

"I rented it. I like the black windows. Makes me feel like a super spy. Those guys could be standing right outside the window and they still couldn't see us. They might hear us but they wouldn't be able to see us. I think I outsmarted them. So, what did you do today?"

Between bites of food, Ted brought Maggie up to date. "Are you sure you lied about being horny?"

"Yes, I'm sure. Well, maybe not a hundred percent sure, but unless we go for it right here in this truck, it ain't gonna happen. That's for later anyway. I went off on my own today. Went to see Isabelle Flanders. She didn't give anything up. She was up to her ears in decorating her new offices.

My gut instinct tells me she's just what she says she is, an architect trying to make a comeback after a bad spell. She was very nice. She didn't even bad-mouth Rosemary Hershey. And she only had nice things to say about Bobby Harcourt, who she was engaged to for a while."

"Something is going on with the Hershey woman. You should have seen her. She looked like something the cat dragged in and then dragged back out. She is one hateful woman, I can tell you that. You know what I think, Maggie? I think she went to Quinn's law firm because she didn't want to alert the previous attorneys that something might be going on. She has no clue about those vigilante women out there at the farm. That means, without knowing it, she fell right into their trap and they didn't have to work at it."

Maggie finished the last of her sandwich and then chomped down on the pickle. "I think you're right, Ted." She kissed him on the cheek, snatching what was left of his sandwich before he knew what was happening. "You should have gotten some dessert. I like something sweet after I eat."

Ted thought he was being crafty. "How sweet?"

"Don't go there right now, Robinson. I thought you were going to call the cops."

"OK, OK." Ted dialed the precinct, gave the address and said, "I'm a neighbor of Ted Robinson. I was coming up from the laundry room and saw three men pick the lock on his apartment. They went inside and they're still there. You don't need my name; I don't want to get involved." He rattled off the apartment number. "I'm keeping track of the time and will tell Mr. Robinson I called. He's a big-shot reporter at the *Post*, in case you don't know. He works on top-secret stuff so you might want to keep that in mind. Don't be stupid and use your siren either."

"Big-shot reporter!" Maggie sniffed when Ted ended the call.

"About that horny business . . . What are we going to do about that?"

"Nothing. Ooh, look, I think I see the cops. Boy, that was quick. Careful now, the windshield is tinted but it isn't black like the other windows. Duck down and peek out."

"What should we do while we're waiting?" Ted asked, unwilling to give up the idea of sex in the back seat of the SUV.

"We could think about partnering up for a double byline. Robinson goes before Spritzer, so you get to go first. We share all info one hundred percent. I can do a lot of the legwork. There are five women to keep track of—and, of course, Rosemary Hershey. You can't do it all, Ted. And let's not forget Jack Emery. We can make out an assignment list and check back with each other at the end of the day. Shhh, look! Your guests are leaving. Guess the locals have a little authority after all."

Both reporters watched as the three special agents walked down the street to their car. The two cops stood, hands on hips, until the car peeled away from the curb, tires screeching.

"That's one for the good guys. I bet they put bugs in my apartment. Those guys are vicious. Now I'm going to have to get one of those gizmos that detect listening devices."

"You can do that tomorrow. So what's your answer?"

Ted sighed. "Yeah, OK, but my name goes first."

"OK. Want to come home with me, Ted? I'm getting warm all over. You better check on the cats first, though."

"Hussy," Ted said happily as he jumped out of the SUV to sprint toward his apartment building.

Maggie's fist shot in the air the minute Ted got out of the SUV. Yep, sex was a girl's best friend. She started to laugh and couldn't stop. Men were so predictable. Ted was sweeter than chocolate candy.

Fifteen

Isabelle Flanders stood in the doorway to her office, her eyes misty with happiness. Everything was so perfect, so modern, so beautiful. In her wildest dreams, she'd never expected to have an office like this one. Her old office, *before Rosemary Hershey*, had been a quarter of this size, crowded, the staff always getting in each other's way, stumbling over boxes, babbling and joking about the cramped quarters, but it had all been in fun. In a desperate move to find more space, one of her staff had hung wires and hooks so they could hang stuff from the ceiling. The staff had been wonderful, everyone compatible except for Rosemary, who'd had her own agenda. Of course, Isabelle hadn't known that at the time. It had been a working office that provided results for anxious clients. And a place for an after-hours tryst or two with Bobby Harcourt. That was a long time ago. *Don't go there, Isabelle.* Easier said than done.

Isabelle sniffed at the newness of the place. The

green plants and the fresh flowers were the last things delivered before she'd left the office at eight o'clock the previous night.

Today, she was open for business. As she walked across the blue-green marble that the tile man said was the exact color of the Mediterranean, she looked toward her new receptionist, whose name was on the tip of her tongue, and waved. The rich mahogany paneling gleamed in the subdued lamplight. Lights would have to burn all day because there was no window in the reception area and no way to install one. Her own office had wraparound windows, dove-gray carpeting, and vertical blinds with elaborate cornice boards on all the windows. Her desk was one of a kind, her drafting table her own, the one she'd started out with *before Rosemary Hershey*. It was the only thing, besides the stool, that she'd kept from the days *before Rosemary Hershey*. She positively itched to sit on the high-backed stool, pencil in hand, fresh paper in front of her, ideas ricocheting around her head.

It was playtime, nothing more. She had no clients, no ideas, just a beautiful office where she could talk on the phone, doodle and stare out the window, hoping and wishing for vindication.

These offices were part of her revenge, nothing more. When the Sisterhood finally vindicated her, she would move on. These elegant, scrumptious quarters were not for her. This simply wasn't who she was. She was a hands-on architect. She had a plan for what she called *after Rosemary*. She was going to open a small one-man office, work her tail off the way she had when she first started out. She'd work long hours, go home bone tired, then wake up and do it all over again. She'd do it on her

own, with no help from anyone. If things got
tough financially, she'd sleep and shower in her office. She'd done that in the early days and had
been happier than a pig in a mudslide. She could
do it again. More important, she *wanted* to do it.

She hoped that word of mouth would get her
new clients. She could advertise in the local papers. She knew in her gut she wouldn't starve. If
she could pay her bills, be contented and happy as
well as at peace, she couldn't ask for more.

Her thoughts carried her back in time to the aftermath of the trial and her downfall. She'd buck-
led, but managed to get up and forge ahead by
taking care of herself and earning a meager living.
She'd started to exercise—running, jogging, working out—so she wouldn't dwell on the past. The
physical exertion had kept her sane.

Isabelle looked around the pricey office and
laughed. She knew she could keep this place if she
wanted to go on the hook for rent so high a family
of four could live off it. "Not in my game plan," she
muttered to herself.

Her new partners, whom she barely knew, would
take over these top-of-the-line offices when she
walked away. This time, though, it would be different. When she walked away, she would be doing so
by her own choice and not because Rosemary
Hershey forced her to.

Isabelle shrugged. Time to start her day. The
first thing she'd always done was buzz her secretary for coffee. Well, she could do that now, just as
soon as she figured out how to work the elaborate
telephone console, which had more buttons than
a 747 aircraft. She hoped there was a manual somewhere. In the interests of expediency and a need

for immediate caffeine, she opened the door and called to Janice to fetch her a cup of black coffee. "Grind the beans," she called out. "Please. My cup is the one with the red strawberry on the side with my initials." The oversized cup had been a gift from Bobby. It was a silly thing but she liked it because it held almost half a pot of coffee. It was probably a soup cup and Bobby hadn't known the difference. She'd kept it, though, because she was sentimental. She should have thrown it away a long time ago. It wasn't like she had used it on a daily basis, if at all. Too many memories. And yet it was the first thing she'd brought with her when she moved her things into these offices.

She paced, making a track in the new plush carpeting as she waited for her coffee. "I wonder what happened to my fica tree," she mused. Everyone used to laugh at her when she would hang sticky notes on the leaves. Did it die? Did Rosemary take it? Did *anyone* take it? There was a perfect spot for a new tree right next to her drafting table. Maybe she should look into getting one. She ruled out the idea almost immediately. She wasn't going to be here long enough to need a tree. This is just playtime, Isabelle, she warned herself. Don't, whatever you do, get attached to anything in these offices.

All dressed up and nowhere to go, she thought as she accepted the cup of coffee from her secretary. She smiled, liking the feel of the cup in her hands. She carried it over to the little stand next to her drafting table. She sat down, picked up her pencil and moved into another world. She reached for a sticky note, scribbled something on it, moved to the left to hang it on the tree but of course the tree wasn't there. Isabelle bit down on her lower lip when her eyes started to burn. She was about to stick the note on the side of her drafting table when the door opened and her secretary said, "There's a delivery for you, Miss Flanders."

"OK, just put it anywhere," Isabelle replied without turning around.

The deep voice sent chills up her spine. "Looks like I'm just in time. Hold that sticky note for just one more minute. There you go!" Bobby Harcourt said as he set down a fica tree in full leaf right next to her drafting table.

"Bobby!"

"That's me. I wanted to welcome you back into the fold." His voice became anxious. "If you'd rather not have it, I can donate it someplace else."

Isabelle turned around in her chair. She was glad she was dressed up, every hair in place, makeup subdued and not overdone. Even her perfume was subdued. "No, no! You just caught me by surprise. I wasn't expecting . . . *you.* Thanks for the tree. I was sitting here a few minutes ago wondering what happened to the old one. Do you know?"

Bobby dusted his hands and then wiped them on a snow-white handkerchief that he pulled out of his pants pocket. "Only by hearsay. It's not worth talking about. Nice offices, Isabelle. Good luck. Good to see you again."

Bobby was almost to the door when Isabelle called him back. "Wait, Bobby. Sit down. Would you like some coffee?"

"Are you sure you want to have coffee with me?" His gaze traveled to the large cup with the strawberry on the side. "Yes, I would like a cup of coffee. I was in a hurry this morning and didn't get a chance to hit Starbucks."

She should have thanked him for the tree and let him walk out of the offices. That's what she *should* have done. Instead, she walked over to the door and called over to Janice. "Bring a cup of coffee, black, one sugar, for Mr. Harcourt, please."

"You remember I take it black with one sugar?" Bobby asked in amazement.

"I remember *everything*, Bobby. Thanks for the tree. Makes the office complete now. How are you? It's been a long time. I really haven't kept up with what's going on in our business. Are you doing well?"

Bobby laughed. Isabelle felt her insides start to crumble at the sound. How she loved his laugh. Her voice became testy. "Did I say something funny?"

"No. I really don't know how to answer the question. I'm fine. I'm thinking about going out on my own again. My partner and I are dissolving our partnership and we're going to go our separate ways. I imagine it's going to get a little rocky as time goes on, but I miss being my own boss."

Thank God for small favors. He hadn't mentioned his wife's name.

"Are you sure that's what you want to do? When you're in business for yourself, the buck stops with you. You're responsible for everything. But then, I guess you know that."

"I liked that part of it. But to answer your question, yes, I'm sure. I just wanted to stop by to wish you good luck. Thanks for the coffee."

There was a lump in Isabelle's throat. "Nice seeing you again, and thanks for the tree."

Bobby shrugged. His hand was on the door-knob when he turned around. "Why wouldn't you see me when you were in the hospital?" he asked. "Why did you cut me out of your life like that? Where did you go afterward? I'd really like to know, Isabelle, so I can make sense out of what happened to me. That trial . . . that circus . . . I tried calling you, I chased after you . . . Why?"

"The past belongs in the past. I've moved on. It just took me longer than it did you. What happened to *you* was a woman named Rosemary. You believed her instead of me. There is one thing I would like to tell you, though. I wasn't drinking. You know I don't drink at lunchtime. Never. I did, however, swig down a lot of cough medicine. It never occurred to me that there was alcohol in it. I wasn't driving the car, Bobby. I was too damn sick to drive that day."

"What are you saying, Isabelle? Jesus Christ, what are you saying?"

"I'm saying goodbye, Bobby."

Isabelle ran over to the door, pushed him through, and then closed and locked it behind him. Her breathing was so labored that she had to sit down and put her head between her knees.

Maggie Spritzer looked around Squire's Pub and made a face. "This is definitely a guy's place. Why are we here, Ted?"

"To eat. What? You wanted to go to a tea room and have cucumber sandwiches? I need to eat real food. It's called sustenance. We need to talk and we need to make a plan and we need to do it right now. I have this itch between my shoulder blades which tells me things are on fast-forward. I say we hit them hard. We get right in their faces and tell them what we suspect. But we say it as fact, not suspicion. Since we're both reporters that means they are going to try to spin us." The waitress appeared, pad and pencil in hand. "Double bacon cheeseburger, fries and a large Coke, plenty of ketchup," Ted said.

"I'll have the vegetable platter with the two dipping sauces. A glass of water with a twist of lemon. You're going to die at an early age if you keep eating like that," Maggie said.

"I only eat like this at lunchtime. As I was saying, they're going to try to spin us. We can't let that happen. I want you to take another crack at Isabelle Flanders and Rosemary Hershey. I didn't get anywhere with either one of them. Something is definitely wrong with the Hershey woman. She looks like she's falling apart. That tells me there was something fishy about that old lawsuit. I think she lied and walked away with millions while one of the Pinewood ladies, Isabelle, got taken to the cleaners. The grandmother and the little boy didn't do so well, either. Think about it. Flanders lost her license; she went into hock up to her eyeballs trying to defend herself. She lost everything. I can't find out anything in her background, which is fairly current, that would allow her to hit the big time like she's doing right now. That has to mean she's got a backer. Who else but Myra Rutledge, who has as much money as Bill Gates? Tell me this doesn't make sense."

"It makes sense. So, what you're saying is those

ladies out at Pinewood are going to go after Rosemary Hershey to make her pay for what she did to Isabelle Flanders."

"Right. Now, if I was as insidious as I think those Pinewood ladies are, I think they're going to play with Hershey's head, make her look over her shoulder every second and then close in for the kill so that she confesses. But here's the clunker. Hershey went to Nikki Quinn's law offices. I'm sure she has no idea about those ladies out at Pinewood, of which Nikki is a member. By the way, Hershey's husband used to be engaged to Isabelle Flanders."

"Well, shoot, I didn't know that. Whoa. Our plot thickens. What happened?"

"Don't know. All of a sudden, Bobby Harcourt marries Rosemary Hershey. Flanders drops out of sight after the trial. She couldn't work at her profession, lived on the poverty level. Until now. Take Bobby, too. In my opinion, he's a stand-up guy. You might be able to worm something out of him. He's probably in the dark about everything. Clue him in, but be careful."

"OK. What are you going to do?"

"I'm going to try and hook up with the black woman, Alexis, and the Japanese girl. The trucker is up for grabs. You told me last night that when you called Myra Rutledge she said she wasn't interested in giving out interviews."

Maggie reached for the vegetable plate that the waitress was holding out. "Did anyone ever tell you that Myra Rutledge is best friends with Judge Cornelia Easter?"

Ted bit down on his burger, chewed, swirled the

food to the side of his mouth and said, "No. Do you think that's important?"

Maggie wagged a carrot stick under Ted's nose. "Don't know. I think it's one of those things you keep tucked away at the back of your mind. What are you going to do about going back to your apartment?"

"I checked on the police report early this morning. I got those guys' names off the report, and filed a restraining order against all three of them. I'm going to paste it on my apartment door. Short of hiring a bodyguard, what else can I do?"

"You can start being careful, Ted. Do you really think this is a big story?"

"A baby Watergate. Trust me. The ladies of Pinewood are breaking the law and those goons are protecting them. Tell me that's fair. You know what really gets me, Maggie. Those women are professionals. They're so goddamn slick they make my eyes water. They don't leave a clue behind. Jack Emery is in this up to his ears. How else do you explain the National Security Advisor getting beaten to within an inch of his life? And how did the first three goons get beaten up and dumped in the NSA's backyard?"

Maggie dipped a celery stalk into some ranch dressing. "Don't look now, but your old buddy Emery just walked through the door."

"Is he coming over here? If he is, keep quiet and let me do the talking."

"Well, sure, boss. You're the shark here." Her sarcasm went unnoticed by Ted.

"Don't you think it's a little strange for Jack to show up here after my confrontation with Nikki last night?"

"Let me be the voice of logic. How did he know you'd be here, Ted?"

"Because this is where I usually have lunch and he knows it. Is he headed this way?"

"Yep." She motioned to the waitress. "I'll have a piece of your sinful decadent chocolate cake. With a dollop of whipped cream." Ted passed on dessert and rolled his eyes. "I can eat cake because unlike you, I ate veggies for lunch," said Maggie with a grin.

"Mind if I join you guys?" Jack said as he shrugged out of his raincoat.

"No, I don't mind," Maggie replied.

"Well, I mind," Ted said.

Jack sat down anyway.

Maggie got up and said, "While you guys snap and snarl at each other, I think I'll visit the rest-room. Don't anybody eat my dessert."

Ted leaned back in the booth, his eyes narrowing as he glared at Jack. "You following me or what?"

"No, I'm not following you. Why would I do that?"

"To report to those ladies out at Pinewood, that's why. Guess what, you son of a bitch, my boss has agreed to a full court press when the time comes. He's behind me and Maggie a hundred percent. We're closing in, *buddy*. Those guys were waiting for me again when I got home last night. They had the chutzpah to let themselves into my apartment. That's goddamn fucking breaking and entering and I don't give a shit what color their shields are, gold or otherwise. A man's home is his castle. Maggie spotted them. I called the cops and they rousted them out and this morning I got a restraining order against all three of them. My boss is royally pissed. I'm pissed, too, Jack."

"Can't say that I blame you. Be careful. They'll waylay you somewhere else if you piss them off. You know they're a law unto themselves."

"Now, how would you know that?"

"My DA's instinct, that's how. Come on, get off your high horse and talk to me. I didn't lie to you, Ted."

"Yeah, you did. You're just better at it than Nikki is. The lady still blushes and she blinks a lot when she lies. I pick up on shit like that because I'm a reporter."

Ted looked up at the waitress holding a plate with a piece of chocolate cake. "Wrap it up to go, OK?" He flipped some bills on the table.

Jack half stood, his eyes and voice miserable. "What the hell do you want from me, Ted?"

"Just the truth, Jack, just the truth."

"I told you the truth."

Ted turned around and walked back to the table. He smacked both palms on the tabletop and said, "You know what, Jack? You are so full of shit, your eyes are turning brown."

"Fuck you, Ted, and the horse you rode in on."

Maggie appeared out of nowhere. She reached up to take the to-go bag from the waitress. "You're both acting like stupid little schoolboys. Grow up and act like the men you're supposed to be."

"Stay out of this, Maggie. This is between Jack and me."

Jack knew when to keep his mouth shut. He just stared at the feisty young woman. He was stunned a moment later when she turned and came right up to his face. "If I *ever* find out you snookered

Ted, I'll hunt you down and I'll personally slice off your dick. You hear me, Jack?" she hissed in his ear.

Jack looked into Maggie's menacing eyes and nodded. He could already feel the pain.

Sixteen

Ted wondered at how cold it had become since he and Maggie entered Squire's Pub. Where was the sunshine and blue skies he so hungered for?

Maggie, dessert bag in hand, steered Ted around the corner to get out of the wind. "I'm going to try to track down Rosemary Hershey. Listen to me, Ted. There's no way we're going to be able to follow all those women from Pinewood. If you're certain Hershey is on their to-do list, then it makes sense to stick to her. Eventually, they'll show up to do . . . whatever it is they plan on doing, and *bam*, we nail them all at one time. How does that sound?" Not bothering to wait for a reply, she rattled on. "As soon as I locate Hershey and see that she's going to stay put for a while, I'll try to get Isabelle Flanders in my crosshairs. If you tackle Bobby Harcourt, we just might have something to discuss tonight. Your house or mine?"

Ted decided he liked the way that sounded. "I have to check on Mickey and Minnie. My place if you aren't afraid of unwanted, unwelcome visitors. I'll even put clean sheets on the bed. I was going to do that today anyway, so don't go getting excited at the prospect of ravaging my body. You have to stop thinking I'm easy. I'll try to track down Bobby. My place at seven, then? I'll buy dinner at the Boston Market."

"Deal," Maggie said, high-fiving him. She was gone a minute later.

Ted stood on the corner for a moment before he crossed the street. With Maggie Spritzer on her trail, he almost felt sorry for Rosemary Hershey.

Her teeth bared, Rosemary ripped at her astrology books. There wasn't one promising word in the whole week's forecast. Wild-eyed, she looked around, wondering why her world was crumbling around her. Why now? Why out of the blue like this? After so long, wasn't it better to let sleeping dogs lie? At her feet was the latest mailing, an article and a picture of the elder Mrs. Myers wiping at her eyes before she made a comment for the carnivorous press. "There is no justice for people like me. Just people like *her*." The article went on to say how Mrs. Myers had pointed to architect Rosemary Hershey. Then there was another quote from Mrs. Myers. "I didn't believe a word that woman said on the stand. It's my opinion, and I am entitled to my opinion, that the woman committed perjury. That's all I have to say."

Rosemary glared at the paper with its yellow

highlighted quote. Somebody knows, she thought. Somebody who was now stalking her. It had to be Isabelle Flanders. The Myers woman was too old, and all talk anyway. Old people didn't play mind games. It could only be that bitch Isabelle.

She sat down and nibbled at her ruined manicure. She should call James. Maybe the cards had changed. Was Mercury still in retrograde? Too bad there wasn't someone she could call up to ask, since she'd just mangled her astrology books. She ground her heel into the paper on the floor until it was nothing more than slivers of paper. She couldn't take this anymore. There was no way she was going to let Isabelle Flanders ruin her life.

Rosemary was like a charging bull when she stomped her way out of the office, not saying where she was headed, leaving her staff bug-eyed at her strange behavior.

Maggie, her engine running, followed the wild-eyed architect when she sped off in her Mercedes sports car. For ninety minutes she followed her until they reached a gas station, where Hershey caused a scene that called for police intervention. From there she tailed her to Nails Are Nice where, even from her car, she could hear Rosemary screaming at the Vietnamese manicurist who, bowing and fluttering, tried to explain that the shop was busy and that Missy Rosemary had no appointment.

Deciding this was too good to miss, Maggie got out of her car and went into the salon. Pretending to pick out nail polish, she listened to the tirade.

"Well, you'll never see me here again!" Rosemary

screeched. "Don't I tip you well? Didn't I refer customers to you? Why can't you squeeze me in? Look at my nails! Well?"

"Missy Rosemary, you do not have the appointment. You come back later. We fix your nails at four o'clock."

Maggie plunked down five dollars and fifty cents for a bottle of Strawberry Slush nail polish. She was out the door and in her car in seconds, ready to follow the architect again. Finally, muttering and cursing, Rosemary ran back to her car.

Ten minutes into the drive, Maggie knew Rosemary was headed for Isabelle Flanders's office. For a few brief minutes, Maggie actually toyed with the idea of alerting Isabelle to her approaching visitor. She negated the idea almost immediately. This was one conversation she wanted to hear. On the other hand, she'd already gambled twice—at the gas station and the nail salon. Even though Hershey was in a tizzy, sooner or later she'd put two and two together and remember that she'd seen Maggie twice already. Undaunted, Maggie pulled ahead and hit the gas pedal. She arrived in the parking lot behind Isabelle Flanders's office a good five minutes before Rosemary—just in time to stuff her red hair under a baseball cap, add a pair of plain glasses, and change into a light-blue windbreaker. What she hoped to accomplish with this limited disguise was beyond her. *Go with the flow*, she told herself.

Maggie bolted from her car the moment she saw Rosemary swerve into the lot and come to a screeching halt. She made a beeline for the entrance, showed her press credentials, signed her name in an illegible scrawl then scooted across the lobby and made the elevator just as the door was about to close. Winded, she leaned against the wall to watch the numbers overhead. When she reached Isabelle's floor, she tried to look dignified as she opened the plate-glass doors. She smiled at the receptionist and said, "I'm early and I'm waiting for my mother to join me. I'll just sit over here till she arrives. You know mothers, they're always late."

The receptionist nodded and smiled.

The plate-glass doors didn't just open. They blasted apart like two linebackers had shouldered them. Maggie had no chance to admire the pricey decor before Rosemary stomped her way to the receptionist's desk. "I'd like to see Isabelle Flanders."

The pretty blonde looked up and smiled. "Your name? Do you have an appointment?"

"My name is Rosemary Hershey and no, I do not have an appointment. Where is her office?"

"If you'll take a seat, Miss—"

"Don't tell me to take a seat. If I wanted to sit down, I would. I want to see Isabelle right now. Where is she?"

"Miss Hershey, you can't go back there. I'll have to call security," the receptionist said, getting up to follow Rosemary down the hall. Maggie was up in a flash, sprinting after them. The gods of luck were on her side as she ducked into a door right before Isabelle Flanders stepped into the hall to see what the commotion was all about. Maggie closed the door softly but she could still hear the architects' raised voices.

Maggie's eyebrows shot upward when she heard Isabelle say, "Either calm down and talk civilly or I will call security. You might want to think about how that will play out on the evening news, Rosemary. Lower your voice this instant."

The door closed. Maggie could see the receptionist making her way back down the hall. In the blink of an eye she made the decision to listen outside Isabelle Flanders's door. Since Isabelle's offices were the last two rooms at the end of the hall, it was unlikely anyone would be coming this way. If she got caught, Ted would just have to eat his Boston Market chicken all by himself.

Her ear pressed to the door, her eyes on the hallway, with two slips of paper on the floor at her feet, Maggie listened to the caterwauling going on inside Isabelle's office.

"What are you doing here, Rosemary? I don't want anything to do with you. You're a liar, a cheat and a thief. You got what you wanted; you ruined me. You got Bobby, too. I don't have anything else to give up to you. I want you to leave and I don't want you bothering me ever again."

"You fucking bitch! Like I care what you want! Why are you hounding me like this? Do you think if you resurrect that garbage you can make it back to the top? It's not going to work. Don't think that sending me newspaper articles every day is going to change a thing. You aren't going to get away with this. I'll get you once and for all!"

Hands on her hips, Isabelle glared at her adversary. "What *are* you talking about? I think you should leave before one of us does something we'll regret."

"Oh, you're going to regret it all right. I'll show you! Who do you think you're messing around with? Didn't you learn a lesson the first time? You

can't scare me, Isabelle. Where'd you get all this?"
Rosemary said, waving her arms around her.

"It's none of your business where I got *all of this*.
I certainly know who I'm messing around with.
How could I ever forget? You were driving that day,
Rosemary. You had two glasses of wine at lunch.
You ran the stop sign. You killed that family; not
me. You stole my designs and put your name on
them. I got my memory back once it was all over. If
I was going to do anything to you, I would have done
it back then. That's all in the past. I've moved on. I
suggest you do the same thing. Oh, and one other
thing, Rosemary. The dandiest thing happened to
me when I got my memory back. I became psychic.
I have these visions. I see things. I hate to say I can
predict, but guess what? I can. I'm not going to tell
you what I see in regard to you, because you won't
be able to handle it. It's not pretty, Rosemary."

Rosemary felt her knees start to buckle. "Psychic!
Yeah, right! Don't think I'm going to fall for bunk
like that. Bobby is probably telling you all kinds of
things just to get back at me. He knows I'm sick of
him. He can't be without a woman so he came
slinking back to you and you fell for his slick line.
You want him back, is that it?" Rosemary screamed.
"Go for it."

"Bobby belongs to the past, just the way you do,
Rosemary. I don't want anything to do with either
one of you. If you're worried about your husband,
I'd like to make a suggestion: look in the mirror.
You look . . . deranged. I'm only going to say this
one more time. Leave or I'll call security. Do not
come here again. I mean it, Rosemary."

"Deranged! Is that what you said? You wish! I
know what you're trying to do. It wouldn't surprise

me one little bit to know that Bobby is helping you. I'm going to the police. Let's see how you like going a few rounds with them . . . again. I've also consulted an attorney. Be warned, Isabelle, get off my back and stop with the harassing mail."

Outside the door, Maggie decided the discussion she'd been listening to was about to come to a close. She whipped around and ran down the hall. Just before she headed out the door, she shouted to the receptionist. "I think my mother must have forgotten our appointment. I'll call to reschedule when I find out what happened to her. Bye!"

Rosemary Hershey peeled out of the parking lot, hit the curb and took the curve on two wheels. Maggie was right behind her but using all four wheels of her car.

Where was Hershey going? Was she just blowing smoke by saying she was going to go to the police? If Maggie were a betting woman, she'd bet no. No sense in opening herself up to more angst. Maybe she was going back to the office or home. Maggie gambled and headed for the office. She parked at the far side of the lot and felt like cheering that her instincts were on the money when, only a few minutes later, Rosemary barreled into the lot, tires screeching. She parked and didn't even bother locking the door. How perfect was *that*?

Maggie waited a full five minutes before she opened the car door. Her adrenaline pumping, she got out of her car and nonchalantly sauntered over to the Mercedes. She hoped she didn't look as apprehensive as she felt when she opened the door and slid into the driver's seat. So, this was a

Mercedes. Humph. She'd take her Honda and her good gas mileage, not to mention the comfortable driver's seat, over this car any day.

Maggie quickly pawed through the contents of the glove compartment. Nothing useful there. Two pens, a notebook, a road map, a packet of tissues, some chewing gum and a flashlight. The console between the seats held nothing but a cigarette lighter and an unopened pack of cigarettes. "Well, this was a bust," she muttered. But maybe not. People usually kept their stuff in the trunk as opposed to the inside of the car so people like her couldn't go through their things—or, worse, steal them.

With a fancy car like this, there should be a button to pop the trunk somewhere; but then again, maybe the trunk had a separate key. She looked over the busy dashboard until she found the button she was looking for. Careful not to draw attention to herself, Maggie climbed out of the car, walked around to the back and raised the top of the trunk. The mother lode. Yessiree. Golf clubs, golf shoes, tennis racket, sneakers, gym bag. Six bottles of Evian water. A bag of nutrition bars. Cosmetic bag. A brown accordion file and a briefcase.

Maggie didn't think twice. She picked up the file and the briefcase. At the last second, she helped herself to a bottle of water. She slammed the trunk shut and moved over to her own car, her heart slamming against her ribs. No one called her name. No one shouted for her to stop. She was safe. And she'd done it in broad daylight. "Eat your heart out, Ted Robinson," she mumbled as she drove out of the parking lot, her foot shaking on the gas pedal. It looked like she just might get to eat that

Boston Market chicken after all. The thought of digging into the mashed potatoes and gravy left her almost giddy.

Rosemary Hershey's heart pounded in her chest as she made her way to her office. Isabelle Flanders, a psychic! How ridiculous! Isabelle said she wouldn't like what she could see. What the hell did that mean?

"Psychic, my ass!" she muttered. But oh, God, what if she was telling the truth? In the past, Isabelle had never been a liar. Actually, she was one of those in-your-face, tell-it-like-it-is kind of people. Fear unlike anything Rosemary had ever experienced coursed through her now. She could feel the panic start to set in.

Deranged. Isabelle said she looked deranged. Rosemary ran to the little lavatory at the side of her office. She turned on the light and gasped, horrified, at the reflection glaring back at her.

She needed a plan. A foolproof plan of some kind. And she needed to put that plan into effect right now before what was left of her world washed away. *Think. Think. Think.* She fought her panic as she looked around. Everything she had, or ever hoped to have, was because of Isabelle and her own ingenuity. That included Bobby. She wished now that she'd treated him better, been a better wife.

Bobby was idealistic, full of principles and integrity. He was just like Isabelle in that respect. Bobby always tried to see both sides of everything. And exactly what was that going to get him? Freedom, that's what he was going to get. Freedom to go back to Isabelle Flanders.

Rosemary washed her face and combed her hair. She didn't look one bit better, nor did she feel better. Her head up, her shoulders back, she marched into the drafting room where a team of young architects were hard at work on the new designs for the farm out at McLean. She walked around, peering over her employees' shoulders. Suddenly she jabbed a finger at the design in front of one young architect.

"Ceil, what the hell is this?"

Rosemary could see the young woman's shoulders start to quiver. "It's . . . it's a barn, Rosemary."

"A barn! A goddamn barn! Anyone can design and build a barn. We're known for our innovation. I want spectacular. I want eye-popping. This," Rosemary said, jabbing her finger at the barn, "is not what I want. Time is running out. These designs have to be submitted by the end of the week. To you that means noon on Friday. The winning design is going to be chosen Sunday evening at the Silver Swan dinner. There is no way I'm submitting this . . . this *crap*!"

Rosemary continued with her tirade as she walked around the room. "I can't believe I pay you what I pay you. A ten-year-old could do what you've just wasted a week doing. I'm going to tell you this once, get your asses in gear, scrap this garbage and design something that will make us all proud. If you can't cut it, leave. The pickings are pretty slim out there at this time of year and this office won't be kind in its references, either, so please take that into consideration. I want you here twenty-four-seven. Order in. You get one trip home for a change of clothing. Bring your own towels and use my shower. The next time I walk through here I want to see results. *Results*, ladies and gentlemen."

Seventeen

Myra called the meeting to order. The women fell quiet.

"We need an update, girls. Nikki, let's start with you."

Nikki smiled. And then she laughed out loud. "Can you imagine Rosemary Hershey walking into my law firm and saying she can't schedule another appointment until she consults the stars? That's exactly what she did. Aside from the fact that Bobby Harcourt filed for divorce and filed to dissolve his partnership with Miss Hershey, that's about all I can report. She wanted to know if she could get alimony. She refuses to buy him out at the price he wants. That's another way of saying she wants it all. She has no intention of allowing him to buy her out. It's stalemate. We're going through the motions, filing the appropriate papers when we get around to it. We're just stalling her. She calls the office every ten minutes for progress reports. That tells us she's a control freak.

She looks like she's under a great deal of stress. Dark circles under her eyes, her hair looks like the bad end of a mop. Her nails are chipped and cracked, her clothes mussed and rumpled.

"The attorney we assigned to handle her case summed it up this way. Rosemary sees herself losing control and she doesn't like it. Nor does she take suggestions well. She's used to jerking everyone's strings, not the other way around. She's actually worried about appearances, how her little community of architects will view her once they find out Bobby filed for divorce and wants to dissolve the company. During her last phone call she said she was going into the spin mode. Knowing the woman's background the way we do, it could mean anything." Nikki laughed again. "The only thing she *didn't* have a problem with was writing out the retainer check for twenty-five grand. Oh, one more thing Opal, the attorney handling Rosemary's case, said that the lady—and she used the word lightly—was original sin in a pair of slut shoes."

Kathryn laughed out loud, the others joining in. "So the lady jumped him, humped him and then he dumped her! How fitting!" she guffawed.

Isabelle's cheeks flamed. She hated hearing anything negative that pertained to Bobby Harcourt. "She's on the edge, that's for sure. No one was more surprised than I was when she showed up at the office. Of course she blames me. And Bobby. She's way off base in that regard. She's never been frightened before but she's frightened now. She was shaking all over. I loved seeing her like that because I lived that way for years. I'm glad she's experiencing a little of what I went through—and all because of her greed."

"What goes around, eventually comes around," Alexis said.

"Yoko, do you have anything to add to what the others just said?"

"In my opinion, Miss Hershey is a walking time bomb. Her eyes glitter with greed. The animosity between the couple was obvious; I felt uncomfortable. Mr. Harcourt was very professional. A gentleman. It is hard to imagine the two of them together."

Kathryn's face registered disgust. "It's a business arrangement. Dollar signs are the bottom line."

Isabelle said, "That might be the way it is now, but that's not the way it was in the beginning. Bobby was so hot for her he couldn't see straight."

"Guess he got a wake-up call along the way, eh?" Kathryn said. "Furthermore, the man hasn't been born that you can trust. He strayed, he played, and now he has to pay. Not that we're going after him. He's all grown up and can clean up his own mess. Alan used to say you never know what you have until you lose it. Bobby Harcourt is experiencing that now. You were the best thing that ever happened to him, Isabelle, and don't you ever forget it."

Isabelle locked her gaze with Kathryn's. "Don't worry, I had my day in the sun with Bobby. You can't go home again, I know that. If there's a white knight in my life somewhere, he'll find me on his own. So, where do we stand?"

Myra took center stage. "My dinner party at the Silver Swan is right on schedule. We'll announce the winning entry right after dinner. Isabelle, did you bring your designs?"

Isabelle leaned over and picked up two long cylinders. She slid them across the table toward

Myra, who nodded as she turned around to hand both cylinders to Charles.

"Yoko, are you ready to go into phase one of Rosemary Hershey's punishment? If you make one mistake, none of the rest of it will work. Can you do it?" Myra asked.

All eyes turned to Yoko. She met the sisters' gaze with unflinching intensity. "I can do it. I might need to . . ." she sought for the word she wanted, "tweak, yes, tweak my part just a little. Do not worry."

"That's good enough for me, kiddo," Kathryn said, slapping Yoko on the back. Yoko grinned from ear to ear. Praise of any kind from Kathryn was well worth waiting for.

Myra looked down at her notes. "Kathryn and Alexis, are you both ready to do your part?"

Kathryn made gnashing sounds with her teeth. "I am so ready, you wouldn't believe."

"Me too," Alexis agreed.

Myra turned around to Charles. "Have you done your part, Charles?"

"Not yet, Myra. For something of this . . . ah . . . magnitude, one must wait till the proper moment. If I jump the gun, it won't bode well for our girls. I don't anticipate any problems, though. Trust me, things will fall into place at the proper moment."

"I like to hear that, Charles. I always feel confident when you're at the helm," Kathryn quipped.

Myra looked up at the three television monitors that sat side by side. Lady Justice in all her majesty towered over the table. "Nikki and I will not be actively participating in this punishment. It's obvious that Miss Hershey will recognize me. We can't be sure that she doesn't know Nikki, even though she's dealing with another attorney in her firm.

Just let me say I have every confidence in all of you. In the meantime, we will continue with our mail campaign since it seems to be working."

Nikki eyed the women. She wished she knew more about psychology. Driving someone over the edge was something she wasn't exactly comfortable with. Still, the plan seemed almost foolproof. All she could do was wait in case she was needed.

"If there is no other business, I suggest we adjourn and meet up again on Friday," Myra said.

It was almost twilight, that mysterious time of day that surrounded the city in a grayish-purple light and would eventually lead to a black night. It was a time to be indoors where it was safe and cozy.

Maggie Spritzer ran up the steps to Ted's apartment building. She had a bad moment as she fumbled with the key, struggling to fit it into the lock, when she thought she heard someone call her name. No one in this neighborhood knew her. She'd just spoken to Ted, who said it would be another hour before he'd head home. Her heartbeat raced as the key finally made contact and she was inside. She turned around to look outside, but she couldn't see anyone. The wind, she decided. Still, the sensitive spot between her shoulder blades twitched like mad.

Never a coward, Maggie ran like hell, taking the stairs two at a time until she reached Ted's floor. At the top, winded, she wondered why she hadn't taken the creaking elevator. Because she didn't want to be in such a confined area, that's why. Sometimes, she admitted, she *was* a coward.

Outside, she'd been freezing. Now she was dripping from her sprint up the stairs carrying her fully loaded backpack. When she dropped it to the floor, Mickey and Minnie got busy sniffing and trying to paw at the stiff canvas.

Maggie dropped to her knees, not from exhaustion but from fear. She hated it that she was shaking. She picked up Mickey, or maybe it was Minnie, and tried to cuddle the fat, bushy-tailed cat, but it strenuously objected and sprang out of her arms. The other cat took that moment to leap into Maggie's lap and immediately started to purr her pleasure.

When Ted finally walked in the door, Maggie was still sitting cross-legged on the floor, cuddling with the cat her lap. Tears streaked her cheeks.

Ted dropped the shopping bag and ran to her. "What's wrong? Did something happen? Talk to me, Maggie."

"It's just me, nerves of steel. I spooked myself. I thought I heard someone call my name when I got here. I'm sure it was the wind."

Ted sat back on his haunches. "Did anything out of the ordinary happen today? Are you sure you're OK?"

Maggie looked over at the man who was staring so intently at her. She realized right then how much she liked him. Maybe *liked* was too tame a word. For all her breeziness, her sharp tongue, her blasé attitude, she truly, truly cared about the reporter. She didn't mean to say anything but somehow the words just tumbled out of her mouth. "I'm in love with you."

Minnie hissed and snarled as her owner's jaw dropped.

Ted grappled with the words he'd just heard. Well, this certainly changed things. This was where he was supposed to acknowledge the words and return them. That's what Jack Emery would have done. Then he remembered that he hated Jack's guts and that applied to his advice as well. He decided to go for something romantic. "So, do you want to get married?"

Maggie wrinkled her nose. "You're supposed to tell me you love me, too, then you get on your knees and propose. That's the way you're supposed to do it, Ted." More tears dripped down her freckled cheeks.

Ted looked befuddled. "I told you I loved you last week and you said I should keep my emotions to myself. You tell me one thing and then expect something else. I can't read your mind. Is that a yes or a no?"

"I don't see you on your knees, Ted. How can I take you seriously if you don't get on your knees? How much do you make a year?"

Ted blinked as he dropped to his knees. Jack Emery would never get on his knees, even for Cindy Crawford. *I hate you, Jack.* Ted reached for Maggie's hand because he thought that was what he was supposed to do. "Will you marry me?"

Maggie tilted her head to the side. "Yeah, but not right now. Let's eat. You didn't tell me how much you make. We need to get that straight. I pay rent, you pay rent. We need to buy a house and a family car. I'll manage the checkbook. No more eating out every night. One or the other of us will cook. We'll take turns cleaning the house, too."

Ted wondered where the romance was going to

come in. Stud Muffin Emery would never agree to these terms. *I hate you, Jack!*

"So, do we have a deal?" Maggie asked as she started taking their dinner out of the bags.

Ted reached for the silverware. "Is that how you think of it, Maggie? A deal? I thought marriage was something special. You know, romance, flirting, caring about one another, helping one another, cuddling, putting up the Christmas tree together, buying toys for the animals, lots of kissing, lots and lots of sex."

Maggie held the carving knife over the chicken. She looked up at Ted, her expression unreadable. She laid the knife down on the table. "I don't understand you, Ted. The scenario I presented to you is what I thought you could handle. You blow hot and cold. It's like you have to consult someone or something before you can even make a decision. Now, you spring yours on me—which, by the way, is the way a marriage is supposed to be. It wasn't hard to fall in love with you. It won't be hard to fall out of love, either. We need to come to some kind of decision before I cut up this chicken."

"Maggie, I want whatever you want. Let's put this all on the shelf and talk about it when we aren't both so stressed out. Can we agree for now that it's enough to know you love me and I love you and we'll work on the rest of it?"

Maggie smiled. "I'll agree to everything just as soon as you tell me how much you make."

"Fifteen grand a year more than you do. I've been there longer, Maggie."

"No problem. I just needed a mental picture of how much we could afford when it comes to a house. White or dark meat?"

Ted blinked. "Both," he said smartly.

Both reporters ate the way they did everything: with gusto. From time to time, one of them would wave a fork around while trying to make a particular point.

"Now that we've made a commitment to one another, I guess I can tell you something no one else in this town knows but me."

Ted was suddenly all ears and eyes as he waited for what he knew was going to be earth shattering. The fact that his lady love was about to share something momentous left him almost teary-eyed. Suddenly he felt like he could take on the world. "What?" he whispered.

"There's an organization in this town that boasts eight hundred members. Nothing goes on inside or outside the Beltway that these members don't know about. Eight hundred members, Ted. Most of the members are active, meaning they pay their yearly dues. They meet once a month, always at a different location and usually at some church hall."

"Who? What? Why? How do they manage to keep it a secret? And how did you find out? Is one of the members your snitch?"

Maggie was busy picking slivers of chicken off a wing and slipping it to the cats. "I want your word that what I tell you stays with you. The journalist's oath, Ted."

"You got it. Come on, tell me."

"The organization is called the Beltway Divas, made up mostly of housekeepers, daily and weekly domestics, and nannies. They know everything that goes on in this town, Ted. *Everything.*"

Ted tried to look impressed. "Uh-huh."

"Uh-huh? That's all you can say? I think I'm the only one who knows. Violet, my twice-a-week cleaning lady, told me all about it. The reason she told me is she got sick and I took care of her. She wanted to do something for me. So she told me her secret. Now she's my spy. She pretty much works under the table and has no health insurance. I took her to the doctor, let her stay in my spare room, made her soup, made sure she took her medicine. She's a very nice person. She told me stories that would curl your hair. That's what they do at their meetings, tell stories about all the politicians and the power brokers they work for. They tape all the meetings and want to write a book. The only problem is that when they hired them, their employers insisted the live-in housekeepers and nannies sign documents saying they would never divulge anything they saw or heard while in their employ. I figure I could act as their agent, proofread the text, hire them a ghostwriter. I could probably make enough to get a big chunk of money to put down on a deposit for a house. I'll get serious about it when I talk to a lawyer. I'd need a chunk of free time, which I don't have right now. It's definitely on my agenda, though. For now, it's almost like having money in the bank.

"I also have a quasi list of people that Rosemary Hershey slept with. I don't even know if we need to speak to any of those men, but I have the list, thanks to Hershey's cleaning lady, who she treats like dirt. The woman couldn't wait to give it up to Violet. Say something, Ted."

"I don't know what to say other than that I see lawsuits all over the place. I thought you had a . . . *bombshell.*"

Maggie looked crushed. "How's this for a bomb-shell? Rosemary Hershey's weekly cleaning lady quit on her this week. It seems Rosemary called her to come in an extra day to clean up a mess of sorts. When she got there and saw what it was that she was supposed to clean, she quit on the spot. It seems everything in one of the bathrooms was blocked up—the sink, the tub, the shower, the toilet. The whole bathroom looked charred and something rather large had been burned in the tub. Rosemary's explanation to the cleaning lady was that her husband did it to spite her before he moved out."

Ted nibbled on the remains of a chicken leg as he tried to digest the information Maggie had just shared. "Sounds like Miss Hershey needs a plumber. So what does this mean to us?"

"I don't know, Ted. I told you everything that happened today. Those ladies of Pinewood have Hershey on the run, that's for sure. When I was at Flanders's office, Rosemary kept referring to articles she was getting in the mail. They must be sending her stuff from the old trial. It's spooking her. She's acting out of character. Did you find out anything from the husband?"

Ted finished off the chicken leg and picked up the other one. "Not much. He really is a stand-up guy. His personal life is none of my business, so I couldn't dwell on it. He was busy but he gave me ten minutes. He's concentrating on the designs he's going to submit for the McLean horse farm. The guy is into it. He casually mentioned that he was in the process of dissolving his partnership with his wife and that he'd filed for divorce. Bobby Harcourt wouldn't say one bad word about Isabelle

Flanders. In fact, he told me he personally delivered a fica tree to her offices. I told him I heard the smart money says it was a tie between the two of them. His comment was, 'Then I'm in good company.' End of interview. Where does that leave us?"

"Right where we were this morning. I'll stay on Rosemary and you concentrate on the ladies of Pinewood. Which of us is covering the dinner at the Silver Swan?"

"Probably you. Are you sure there was nothing in Hershey's files?"

"I'm sure. I went through everything, page by page. There was nothing there that can help us. My gut tells me that whatever is going to happen is going to happen right after that dinner."

Ted tossed the picked-clean chicken leg on to his plate. "I think you're right . . . honey."

Eighteen

Alexis brought her Mini Cooper to a stop. She took a moment to look around at the neat, tidy nursery that Yoko owned. The windows of the long line of greenhouses sparkled in the late-morning sun. Knowing Yoko as she did, she expected no less than perfection. She climbed out of the car and headed for the flower shop.

A bell tinkled overhead when Alexis opened the door. Yoko looked up from the flowers she was arranging, alarm spreading across her face when she saw Alexis.

Alexis smiled. "This is nice, Yoko. Being surrounded by beautiful flowers and plants all day has to give you a good feeling. Are you busy?"

"Not really. Valentine's Day was our busiest time. Things taper off after that. My workers are busy in the greenhouses with the seedlings so they'll be ready for the first spring rush. Would you like some tea, perhaps coffee? We can go to the back, in my workroom, and one of the girls can handle the register and phone. Is something wrong?" Yoko whispered.

"No, nothing's wrong. Myra asked me to bring something to you. Today is Friday and she needs you to deliver it this afternoon. I brought some things for you, too. Can you get away?"

"It will not be a problem. Coffee or tea?"

Alexis looked around at the fica trees by the front windows, the tall rubber plants and an extremely large banana tree with three green bananas hanging off it. "Is there a market for banana trees?"

Yoko giggled. "Unfortunately, no. It was an expenditure of my husband's. I just keep moving it around. Do you see anything you like?"

Alexis smiled. "I like it all. One of these days I'm going to have my own house with all kinds of flower gardens. I'm partial to English gardens. I have—had—tons of catalogs before . . . you know, before. Depending on the size of my yard, I plan on some statuary, a fountain and tons and tons of flowers. I want the gardens to scream my name. You know: Alexis Thorne lives here and she loves flowers. But that's somewhere down the road and I try not to think about it too much." She sighed as she followed Yoko through a door that led to a massive work area. Everything smelled earthy and pungent.

Yoko opened a mini refrigerator and popped two bottles of root beer. She handed one to Alexis. They clinked their bottles in a silent toast. Yoko motioned to a high stool. "Now, tell me what it is you brought me."

"Everything is in the car. Myra wants you to deliver a set of blueprints to Rosemary Hershey's office. You'll be going as Mrs. Kim Yee again, so I brought a new outfit for you to wear, along with Myra's bag of diamonds. I haven't had root beer in years and years. This is really good."

Yoko leaned forward. "Whose blueprints are they?"

"I'm not sure, but if you want my guess, I'd say they're Isabelle's. You are to tell Miss Hershey that as you were leaving Mr. Harcourt's office he asked if you would mind dropping off the prints, since it was on your way, and you agreed. Other than that, I know nothing. Listen, I'd love to stay and hang out here but I have to get back to the farm. I'm expecting a lot of deliveries. My red bag is almost empty and we can't have that, now can we?"

Yoko giggled. "Absolutely not. I'll walk you to the car."

Outside in the bright sunshine, Alexis popped the trunk of the Mini Cooper. Between the two of them they managed to carry the blueprint cylinder and the various boxes and bags that Myra had said Yoko would need.

Alexis was about to close the trunk when Yoko looked at a pile of pink froth in the corner. She pointed, her eyes alight with laughter. "Is that what I think it is?"

"It's for my red bag. I got the idea when you told me what you saw in Rosemary's closet. You know, all those ballerina costumes. I thought having one in my bag might come in handy. I had this crazy idea . . . never mind."

"Oh, for a minute I thought you . . . you had a date . . . you're right, never mind."

Maggie Spritzer was right behind Rosemary Hershey as she stalked her way out of the Publix super-market having just created a scene with James, the tarot card reader. What the hell was *that* all about? Maggie wondered.

She didn't bother trying to hide or sidestep the architect this time. She could have been lit up like a neon sign and Rosemary wouldn't notice her. The manager of the supermarket had threatened to call the police and ordered Rosemary to leave the premises.

Rosemary drove erratically, running yellow lights and driving over the speed limit. Where were the cops when you needed them? Maggie didn't sweat the situation, knowing Rosemary was headed for her office because it was her sanctuary.

Ten minutes later, Maggie mentally patted herself on the back when she saw Rosemary's Mercedes in the parking lot of her office. She managed to park two spots away. She hoped the architect hadn't locked the car door this time so she could replace the things she'd taken out earlier. All she could do now was wait and use up some of the time calling some of the politicians and power brokers on her list. People who, according to Violet and the other Domestic Divas, Rosemary had slept with. She'd ask for a comment. She slid a CD into the player and leaned back against the headrest, her eyes never leaving the entrance to the building as she proceeded to make one phone call after another.

Little did she know that by making her phone calls she was aiding the ladies of Pinewood in their quest to bring Rosemary Hershey to justice

Inside, Rosemary Hershey stomped around her offices, cursing and yelling at her employees. "Today is Friday! Friday, people! Those designs were supposed to be finished last night! Are they finished? No!" she screeched. "They are not finished! That . . . that *crap* is not going anywhere. You call yourselves architects! You're a disgrace to the profession. You're all fired! Now, get out of here. You take nothing but your personal belongings. Now means now, people! Go! That goes for you, too," she said, shaking a finger at her secretary and receptionist. "And don't think you're going to collect unemployment either! I'll fight it!"

When the office cleared, Rosemary walked around trying to figure out if anyone had managed to smuggle anything out. She started to cry as she made her way back to her office with the sheaf of blueprints in her hand. There was no way she could go to dinner at the Silver Swan now. If she showed up with no entry, she'd look like a fool. The prints were supposed to be ready at four o'clock to be picked up by a messenger who would then transport them to Myra Rutledge. That wasn't going to happen now.

Crying and blubbering, Rosemary paced her offices. She was in this pickle because of Isabelle Flanders. She should kill her. But killing her was too good. She knew in her gut that Isabelle was going to win on Sunday night. She'd be back on top, with Bobby at her side, just the way it was before the accident. She'd like to kill Bobby, too.

Rosemary started to cry again. She wasn't going to kill anyone. She already had three deaths under her belt and didn't need to increase that number. Maybe she should cut and run. Maybe it was time to clear out, leave everything behind and start over somewhere else. It wasn't too late. She was still young, still beautiful. She could get a facelift, repair the damage these past weeks had wrecked on her person. All she had to do was go home, clean out her safe, pack her clothes and leave.

The phone rang. Rosemary waited and then remembered she'd fired the receptionist. She picked it up and barked a greeting. She reared back, panic rushing through her at the voice on the other end of the line.

"This is Connor Daniels, Rosemary. Listen to me, young lady, and listen carefully. I just had a call from some reporter at the *Post* asking for a comment about our affair. My question to you is: who did you blab to? I won't tolerate this, Rosemary. I have a family and I don't want any kind of scandal. You better take care of this, and I do mean immediately, or I'll be forced to use other measures. We had an agreement. Are you listening to me?"

Rosemary clenched her teeth. "Yes, I'm listening, Connor. I'm not the kiss-and-tell type. You need to look to your own end. Don't ever make the mistake of threatening me again. If I wanted to blackmail you or get even with you over something, I would have done it a long time ago. You do remember all those dirty little secrets you used to whisper in my ear, don't you? You used to love pillow talk. Don't call me again, and like I said, don't threaten me. I kept a diary. Enough said. Goodbye, Connor."

Rosemary was shaking so badly she had to sit on her hands to stop them from trembling. When the phone rang again she almost jumped out of her skin. Connor wouldn't be stupid enough to call back. Her arm snaked out. Her greeting this time was more subdued.

"Rosemary, this is Dwayne Hickman. I just got a call from some reporter at the *Post* asking for a comment about . . . our past relationship. Of course I denied everything other than having worked with you on our beach house. What's going on? If this gets out it is going to hurt you as much as me. I have teenagers. I want you to take care of this, Rosemary. Whatever you do, don't underestimate me when it comes to protecting my own. I want to hear you say something, Rosemary."

Rosemary thought her head was going to twist right off her neck. "If I knew what to say, Dwayne, I'd say it. I don't know how it happened. No one has been in touch with me. I never, ever, confided in anyone about our little affair. You do like to babble when you've had too much to drink. Don't blame me for this. I don't have anything else to say to you."

She slammed the phone back into place. She ran to the lavatory, closed the door and then slid down to the floor. She hugged her knees to her chest. Hard, bitter sobs ripped from her throat. She could hear the phone ringing off the hook. How long, she wondered, would it take for the reporter to go through her list of paramours? All day, she decided.

Just a few minutes ago she'd had a plan. What was it? Did she even care what it was? Rosemary curled into the fetal position and went to sleep.

Outside the lavatory, the private phone rang and rang and rang.

Promptly at two-thirty, mindful of the time, Yoko got out of the chauffeur-driven town car. Carrying the blueprints in their colorful container, she went into the building feeling like she'd entered an alien minefield. There was no sound, no sign of a human being. She looked over at the fish tanks that lined the walls. The fish moved from one end of the tanks to the other in lazy, graceful motions. It was way past lunchtime. Where was everyone?

Yoko licked at her dry lips as she crossed the small waiting area to the hall leading to the main offices at the back of the building. As she walked along, she called out Rosemary's name. She kept calling until she got to the doorway of Rosemary's office. Then she stood in the doorway, chills racing up and down her spine. Something was wrong. Suddenly she decided she didn't want to be here, but she was here and she had to follow through. She called out again. When the door of the lavatory opened, Yoko took a step backward. She hoped her expression didn't betray what she felt at the sight of the architect. No one alive looked like this. Then again, no dead person she'd ever seen looked like Rosemary Hershey, either. Yoko fought the urge to run.

She pasted a smile on her face and said, "Miss Hershey, Mr. Harcourt asked me if I would mind delivering this to you on my way home. I said I didn't mind. I apologize for coming straight through here, but there doesn't seem to be anyone else in the building. Mr. Harcourt seemed quite anxious that

you have this before four o'clock." She held out
the colorful cylinder.

Instead of stepping forward to reach out for it,
Rosemary backed up. Suspicion ringing in her
voice, she asked, "What is it?"

"I do not know. Mr. Harcourt just said you
would need this by four o'clock. He did say he
hoped it would put a smile on your face. I must
leave now."

"Wait. Wait. Bobby actually said that?"

"But of course. It was nice speaking with you
again, Miss Hershey. I'll just lay this on your desk.
Goodbye."

Rosemary rubbed her hands together as she
chewed on her lower lip. She eyed the cylinder
and then the phone when it started to ring again.
She ignored the phone as she gouged at the round
clip holding the contents of the tube secure. She
broke two nails as she tried to pry it off. Finally, she
used a letter opener. The lid shot in the air but
Rosemary barely noticed. The phone continued to
ring. She yanked at the contents and pulled out a
thick wad of blueprints, which she carried over to
her drafting table and spread out for easier view-
ing. The Barrington farm. She let her gaze travel
down to the bottom right-hand corner where it
said: ROSEMARY HERSHEY, ARCHITECT.

"Oh, God! Oh, you dear, sweet man! You did
this for me!"

Rosemary flipped the oversized sheets, marveling
at her husband's expertise. She literally swooned
with happiness. "Bobby, Bobby, Bobby, this is too
wonderful for words. You came through for me.
Thank you, thank you. I'll find a way to make this
up to you. I will, I swear I will."

The phone continued to ring. Finally, she picked it up, listened for a moment, then said, "Go to hell, you weasel!" It began to ring again the moment she broke the connection. Finally, she yanked the wire out of the baseboard jack.

She was back in the game. Without a doubt she was holding a winning hand. The designs were pure genius. Pure Bobby. Wonderful, sweet Bobby who had just saved her skin.

Rosemary spent the next fifteen minutes hunting down a new cylinder for the designs that bore her name. She spent another ten minutes typing up her submission letter. She was just about to clamp the lid on the cylinder when she realized she needed to make a copy of the prints, and used up another ten minutes doing that before it was time to slide the original into the cylinder. She knew the phone was still ringing because she could hear a faint fuzz, even though she'd ripped the cord out of the wall.

Rosemary felt giddy as she gathered up the blueprint container and carried it out to the waiting room to wait for the messenger who was due to arrive at four o'clock.

While she waited, she picked through the stack of mail that was sitting on the receptionist's desk. She sucked in her breath when she saw the two familiar white envelopes. She didn't have to open them. Why torture herself?

Why did Bobby give her his designs? She smiled at what she thought was the answer. Going out on his own he had limited time. Mrs. Yee must have hired him, which wouldn't leave him much time to work on a design for the horse farm. Whatever it was, she was the happy recipient of his generosity.

She made a mental note to send him a colossal Christmas present as a thank you.

The messenger was a young kid with saddlebags on his bike. He reached for the blueprints, ripped a receipt off a pad, initialed it and took off.

Nineteen

Jack Emery twisted sideways to throw another log on the fire. It was a pure reflex action on his part because he didn't want Nikki to see the shock he was feeling at what she'd just told him. Sometimes, like now, he wished he'd never agreed to be a silent partner to the ladies of Pinewood. He dusted his hands as he squirmed back into position. He wished he could turn the clock back to a time when he was just a struggling ADA in love with a rich girl who just happened to be a lawyer. Before . . . before so many things that haunted him these days.

"Why so serious tonight, Jack?" Nikki asked as she traced her index finger up and down his cheek.

Jack tried to shrug but it was hard since his head was in Nikki's lap. They were propped up in front of the fire on mounds of pillows. They'd just toasted weenies and marshmallows and were on their second bottle of wine. The evening had started out with such promise but now the glow was gone and even drinking three bottles of wine wasn't going to bring the mood back.

"No particular reason. I saw Ted today at Squire's Pub and he thumbed his nose at me. I'm having a hard time with that. You know how I feel about friendships. They're hard to come by and should be treasured. He wants to take a poke at me so bad to make himself feel better."

"Jack, the reason Ted keeps going to the pub is to see you, not to eat. He knows you go there all the time. Sometimes people don't know how to say they're sorry. I think Ted is as miserable as you are about your friendship. You could step up to the plate and make nice. You're not playing in a sandbox these days. You're all grown up, so start acting like the grownup you are." When Jack didn't respond, she continued. "Why do you guys have to turn everything into a pissing contest? So what if you blink first? So what? The next time, and there will be a next time, Ted will blink first, and you'll be even. But that's not all of it, is it?"

Jack tried to shrug again but was unsuccessful. He rolled away and propped himself up on one elbow. "No, that's not all of it."

Nikki's tone sharpened. "Is it what I told you about Rosemary Hershey that's bothering you? She killed three people, Jack. She ruined Isabelle's life. She has to pay for that."

"The law . . ."

Nikki's tone took on a hard edge. "Don't talk to me about the law, Jack. Hershey was tried and acquitted. Three people are still dead. A little boy is growing up without a mother and a father. His grandmother is elderly. What's going to happen to that child when she passes on? Isabelle can never get back her lost years or her reputation. The law isn't going to do a damn thing for those dead people, for that little boy or for Isabelle. You and I both know the law is seriously flawed. The prosecutor didn't do his job. If he had, Hershey would have been found guilty—and don't even think about blaming the jury."

"You made your point, Nik. I can't change the way I think, OK? Driving someone crazy is . . ."

"A bit over the top? Would you rather we had made it an eye for an eye, that kind of thing, which of course would mean we would have to kill her? We aren't murderers."

Jack watched a shower of sparks shoot upward in the fireplace. Normally he loved the snap and crackle of a good fire, but he wasn't enjoying this one. "Hell, no!"

Nikki stood up. "If we keep this up, one of us is going to say or do something we'll regret. I'm going back to the farm. Tomorrow is going to be a busy day for us and I don't want to give Myra any cause for worry. As it is, I think she pretty much knows what's going on between us."

Jack didn't get up. He felt like he'd just been punched in the gut. He hated being Nikki's dirty little secret. The room was almost dark apart from the flames from the fire. He could see tears glistening in Nikki's eyes before she turned and headed for the front door. He should get up, walk her to the door, kiss her good night. That's what he should do. He rolled over onto his stomach and banged his head on the floor. When the door closed behind Nikki he wanted to throw a tantrum the way he had when he was a little boy. She hadn't even said good night.

Jack mumbled and muttered to himself as he cleared up the dishes, corked the wine bottle and carried everything to the kitchen. He stood with his back to the counter as he looked around. Nikki's domain. This kitchen should have food smells in it but it didn't. It smelled like Nikki, all clean and sunshiny. Once she'd told him he smelled like a mossy glen, all woodsy and pungent. He remembered how flattered he'd been. Hell, he was flattered every time Nikki even looked at him. The fact that she loved him made him giddy.

It was nine o'clock according to the digital clock on the stove. He had nothing to do. The thought of watching television set his teeth on edge. Sleep was out of the question. He was too damn wired to even think about going to bed. If he had a dog, he could take it for a walk. But he didn't have a dog or a cat. Ted had two cats. Maybe he could go over there and . . . and . . . Yeah, he'd pick up a twelve pack and head over to Ted's place. Maybe a pizza. Ted loved pizza. Ted loved food, period.

Forty minutes later, Jack managed to find a parking space right in front of Ted's building. Pizza box in one hand, the twelve pack in the other hand, he used his knee to slam the door of his car shut. A gust of wind shoved him in the back, propelling him forward.

"Good evening, Mr. Emery. Eating rather late this evening, aren't we?"

Jack's blood ran cold. *Shit!* He sucked in his breath, envisioning the pizza flying through the air and the beer bottles crashing down on the sidewalk. He struggled for nonchalance. "Good evening, Special Agent Nevins. How goes it this blustery evening? I thought, and feel free to correct me if I'm wrong, but I thought Robinson got a restraining order against you guys."

"So, Mr. Emery? Restraining orders are just that: restraining orders. They really don't apply to people like me. I can prove the validity of that statement if you care to bring it to a head."

Jack's voice was angry and sarcastic. "That's not my decision, Special Agent Nevins. I'm just bringing dinner and a few beers to a friend. Do you have a problem with that?"

"Not right now, I don't. Later is another story. My predecessors keep asking about you, Emery. I keep telling them you're on the straight and narrow these days. Don't make me out to be a liar."

Jack snorted. "My bullshit meter just clicked on. Are we done now, Nevins? My pizza is getting cold."

"Then I suggest you go inside and eat it. Give Mr. Robinson my regards."

"I'll be sure to do that."

At Ted's apartment door, his hands full, Jack kicked at the scarred, paint-chipped door. Ted opened the door, Mickey and Minnie circling his feet. He eyed the pizza and the beer.

"I already ate, and I don't drink with people who lie to me," Ted growled.

"Cut the shit, Ted. I came over here to blink, so will you let me blink, for Christ's sake? Shut the damn door and lock it. Your shadow is still out there. We had a nice little chat."

"Don't try to con me, Emery. I got a restraining order against those goons."

"Yeah, yeah, he said that, but he also said restraining orders applied to other people, not the likes of him. You know that gold shield puts him in another category. He dared me to bring it to a head. Of course I declined. Dishes and napkins would be nice."

Hands on hips, his eyes suspicious, Ted demanded, "What do you want, Emery? It's late and I'm not in the mood for your shit."

"Fine, we'll eat without dishes and napkins. I came here to apologize and to explain."

Ted reached down to take a slice of pizza from the box. "Like I'd really believe anything you have to say."

"Goddamn it, Ted, sit down so I can say what I came here to say. Then, and only then, will I leave. Yeah, OK, I lied about me and Nikki. I never would have believed I was one of those guys who could only love once. I saw myself going through life miserable, with no wife, no kids, no house to call home. I decided I had no other choice but to go along with Nikki because I wanted her in my life, not outside it. I made the decision to . . . to look the other way, to ignore what I thought I knew. I don't expect you to understand that, Ted, but that's what happened. I want to marry Nikki one day. I have trouble knowing what I know, but I also have trouble with the law sometimes. OK, so now I'll leave."

"What are they up to now?" Ted asked.

Jack shrugged. "The deal Nikki and I have is don't ask, don't tell. Not a clue. It works for me and for Nikki, Ted, because we don't mix what she calls her business with our pleasure. I want to keep it that way. I also want you to know that I will not get in your way if you manage to nail any of this down," he added, lying through his teeth. "The ball's in your court now. Do you want me to leave?"

Ted eyed the last piece of pizza in the box before he snatched it. "How do I know you're telling me the truth? How do I know this isn't some snow job? You can spin with the best of them."

Jack closed the pizza box. "That's a decision only you can make. I hate it when I lose a friend. A good friend, and you've been a good friend, is hard to come by in this world we live in today. I don't want it to be Nikki versus you, Ted. We were lucky that we got back together. I don't want to lose her again, because she's part of me. When you find the right woman, you'll *really* understand."

Ted swigged from his beer bottle. "I asked Maggie to marry me. So I can relate to what you just said. She said yes, but didn't set a date."

Jack jumped up to pummel his friend on the back. "That's great, Ted! Congratulations! Wait a minute. What's that going to do to the byline?"

Ted laughed. "R comes before S. We'll make it work for us the way you and Nikki are making it work. If something goes awry, we'll fall back and regroup. That's down the road, so I can't worry about that now. The ladies of Pinewood are on the prowl again, Jack. They're taking on that architect, Rosemary Hershey. Stuff's going to go down any day now. Maggie and I have been partnering up on this and she's come up with a few things that lead us to believe whatever is going to happen will take place after that award dinner Sunday night. We're on it like fleas on a dog." Ted's voice suddenly turned suspicious. "Why aren't you asking me any questions?"

For an investigative reporter, sometimes Ted

was dumber than dirt. "Because I don't care. I only care about me and Nikki. Get it through your head; I moved beyond all that vengeance crap. It's in your hands now, buddy. But I'm more than willing to place a little wager that whatever those ladies are up to, you aren't going to nail them. They're slicker than greased pigs. Don't for one minute forget that guy out front. Isn't there *anything* going on in the world that you can still get excited about? Let's make it interesting and say fifty bucks."

Ted bellowed. "Fifty bucks! Are you fucking nuts? They're just a bunch of women playing at being vigilantes."

Jack laughed so hard his sides started to hurt. He gasped, "My point exactly! They have their asses covered six ways to Sunday."

"OK, smart-ass, you're on for fifty bucks. I'm gonna love taking your hard-earned money. To show you what a fine upstanding guy I am, I'm going to tell you a secret. Did you know there's a secret organization in this town that boasts eight hundred active members? They know everything," Ted said, repeating Maggie's words. "They know things that are going to happen before they actually happen." Ted wiggled his eyebrows. "And they're all women! All eight hundred of them!"

"Are you saying the ladies of Pinewood belong to this secret organization?" Jack felt befuddled at what he was hearing.

"Hell no. Well, maybe, but I don't think so. They call themselves the Beltway Divas."

"What's that mean to me, Ted? Are you telling me these eight hundred women represent the eight-hundred-pound gorilla?"

Ted rolled his eyes. "It could mean nothing or it could mean something. Just wanted you to know there was such an organization. Maggie cracked it and is now an honorary member." Ted wondered if he was telling a lie. Who cared? Jack needed to sweat a little.

Jack got up and slipped into his jacket. "You deal with it, Ted. I'm going home to bed. I have to be in court early. I work for a living, remember?" Jack shuffled his feet for a moment. "I'm glad we got squared away, Ted. Congratulations again. Tell Maggie I said so. When you're ready, let's go to dinner to celebrate." He clapped Ted on the back and raced Minnie and Mickey to the door.

"See ya," Ted said as he closed and locked the door. "Like I believe one damn thing you said, Mr. District Attorney!"

The evening air was almost balmy. Jack crossed his fingers that he would make it to his car without a dialogue with Special Agent Nevins. He felt lucky as he unlocked his car door. Before he could settle himself in the seat he could see the agent lumbering toward him. "Have a nice evening, Mr. Emery."

"Fuck you, asshole," Jack mumbled under his breath as he turned the key in the ignition and then hit the lights. He peeled away from the curb, his tires screeching.

As he drove through the deserted streets, Jack wished he could figure out what the gold shields were doing on the scene twenty-four-seven. Were they *protecting* the ladies of Pinewood? Knowing everything he now did, it was the only thing that made sense. That meant the ladies of Pinewood had *carte blanche* while they were in vigilante mode. What the hell was wrong with this picture?

By the time Jack arrived home, found a parking space and walked a block to the house, he still couldn't decide if he should call Nikki to alert her to what Ted had just told him. Maybe he should fade into the woodwork and just be the keeper of the secrets on both sides. He'd never been very good at straddling fences and there was no reason to believe he would be good at it now.

As he fumbled with the key in the lock he could feel the fine hairs on the back of his neck move. Nerves, he told himself. He used his shoulder on the door to push it open, then froze when he heard a voice he recognized. One of the first string of gold shields. One of the ones without a spleen these days. Quick recovery, he thought. If memory served him right, it had taken Ted *forever* to recover. Maybe this guy was in better shape. Carrying around one of those special gold shields could puff up anyone. No one was going to intimidate him, especially some jerk-off without a spleen.

"You better not be trying an end-run here, Emery. I just want you to know I have a personal stake in nailing your ass to the wall these days. Your nose drips and I'm going to haul in your ass."

The door wide open, Jack walked down the steps. "OK, you said it. You can stay here from now till the end of time and it isn't going to bother me. You want personal, I'll give you personal. You come within spitting distance of me and I'll have my buddies cut off your dick and I'll personally shove it up your ass. Now, *that's* personal. Go find a rock and crawl under it, you slug."

"Good night, Jack."

"Screw you, and don't go calling me Jack. Only my friends call me Jack."

Inside, with the door locked and bolted, the alarm set, Jack headed for the second floor where he stripped down and pulled on pajamas. He padded downstairs in his bare feet, added another log to the fire, and popped his last beer of the evening.

Call Nik or not call Nik? Why was it suddenly so hard to make a decision?

Twenty

Nikki Quinn woke up feeling out of sorts. She lay quietly, her gaze on the rocking chair across the room. Out of the corner of her eye she could see that it was moving. "Kind of early for a visit, isn't it, Barb?" Nikki asked as she rubbed sleep out of her eyes.

"I suppose. The sun will be up in a few minutes. I like to watch the sun rise more than I like to watch it set. Something about a new day as opposed to ending the day. You OK, Nik?"

"Define OK."

"Oh, you know, all's right with the world. All's right with Jack and the group. If you want to talk about it, I'm a good listener. Are you nervous about tomorrow night?"

Nikki sat up and wrapped her arms around her knees. "All of the above, I guess. I sort of had words with Jack last night. It wasn't an argument or anything like that. I left before that could happen. I waited till two o'clock this morning for him to call but he didn't. Even though he's more or less one of us, he still has trouble with his conscience. He really is one of the good guys, Barb. That's why I fell in love with him."

"I guess if I wanted to translate what you just said it would mean if push came to shove you aren't sure if Jack would push or shove. How'm I doing?"

"That pretty much sums it up." Nikki reached for the pillow beside her. She gave it a resounding smack.

"Here comes the sun. I think it's going to be a beautiful day. Try to think beautiful thoughts. What's on your agenda?"

"You boggle my mind, Barb. Don't you know what's going on? Aren't you all-seeing and all-feeling? Help me out here." She was rewarded with a tinkling laugh. The rocking chair grew still and then Willie, her stuffed bear, was in her hands. How warm he felt. How comforting. Nikki brought the bear to her cheek and closed her eyes. "God, I miss you, Barb. I'd give up every single thing in this world that I own or ever hope to own to have you back. I mean that." Her eyes filled with tears when she felt something soft brush against her cheek.

"I'll always be here, Nik. Just call my name. Hey, remember that song? C'mon, lighten up, it's going to be a beautiful day. I want you to stay alert and on your toes. Promise me, Nik."

Nikki swallowed hard. "I promise. Is something going to go wrong, Barb?"

"It could if you don't stay alert. See ya, girlfriend."

Nikki buried her head in her pillow and cried. When the sun was fully over the horizon, she crept from her bed and headed for the shower. A beautiful day for beautiful thoughts.

Downstairs, Myra was sitting alone at the kitchen

table, a cup of coffee in front of her. Her voice rang with cheerfulness. "Good morning, dear. I hope you slept well."

"So so," Nikki said as she poured herself a cup of coffee. She picked up a mini gooey sweet roll and stuffed the whole thing in her mouth. "I love sweets early in the morning. A sugar high early on helps me get moving. Then the caffeine kicks it up another notch, and bam, I'm off and running. Where's Charles?" she asked, looking around as though the former MI6 operative would materialize out of nowhere.

"In the command center seeing to last-minute details. It appears that everything is right on schedule. The others should arrive by noon. There doesn't seem to be much for me to do on this mission. My dinner is on schedule. I feel like I should be doing more."

"Once in a while we have to sit it out, Myra. On this mission, we'd just be in the way. It's not so bad to hold down the fort once in a while. Did Nealy arrive last night?"

"She arrived around midnight. Did we make too much noise? Right now she's out riding but she did peruse the designs and she said one of them popped her between the eyes. She also said she wished she was younger so she could revamp Sunstar Farms. You look tired, dear. Are you sure we didn't keep you awake? Nealy and I can get rowdy when we start with our memories."

"No, you didn't wake me. I hit that bed and was asleep within minutes," Nikki fibbed. She reached for another sticky bun. "Did Charles come up with anything else in regard to Rosemary Hershey?"

"As far as I know, no new information has come

in. Our plans remain the same. I do know that
Charles has someone watching Miss Hershey in
case she decides to make a run for it. If that happens, we'll have to improvise on the spot. I'm not
worried because you girls are so good at reacting
to a setback. Is something bothering you about
this mission, dear?"

"I have this weird feeling something is going to
happen. I'm sure it's my imagination. I get wired
up before . . . when it's time to hit the ground running. Just nerves," she said again.

"Charles said everything is under control. Calm
your nerves and think positive thoughts."

Positive thoughts. Beautiful thoughts. Nikki smiled.
"If you don't need me to do anything, I'm going to
go for a run."

"Run along then."

Jack Emery woke in a foul mood with an aching
back, his legs stiff and sore from sleeping on the
sofa. The last beer had turned into three more
until he finally conked out. He stumbled his way
upstairs where he showered and shaved, his brain
cells working overtime as he contemplated the day
ahead of him.

What really bothered him was that he hadn't
called Nikki. He'd wanted to call her. Meant to call
her after the second beer. Midway through the
third beer he'd hauled out his cell phone and
punched in the first three numbers before he cancelled the call. Those last three beers were a mistake. He should have called. Knowing Nikki the
way he did, he knew she expected him to call. He

could call now and come up with some excuse. Why the hell did he need an excuse?

He reached in his pocket for his cell phone, punched in her number and waited. Nikki was breathless when she answered.

"It's me, Nik. How come you're out of breath?"

"I'm out running. What's up?"

"Wanna go to lunch? I can drive out to Virginia if you can get away."

Nikki's voice was still breathless as she jogged in place. "I would love to but I can't. I waited for you to call last night."

"Yeah, well, I didn't." Brilliant, Jack. "I thought we both needed to calm down a little. More me than you. Look, I'm trying, Nikki. Sometimes . . . sometimes I have a hard time dealing with what you're doing and what I'm *not* doing. We talked about this. Actually, we pretty much talked it to death. I'm going to keep right on having bad moments, so you'll have to accept it."

"What is it about this time that's bothering you?"

"Because it's so over the top, so goddamn bizarre. I don't know, maybe because it was the end of the day, I was cranky, we were talking about Ted. Stuff piled up and I homed in on your activities. At this point, it doesn't really matter, now does it?" He listened to Nikki sigh deeply on the other end of the line.

"It does matter, Jack. The last time, when we went after the National Security Advisor, you helped. How do you explain that?"

"The best I can do is to say I love you. I don't want to lose you. I'm willing to do whatever it takes to keep us together. Look, this will pass. I guess I just want us to be on the same page so there are no misunderstandings later on. I'm going out to get some breakfast. Call me later if you get a chance. I'll probably be home going over some work. Listen, Nik, one more thing. You have too many open ends. There's no way you can get a lockdown on the location. You're going to be wide open. Have you thought about that?"

"We have it covered, Jack. I keep telling you, this is not a Mickey Mouse operation. Thanks for the concern. Love you."

"Love you, too."

Jack looked around for his jacket. Now he knew what it was that was bothering him. Giving voice to his concerns brought it front and center. Which meant he was going to have to act on those concerns.

Outside, he was surprised at how warm it was. Maybe spring was really on the way. He walked briskly up to the main thoroughfare and stopped in the Copper Penny where he ate a monster breakfast of bacon, eggs, pancakes, juice and three cups of coffee. While he waited for his order to arrive, he whipped out his cell phone. He didn't skirt around the issue but got right to the point.

"Harry, it's Jack Emery."

Harry Wong was a skinny, sinewy little man who owned and operated his own dojo in the heart of the District. With a black belt in martial arts, Harry was the logical man to train the local police one day a week. The training was mandatory and the officers who grumbled and complained in the beginning of the training thanked Harry profusely when they reached a satisfactory level of expertise.

Jack had trained with Harry for five years when he was an ADA and had managed somehow to cement a friendship that had lasted to this day.

"What's on your agenda tomorrow night, Harry? I know you told me not to call you again. Hey, buddy, I saw the fitness reports on those new recruits and they made me want to cry. Did you ever see a DA cry? It ain't pretty. Never you mind where I got those reports. I got them, end of story. Your guys need more practice. I hope you just had a bunch of sloppy recruits and you aren't slipping. I'm willing to give you that practice. What do you say? What do you mean, what's in it for you? The chance to help out a friend, that's what's in it for you. I'd do it for you and you know it. Who are you kidding, Harry? You never do anything on Sunday night except watch the tube. OK, I'll get back to you with the details," Jack said when he saw the waitress approaching the table with his food. "Yeah, I owe you, Harry. Yeah, big time."

Jack started to feel a little better now that he'd taken control of his end of the situation. By the time he was finished with his monster breakfast, he was feeling more than a little pleased with himself. He knew he was right. In fact, he was positive that he was right. But his high spirits suddenly took a nosedive when he realized he was aiding and abetting the ladies of Pinewood again. Which meant there was no backtracking now. He was just as guilty now as he was the night he'd helped them with the National Security Advisor. That had been behind the scenes. But behind the scenes or front and center, it didn't make one bit of difference. He was just as guilty as the ladies of Pinewood. His ass would go into the slammer right along with theirs. It was an ugly picture that he didn't want to dwell on.

Right now, though, he had a bigger problem. He had to find a way to elude the guy with the gold shield who was sitting outside waiting while he chowed down. He looked around, trying to assess his options. There were none that he could see.

He'd eaten here a few times but not enough that he knew the layout of the small café. He held out his cup to a roving waitress as he let his gaze rake the eatery. The restrooms were to the left. Kitchen to the right. Where was the back door? Probably somewhere near the kitchen. For sure there was a door in the kitchen, but the fire codes would make it mandatory to have another exit other than the front door. Would Nevins or his counterpart have a view of the back door? Probably, since it was the first rule of surveillance. Always know how your subject could elude you. That left only the restroom and a window. Assuming there *was* a window.

Four cups of coffee demanded that Jack head for the restroom. He left a small pile of bills on the table and made his way across the café. He cursed when he saw the forty-seven coats of paint on the restroom window. It looked like it hadn't been opened for years and years. OK, that left the back exit or the kitchen exit. If he was going to do that, he might as well go out the front door and head back to the house for his car. Maybe he could lose the shield in traffic.

Outside in the early-morning spring air, Jack sprinted for the corner where he waited for the light to change. His destination was one block up and one block over where there was a cop directing traffic. His ID in hand, he walked briskly, knowing his tail was right with him. Too bad he couldn't turn around for a full-frontal look. To do so would alert the shield to his intentions.

Jack slowed his steps as he approached the corner. He waited for the light to turn red, at which point the traffic cop stepped to the curb. He sprinted forward, arriving at the curb at the same time the cop did. He whipped out his ID and hissed, "I want you to detain the tall guy in the dark suit. He's wearing sunglasses. Looks like a Fed but he isn't. Don't let his creds fool you. I put him away ten years ago and he's out now swearing to kill me. I just need a five-minute head start. Can you do it?"

The stocky cop got into the act and mumbled under his breath. "I'll give you a head start when the light changes. I'll hold him. OK, pick up your feet and go!"

The moment the light turned green, Jack ran across the street and then sprinted up one street and down another until he spotted a cab, which he flagged down. He hopped in and yelled, "Drive!"

"Where to, mister?"

"Just drive till I catch my breath. I want to make a deal with you. I don't want the meter running either. A hundred bucks for the next hour and a half. Twenty buck tip."

The driver turned off the meter. "Let me see the money up front."

Jack obliged.

The minute his breathing returned to normal, he handed over a piece of paper on which he'd drawn a crude map. "That's where I want to go. I'm going to need you to wait for me while I check out some things. Relax, I'm the District Attorney. I know what I'm doing. I need to check out every entrance and every exit and I have some measuring to do. It shouldn't take me more than an hour. You OK with that?"

"Yeah. What would you have said if I said no?"

"Then I'd just have to kill you," Jack said cheerfully.

Twenty-One

Rosemary Hershey looked at the clock. Sixty minutes till it was time to leave for the Silver Swan. She was already dressed and made up. She'd done a remarkable makeup job, if she did say so herself. Of course, the hours she'd spent at the spa earlier accounted for much of the way she looked. The massage was heavenly. The facial to die for. The manicure and pedicure exquisite. The new hairstyle was so perfect that she couldn't have asked for a better one. The industrial strength under-eye concealer had worked magic. She still looked thin and a little gaunt, but her pumpkin-colored dress with the matching jacket covered a multitude of flaws—her scrawny arms and loss of one breast size, just to mention a few. The mandarin collar successfully covered her stringy neck. She felt that she was more than presentable. If anything, she'd blow plain old Isabelle Flanders's socks right off her feet.

She still hadn't spoken to Bobby, although she'd

tried calling his cell phone to thank him for giving her his designs to enter as her own. Tonight, though, she'd get a chance to talk to him. If she played her cards right, she could entice him back to the house and *really* thank him. The way she used to. The thought sent shivers up and down her spine.

With nothing to do until it was time to leave, Rosemary walked around her house. She passed the door to Bobby's bathroom with the charred blackened mess still inside. She brought herself up short. How could she bring Bobby back here with that mess? Was there a key somewhere so she could lock the door? Of course there was; she just had to find it. She really needed to get back on track and find a new cleaning lady. Someone, anyone, to clean up that mess.

Her pacing took her to her home office. It was so messy she didn't even want to step inside. She could see the pile of hate mail on her desk. She'd given up opening the mail days ago. Let old Isabelle send her all the crap she wanted. She wasn't going to buckle. The case was over and done with. No one could touch her for anything that had happened in the past. Just let them try and she'd come out swinging with both arms. Feet, too, if necessary.

People died every day of the week. Every single day of the week, traffic accidents killed people. Every single day of the week people profited from those accidents. Isabelle was a slug. A goody two-shoes. Content to piddle along, no long-term goals, going to dinner with Bobby one night a week, having sex on that same one night. Bobby needed more. Rosemary had given him more, too. But in the end he was just like Isabelle, dull and boring with only one ambition in life: pleasing the client.

She'd let those mailings get to her at first. She'd become paranoid, thinking someone was after her. So what if they were? No one could prove anything. Everything was now after the fact. She'd bounced back with a vengeance, thanks to Bobby. She really had to make it up to him.

A horrible thought struck her suddenly. If Bobby had given up his designs to her then he wouldn't be at the dinner because he didn't have an entry. Even if he worked around the clock there was no way he could have completed two designs. Well, that took the ice out of the ice cream. She didn't even know where he was living these days. He didn't return her calls, so how was she supposed to get in touch with him?

Rosemary poked her head into her walk-in closet that looked like the aftereffects of a fifty-percent sale at Saks. Her gaze went to the back of the closet and the rainbow of froth. She blinked. The froth was all part of her planned seduction of her husband. He was still her husband, after all. She could win him back in a heartbeat. She was sure of it. Maybe one of the architects at the dinner would know where Bobby was these days. She wasn't about to give up unless she absolutely had to.

She looked down at the Presidential Rolex on her wrist. The car service she'd hired for the evening should be arriving any minute now.

The long beveled mirror on the closet door beckoned. She posed, she preened, she turned this way and that. Perfect! I'm going to win tonight.

Bobby's designs are spectacular. How could I not win? My speech will be short and succinct. A sincere thank you. I'm looking forward to working on this remarkable project. A dazzling smile for the cameras and then the walk back to her table. More smiles. Lots of handshaking. Everyone congratulating her, even though they didn't mean it. Jealousy was a terrible thing.

Another plaque for her office wall. Maybe she'd make Architect of the Year again. With a contract like this one, how could she not win accolades? Getting the nomination was a piece of cake. She knew exactly what she had to do to get it. Been there, done that.

The doorbell rang just as Rosemary started to walk down the hall. Time to go, she thought happily. The hell with you, Isabelle Flanders. You can't win.

When she'd settled herself in the back seat of the town car, Rosemary wondered why she was still trembling. Nerves, she told herself, something she had a right to feel considering the circumstances. The trembling had nothing to do with Isabelle and the ugly mail she'd been getting these past few weeks. Absolutely nothing.

Myra stood in the doorway of the dining room, welcoming her guests with Charles at her side. She smiled and made small talk as she handed out a seating diagram to each guest. Out of the corner of her eye she could see the governor and Nealy Clay talking animatedly. The mayor and other dignitaries milled around, sipping champagne and sampling the canapés.

Inside, the tables were draped in pale yellow with centerpieces of exquisite flowers. There was a small dais with a podium. A draped easel with the winning entry stood to the left of the podium where Myra would later announce whose designs had won the coveted position. The architects— some friends, some acquaintances—milled around as they talked shop. Elegantly clad waiters walked around with trays of dainty canapés and flutes of champagne.

A small cluster of architects stood at the back of the room extolling the gastronomic delights of dining at the Silver Swan. The selection this evening, according to Isabelle Flanders, was lobster and shrimp scampi, prime rib and chicken cordon bleu. Bobby Harcourt smiled and made a small wager that the lobster and shrimp scampi would be the first choice.

"It looks like we're all seated at table number seven," Isabelle said as she looked down at the table plan in her hands. "You're sitting next to me, Bobby." Under her breath she muttered, "I wonder how that happened."

Bobby grinned. "Pure dumb luck, I'd say."

Ignoring the byplay, a balding Joel Witlaw asked, "Anyone have any inside information on tonight's choice?"

Agnes Simmons, a sixtyish dowager, laughed and said, "It'll go to one of these young bucks here. We've been put out to pasture, Joe. All us old-timers had our day in the sun a hundred years ago. Speaking strictly for myself, while I submitted an entry, I'm here for the dinner. This place is way beyond my means."

Bobby looked uncomfortable at the woman's

words but he knew it was true. The old-timers rarely submitted a unique or original design, preferring to go the remodeling route. Maybe he really did have a shot at the McLean horse farm. He wasn't being conceited when he thought that his only real competition was Isabelle. If she won over him, he'd be happy for her. She deserved to win, too, to make up for the bad years.

"Looks like it's time to take our seats," Agnes Simmons said. "Where's that wife of yours, Bobby?"

Bobby looked around. "I don't know. I haven't seen her this evening."

"She's over there by table twelve. I saw her when she came in," Joel Witlaw said. "I think she's seated with the Pioneers."

Isabelle gathered up her long turquoise skirt and sat down in the chair that Bobby held out for her. She gathered the short, shimmery shawl closer about her bare shoulders and looked up to see Rosemary Hershey glaring at her from across the room. She started to shake. Bobby leaned closer and whispered in her ear. "She can only spoil this evening for you, Isabelle, if you allow it. Don't give her the satisfaction."

Easy for him to say. He didn't know what was going to happen within the hour. How, Isabelle wondered, was she going to choke down the food that was coming her way, knowing what was about to happen? Around her, everyone was chattering, their voices coming at her from all angles. Off in the distance, Isabelle could feel Myra's gaze on her. She smiled and winked. Charles tilted his head slightly, which meant *stiff upper lip.*

Isabelle sucked in her breath as she dug her fork into the delectable salad in front of her. She tried to listen to the small talk going on around her but finally gave up and concentrated on eating. She gulped at the champagne in her glass as though it was iced tea.

"Easy on the bubbly," Bobby whispered. "Why are you so nervous? You're probably going to win. I have a feeling this is your night, Isabelle. The rest of us are just here to see you back on top."

Isabelle placed her salad fork on her plate. "That's really a nice thing to say, Bobby, and I know you mean it. But I think you're the one who's going to take it home. You're a good architect, Bobby, one of the best. You just made a shitty fiancé. The flowers are beautiful," she said, trying to change the subject.

Dinner progressed, served on the fine bone china the Silver Swan was noted for. Isabelle longed for coffee but the plan was that when coffee was being served, Myra would take to the podium, announce the winning architect and then display the winning design already on the easel. But before she did that, she would make another announcement that would rock the room.

Isabelle's heartbeat sped up as she looked around, trying to imagine her colleagues' reaction. She couldn't help but wonder what Bobby would do.

The waiter reached for Isabelle's cup to fill it. She wanted it so badly she could almost taste it but she knew she'd spill it all over the place if she tried to pick it up. She felt Bobby's eyes on her but all she could do was offer up a sickly smile.

Myra rapped a small gavel for silence. The only sound to be heard was the clink of the china cups on the saucers.

"On behalf of the new owners of Barrington Farms, I want to thank you all for coming this evening. I know you weren't given much notice and the owners asked me to convey their appreciation to you for your willingness to participate in this worthwhile endeavor on such short notice. We have a winning design, chosen by Nealy Clay. I'll get to that in a minute. First, though, I have another announcement to make. It saddens me to make it, but I have no other choice."

Isabelle clasped her hands together in her lap. *Here it comes,* she thought. *You can handle it. Take a deep breath and know it's just part of the plan.*

"In going over the designs, it was soon apparent that two sets of blueprints were identical. However, each one had a different name on it. I'm not making an accusation; your architectural board will have to do that. It was obvious that one of you saw fit to place your name on a colleague's work to pass off as your own design. The reason I know this is because Isabelle Flanders submitted her design a week ago. When the duplicate design came in, submitted by Rosemary Hershey, we were forced to go to Miss Flanders's offices to have her colleagues vouch for the authenticity of her work. We were not able to glean anything from Miss Hershey's offices as there were no employees to question. Miss Hershey herself was unavailable for comment. Unfortunately, Rosemary Hershey will have to answer to your board. I would appreciate it if you would now leave the room, Miss Hershey. I would like to apologize to all of you for this unpleasant announcement."

Isabelle, her face whiter than snow, gasped right on cue. She saw a flash of pumpkin color as Rosemary fled toward the door screaming, "She did it to me again! She stole my design just like she did last time! Are you people going to let her get away with this? Well, are you?" She continued to screech as she slammed her way through the double doors.

Dumbfounded at the announcement, the occupants of the room could only gape and stare. Then the room erupted in sound, high and strident.

Myra waited until the door closed behind Rosemary before she spoke again. "And the winning entry comes from Isabelle Flanders!" The audience clapped half-heartedly as Isabelle stood up, a triumphant look on her face.

What the hell was going on here? Bobby looked around as though the answer to his question would materialize out of thin air. When nothing happened, he looked at Isabelle and said, "Congratulations, Isabelle, you deserve to win." A second later he sprinted from the room, the eyes of the audience on his back.

Her legs shaking, her face alive with pleasure, Isabelle walked up to the easel and pulled back the cover. "This is *my* design. Make no mistake about it." Her voice was shaky but it didn't matter. She'd won fair and square. Nealy Clay said her designs were the best she'd ever seen. Even the governor shook her hand and congratulated her. Myra and Charles hugged her as everyone looked on.

Outside the restaurant, Bobby looked around for his wife but he couldn't see her. Then he whirled around and saw her heading straight for him. Screaming at the top of her lungs, she said, "You bastard! You set me up in there! I fell for it, too! How could you do that to me, Bobby? Why did you do it?'

"What the hell are you talking about, Rosemary?"

"Oh, so you want to play dumb, is that it? How much did you have to pay that Japanese lady to bring me those plans? Damn you, how much? You knocking off ten percent on her job? You sent me all that garbage in the mail, too, didn't you? What a scum-sucking lowlife you are. Well, Bobby Harcourt, you just messed with me for the last time. I'll get you for this, you and that stupid woman you're still lusting after."

"Rosemary, what are you talking about? I didn't send you anything. Mrs. Yee did not hire me. I never saw her again after that meeting in my old office. How did you get hold of Isabelle's designs?"

"Don't you mean how did *Isabelle* get hold of *my* designs? Why are you so quick to judge me? You . . . you . . . piece of scum."

"No, I meant what I said. I know you stole her designs the first time. I recognize her work. You found a way to do it again. This time I don't think you're going to get away with it. I know you, Rosemary, I lived with you. I know what you're capable of doing, which is just about anything to get your way. If you want some advice, I'd bail out right now before someone files charges against you. I saw the looks on our colleagues' faces in that room. They weren't pretty. It's all going to come out now."

Rosemary started to cry. "Bobby, wait. Come home with me. I need . . . I need you. I need you to help me."

Bobby turned away. "I have to go back inside."

"Will you come by the house later?"

"No."

"Bobby, please. Don't turn on me, too. Mrs. Yee

brought those blueprints to my office and said you wanted me to have them. They had my name on them. For God's sake, what was I supposed to do? She said they were from you. I thought you were trying to make up and so you did that for me. Please, Bobby, this is not my fault. I didn't steal anything from that woman. Ask yourself how I could do that. An hour of your time, two at the most. That's all I'm asking for. Please, Bobby, I need your help."

Bobby turned and shrugged. Rosemary took it as a yes.

Inside the town car, her mind raced. Who *was* the mysterious Mrs. Yee? A friend of Isabelle's, obviously. God, how was she going to wiggle her way out of this? Bobby would help her. He was still her husband. Surely he wouldn't let her go down for something she didn't do.

Not Bobby. Not ethical Bobby.

Twenty-Two

Rosemary Hershey tripped her way up the concrete stairs that led to her front door. She hummed under her breath as she fit the key in the lock. Bobby was going to make everything all right. In the scheme of things, tonight was nothing more than a little hiccup. Bobby would know what to do. She just had to put her trust in him. Bobby didn't lie. If he said he didn't send the designs via the Asian lady, then he didn't send them. The Asian lady was probably a buddy of Isabelle Flanders and they were trying to do her in. Well, it wasn't going to work.

Isabelle was so stupid. Who in their right mind would put themselves through such a humiliating experience? Bobby would make sure everything came out right in the end. The board would listen to Bobby. The architectural community would listen to Bobby.

"I know I'm on safe ground, I just know it," she said to herself.

Time to get ready for Bobby. First, though, she had to find the key to the damn bathroom. In her haste she forgot to arm the security panel. She also forgot to lock the front door.

It took Rosemary ten full minutes to find the key. As she searched the linen closet and the vanity drawers she gagged and sputtered at the putrid smell coming from the drains. She leaned over to take a better look at the mess in the tub. A slimy coating of mildew covered the entire bed of water. The same slimy mold was in the sink, the shower and the toilet. She remembered reading something not too long ago about mold causing all kinds of sickness. Maybe she would have to move. In her own bathroom she reached for a can of air spray. She squirted and sprayed everywhere until she started to sneeze.

Rosemary zipped around her bedroom, stripping the bed, putting on clean sheets, picking up the piles of dirty clothes and dumping them in the hamper. When things were neat and tidy, she sprayed the bedsheets with lavender. Bobby loved lavender. Bobby loved anything that was the color purple.

She knew his weaknesses and his strengths. She'd play to both of them. How much time did she have? An hour? Forty minutes? He had seen how desperate she was. More like thirty minutes.

Rosemary shifted into high gear as she kicked off her shoes, stripped off the pumpkin-colored outfit and then her underwear. She bundled everything up and shoved it into the back of her closet. Naked, she pushed aside her business suits and found her playtime ballerina costumes. She had them in every color, all with matching ballet slip-

pers. Each outfit came with tights, but she'd pre-
ferred the G-strings when she performed for Bobby
in the early days of their marriage. Which one to
choose? The lavender one, of course, since Bobby
loved the color.

Five minutes later, Rosemary had the ballet shoes
on and laced around her ankles. The G-string was
next, followed by the tutu, the netting flaring out
from her slim hips. Bobby always got an instant
erection the moment he saw her in one of her ballerina outfits, the little ruffled parasol. He'd never
been able to wait for her to finish her childish dance.

Now, all she had to do was wait. She was glad
now that she hadn't changed the locks on the
door. Bobby would use his key, creep up the steps
and then she'd go into her dance. Five minutes
and he would be eating out of her hand.

Sitting on the vanity bench at the foot of the
bed, Rosemary let her thoughts drift to what had
happened at the Silver Swan. No one at that dinner would believe she would do such a thing.
Thank God she'd had the presence of mind to
stand up and make her position known. And who
was that Asian woman? Rosemary started to rock
from side to side on the vanity bench as she
hummed under her breath. Bobby's thirty minutes
were almost up.

Outside Rosemary's house, Maggie Spritzer whispered into the cell phone pressed to her ear, her
gaze never leaving the driveway. She felt reasonably safe standing behind the blue spruce near the
stairs that led to the front door.

"What do you want me to do, Ted? Where's the

husband? When will you be leaving? The temperature is dropping here. Where's the damn husband? Well, I heard her ask him—no, actually she was pleading with him to come here. Guess what? She didn't lock the door. I can see through the side panel and she didn't arm the security system. She really is expecting him. She didn't act like anything was wrong. Listen to me, Ted, this lady is off the wall. She was humming and singing under her breath when she got here. I literally got here five minutes before her town car showed up. Is it your feeling the husband is going to show up?" When Maggie finally wound down, she listened to Ted answer all her questions.

Maggie slapped at her head in frustration. "Let me make sure I understand what you just said. You followed Isabelle Flanders, who hopped in her car, and she was laughing. Laughing? She then went to a gas station, parked and made a call on her cell phone while she laughed some more. She's laughing because she's happy at winning. Are you saying there's something wrong with this picture, Ted? You don't know where the husband is and you don't know if the dinner is over. Is that it? OK, you don't have to get snippy with me. What do you want me to do? The door's open; I could just open it and walk in. All right, all right, I won't do that. Wait a minute, sweet cheeks. I see someone coming this way. Nah, they went right past. OK, I'll stay here for a little while longer. Where is the Flanders woman now? Still at the gas station. No, I am not going to talk dirty to you while we wait this out. Bye, Ted."

*   *   *

Isabelle waited in the Speedway parking lot. It was such a busy gas station that no one paid any attention to her. She was waiting to hear from either Myra, Yoko or Kathryn to tell her what to do.

God, how she'd anguished over her little performance. It was all a blur, but she kept hearing Rosemary screeching at the top of her lungs. She was still congratulating herself on winning when her cell phone rang.

"Are you all right, dear? You were marvelous. So ladylike, so humble. You're halfway to your vindication now, dear. We aren't sure what happened outside when Mr. Harcourt ran after his wife. It's so hard for me to understand how he got tangled up with that Hershey woman," Myra said.

"Bobby is a fine architect with an excellent reputation. If there are any blemishes on his record, it's Rosemary. He'll be fine. You're right, his designs are spectacular." A devil perched itself on Isabelle's shoulder. "But they aren't as good as mine."

"Touché. Everyone is gone. Nealy left a few minutes ago. Charles and I are ready to leave for the farm. I'd like you to stay close in case Kathryn and Alexis need you. You probably should go out to the cemetery just in case, but if you're tired and want to go home, I can have Nikki fill in."

"No, Myra, I'm fine. I'd like to see this through to the end. Do you think Bobby is going to go to Rosemary's house?"

"Actually, dear, Charles overheard several of the architects invite him to some private club and he accepted their invitation, so it's doubtful. I think he's finished with Miss Hershey. Be careful, Isabelle."

"I will, Myra. Good night. Oh, by the way, it was a lovely dinner."

"Thank you. I think everyone in the room thanked me personally. It's almost over now, Isabelle. Sit back and know you will be vindicated in a matter of a few hours."

Isabelle leaned her head back against the headrest. Finally, finally, her own sweet revenge. What more could she ask for?

For starters, finding a storefront somewhere, hanging up her sign saying she was back in business. Oh, she'd follow through on the Barrington farm because that was a labor of love, but after that, she was going solo like she had back in the beginning. Her new partners would be thrilled to have her fancy new office. Starting over was going to be such a challenge, and she was going to do it her own way. Simply.

In just a little while, this whole mess would be over. Just a few more hours and she would be the old Isabelle again. Maybe then she could learn to smile again, to take joy in the little things in life. Just a few more hours.

Jack Emery felt confident he'd lost his tail even though it had taken him well over two hours to do so. He'd changed cars three times, thanks to cooperative friends, and now here he was, hiding behind the biggest tombstone he could find, baseball bat at his side. He had night-vision goggles, thanks to Mark Lane's days at the FBI, his bat and the gun in his shoulder holster, and a taser in his pants pocket. Harry Wong and his friends were secure in one of the mausoleums. He wondered if he should send them home. Gut instinct told him to wait.

Sacred Trinity cemetery gave him the creeps. Even when he was a kid and hell on wheels, he'd never ventured into a cemetery, at Halloween or any other time. His skin crawled at what he could see through the night-vision goggles. Mark said they also had a heat sensor that would pick up body heat if anyone came within a certain distance. Like that was really going to help him with Harry and his crew just around the corner.

"Let's get this show on the road already," Jack muttered as he jiggled around, trying to keep warm. The light mist that was falling wasn't helping his mood at all. He dropped to his haunches, his back against the huge stone that towered over him. Somebody important must be buried here to warrant such an impressive monument.

"C'mon, c'mon ladies, let's get on with it," he muttered.

Kathryn Lucas parked the newly rented car, whose license plate was covered in mud, at the curb in front of Rosemary Hershey's house. She and Alexis got out of the car and walked boldly up to the front door. Both were dressed for the weather in denim and rain slickers. Heavy Frye boots covered their feet. Both wore flesh-colored latex gloves. Kathryn carried the necessary lock picks and was stunned when she realized that the door wasn't locked at all. The security system wasn't armed, either. The women looked at one another but remained quiet as they entered the house. Alexis turned around and locked the door.

"What's that smell?" Kathryn said as she wrinkled her nose. "Smells like burned popcorn or something." She jerked her thumb upward to indicate Alexis was to follow her up the stairs. "Shhh," she said as she tested each step to see if it made any kind of a sound. They were halfway up the stairs when Rosemary's voice rang out.

"I'm in my room, Bobby. I've been waiting for you."

"Boy, is she going to be disappointed," Alexis whispered.

"What's taking you so long, you sweet man?" Rosemary sing-songed. Kathryn wiggled her eyebrows as she clamped her hand over her mouth. She pointed to the end of the hall.

"We rush in on the count of three. You jab her with the needle and we're outta here. If the husband shows up, we're dead in the water."

"One, two, three." Both women rushed into the room and skidded to a stop on the thick carpeting. Kathryn gawked. Alexis gaped.

"I didn't know it was a dress-up party," Kathryn said, pointing to Rosemary's outfit. "From her profile I took her to be a garter belt and panties kind of gal. This works, too, I guess."

"Damn. So that's what those outfits are for. We just thought she was a ballerina or something. In her other life, of course," Alexis said.

"What? Who are you? Where's Bobby? How did you get in here?" Rosemary screamed. She was on her feet in an instant as she looked for something to protect herself with. Quicker than a cat, she sat back down, rolled backward off the vanity bench to land in the middle of the bed where she yanked at the portable phone, brandishing it like a weapon.

"Don't come any closer! What do you want?" she asked, choking with fright and fury. Both women could see her fingers searching out the numbers on the keypad. In the blink of an eye, Kathryn yanked the telephone wire from the jack. Still screeching at the top of her lungs, Rosemary leaped off the bed and backed up toward the bathroom door. Kathryn and Alexis rushed forward, Alexis tackling her at the knees, Kathryn getting her neck in a vise grip. Rosemary lashed out, bringing the portable phone down on the side of Kathryn's face. Blood spurted from the wicked opening on her cheekbone.

"We're your newest nightmare, lady, now shut up. Hit it, girl!"

Alexis jabbed the needle into Rosemary's arm just as she took a second wild swing in her direction with the portable phone.

"Oooh," Rosemary gurgled, wilting and sliding gracefully to the floor. "How can I dance now? I feel so . . . so . . . loose. Bobby likes me to dance for him. He loves purple."

"Honey, your dancing days are over. They bury people in purple," Kathryn snarled. She picked up a hand towel from the bathroom vanity. "This damn well better not leave a scar! How bad is it, Alexis?"

Alexis peered at the gash. "You should get some stitches. Check the medicine cabinet to see if there are any butterfly bandages. Stick one on and let's get out of here. We have to hurry, Kathryn. She's expecting her husband. He *might* show up. Wet a cloth and hold it over your cheek. We can always stop at a drugstore."

"Don't ballerinas wear tights?" Kathryn asked as she did what Alexis told her to do.

"I have no clue, I've never been to the ballet. Oh, dear, she's wearing a G-string. Guess it goes with the dance," Alexis giggled. "Bobby doesn't know what he's missing. Then again, maybe he does and that's why he isn't here." She giggled again as she bent over to sling Rosemary over her shoulder. "Grab the umbrella. It goes with the outfit."

"Oooh, this is so different. Where are we going?" Rosemary continued to gurgle happily.

"You don't want to know. Now shut up," Kathryn said.

"How long does the shot last?" Alexis asked.

"Charles said she'll be in la-la land for a full thirty minutes. We have to have her in place by the time the shot wears off. I have a feeling this chick is going to fight like a tiger once she figures out what's going on. I have to check out the front of the house. Someone might be walking around. People walk their dogs at this time of night. I'll turn off the front light since it really lights up the front and the walkway," Kathryn said. "All clear," she confirmed as she held the door open.

Alexis, with Rosemary wobbling every which way on her back, sprinted forward. Kathryn had gone ahead of her and was already opening the back door of the car.

Maggie Spritzer felt like her eyeballs were going to pop out of her head. She hit the speed dial on her cell phone and waited for Ted to pick up. "You aren't going to believe this, Ted. Two women walked into Hershey's house, bold as anything, snatched Hershey and dumped her in the car. She's dressed in some kind of frou-frou outfit. I saw her bare ass. Yeah, I did. And, she was wearing ballet shoes. Keep the line open. I gotta get my car and try to follow them. Where's Flanders?"

"She's on the move. I'm with her. Don't lose those women, Maggie."

"Like I'd do that on purpose. My guess is they're all going to the same place, so if one or the other of us loses our quarry, we'll know."

Maggie goosed her Honda and tore down the road in hot pursuit.

Jack Emery's stomach heaved when he saw the first car enter the cemetery. He wished he was home in his warm bed. He adjusted the night-vision goggles and his jaw dropped almost to his knees when he saw the truck driver and the black woman get out of the car. Together, the two of them half-carried and half-dragged Rosemary Hershey across the sodden grass toward an open grave. His stomach heaved again at the women's intentions. From his position, he could hear their conversations perfectly. He waited.

"She's coming around, Kathryn. Quick, we have to slide her down into the grave. Damn, I didn't think Charles was going to be able to do this. Fifteen-feet deep. Big enough for three coffins, two big ones, one little one. He's a man of many talents. Think about it, Kathryn, what's he going to do tomorrow, call up the cemetery and say he changed his mind? They'll think he's nuts. Where's Isabelle?" Alexis asked, her voice full of panic.

"I don't know. Come on. Grab hold of that rope so we can lower her down. We don't want her breaking any bones. We're screwing with her mind, not her body."

Jack watched as the two women struggled to push Rosemary Hershey up the mound of dirt and then lower their quarry into the deep grave. Hershey's arms started to flail as she dug her feet into the wet earth. It took all of the women's strength to push her over the side and still hold on to the rope.

"How's it going?" Isabelle whispered as she appeared out of the darkness.

"Damn, girl, you scared ten years off my life." Alexis's voice verged on hysterical. "She's down there. We lowered her with the rope. You missed the best part. She's dressed in a purple tutu and ballet shoes. She kept mumbling about dancing for Bobby. I'm thinking it's something kinky. You can hardly hear her scream from here. You want to say something to her? You know, maybe something meaningful or . . . or something. This is just way too creepy for me." Alexis stopped her frantic babbling just long enough to take a deep breath.

"Well, hell yes, I have something to say to that lying piece of crap." Isabelle crawled to the top of the mound of dirt and leaned over the gaping hole. "Yoohoo, Rosemary, it's Isabelle. We're going to bury you alive unless you tell the truth about what happened when you killed those people. The whole truth and nothing but the truth. We have a bag full of rattlesnakes up here. Start talking, lady, or the next thing you hear is going to be a rattle."

"You bitch! Damn you to hell. I knew it was you the whole time. You were behind those blueprints. You're the one who has been sending me that stuff in the mail. Get me out of here. Isabelle, get me out of here! Bobby will make you pay for this. Pull me up. Please. You win, OK. Please, get me out of here. My God, I could die down here."

"Nah. Stay there. Do you know whose grave this is? I bet you don't care, either, but I'm going to tell you anyway. Mrs. Myers wants her son, her daughter-in-law and her granddaughter buried in the same plot. The one you're standing in. You'll be on the bottom. A foursome. How cozy. Tell us the truth. It's starting to rain, Rosemary. If it rains hard, the grave will fill up and you'll drown. Tell us about the wine you drank that day at lunch. Tell us you were driving and how fast you were going. Admit you ran the stop sign. Admit you stole my designs. Admit all of it and we'll pull you up."

"Wait, wait!" Alexis said. She ran back to the car to return with the purple parasol. She opened it and tossed it downward. She shrugged at the looks of disbelief on Kathryn's and Isabelle's faces. "It goes with the outfit."

"Did you hear something?" Kathryn asked, whirling around.

"Just her screeching. It's starting to rain harder. Makes a funny sound when it hits the cobblestones," Alexis said. She wondered if that was true.

"Yoohoo, Rosemary, it's starting to rain harder. Tell us the truth and we'll pull you out of there. You got your umbrella up? I bet you're cold down there. You shoulda worn the tights instead of the G-string." Alexis turned to Isabelle and Kathryn. "She doesn't sound too scared. She sure has a lot of guts. I'd be out of my mind if I was down there. Where's the tape recorder?"

"It's on top of the mound. It's protected. It's

half in and half out of one of those plastic baggies," Kathryn said.

The three women climbed to the top of the mound again. "OK, Rosemary, this is your last chance. Either you tell the truth or we start shoveling. You'll be covered in mud within minutes. Here comes the first snake. You'll probably die in ten minutes or so. I'm waiting."

Isabelle reached into a plastic bag and withdrew a plastic wind-up snake whose tail gave off a buzzing sound. All thanks to Charles's shopping spree on the Internet, where anything and everything could be purchased for a price.

"Shut up! Just shut up!" Rosemary screamed. "The jury found in my favor. Get over it. Do you want to be a murderer?" She screamed again. "I demand you get me out of here right now! Right this minute. I'm freezing. Oh, God! Get that damn thing out of here. Now! I'm afraid of snakes." Isabelle tossed down a second snake. Rosemary's screams could be heard all over the cemetery.

"I don't much care. No one is ever going to find you. We'll cover you up with a layer of this dirt and the Myers family will be right on top of you. The burial is set for tomorrow morning. Nine o'clock. Now spit it out or I'll jump down there and beat it out of you," Isabelle shouted. "You're trying my patience. I have four more snakes. They don't care who they bite!"

"It bit me! It bit me!" Rosemary shrilled.

The women looked at one another. "Fear is a terrible thing," Kathryn said. "The thing probably wiggled close to her ankle. Let her sweat it."

"She's tough!" Alexis said in awe.

"I'm thinking she doesn't believe us. Maybe it's time to start shoveling," Isabelle said. "You're right, she's one tough cookie. She isn't going to give it up. I knew this was all too good to be true. I'm never going to get my revenge."

"Shhh. Yes you are. She's playing with us just like we're playing with her."

While the women discussed the situation, Maggie Spritzer and Ted Robinson huddled behind a triple gravestone that was six feet tall. "They're going to bury her alive, Ted. They threw rattle-snakes down in that grave. We have to stop this right now! We can make a citizen's arrest. We can call the police. We have them red-handed. For God's sake, do or say something!"

Jack Emery turned up the voice sensor on the small antenna hiding in his ear. Did he just hear Ted and Maggie? Shit! He stuck his head out from behind the angel's wing and strained to see into the night. He was glad now that he'd stuck the taser gun in his pants pocket at the last second. He heaved a sigh of relief when he heard Ted say, "Not yet."

Jack turned back to the women and would have fainted if a gust of heavy wind hadn't knocked him sideways. All he heard was, "The damn rope split. Now what are we going to do? How are we going to get her out of there?"

Isabelle panicked. "She hasn't confessed yet. We need to get her on tape. Otherwise this has all been for nothing."

"Hey, Rosemary," Kathryn called down into the open grave. "The rope just broke. There's no way to get you out of there. It's starting to rain harder and I can see that little parasol is already in shreds.

Tell us what we want to know and I'll lower Isabelle down to pull you up. I'm going to count to five. Spit it out or we're leaving."

"Oh, my God!" Alexis bleated. "That dirt is sliding down there at the end. We have to do something. It'll bury her!"

Twenty-Three

Jack moved back into place. Shit! Shit! Shit! He was semi-protected by the wingspread of the carved angel that towered over him. He reached up to touch it, hoping that alone would tell him what to do. If he didn't move soon, Rosemary Hershey could get buried by a mound of earth toppling down on top of her. If the rope really broke the way the women said it did, they were up the creek without a paddle. If he showed himself, Ted and Maggie would be on him in a heartbeat. He had to think fast and act faster. He wasted a few seconds, listening to the frantic women. When he stuck his head out and around the tombstone he couldn't believe what he was seeing. Someone was dangling over the edge of the open grave. The women had made a human chain in an effort to bring Hershey topside. The rain was coming down in torrents now, which meant they were dealing with pure mud. He could hear the Hershey woman

screaming. The other three were cursing, using
words he'd never heard before.

Jack popped back around the other side of the
angel to see what Ted and Maggie were doing.
Nothing. He whistled. Two heads popped round
the six-foot marker. He whistled again. Both reporters crawled forward. That's when Jack aimed
the taser and fired twice. Both reporters crumpled
to the ground. Twenty minutes and they'd be up
with a vengeance.

Jack hit the ground running.

He had to give them credit. If they were panick-
ing, they didn't let him see it. Anyone else, he
thought, would have screamed and run off at the
sight of him. He could only imagine what kind of
image he presented with the night-vision goggles
and the antenna coming out of his ears. He
dropped to his stomach and inched his way up the
mound of wet mud. Kathryn turned and stared at
Jack and then jerked her head in Isabelle's direction.

"She can't hold on to her. The mud is too slip-
pery."

The heat sensor was going off again. Jack struggled to look through the rain but couldn't see anything. Ah, shit! Where the hell was his brain? If
Ted and Maggie were here, then so were their
shadows.

Jack ripped at a whistle hanging on a chain
around his neck. He blew two sharp blasts as he
yanked Isabelle back from the yawning opening in
the ground. "Get out of here! Take the south entrance and run like the hounds of hell are at your
heels. I'll get her out of here. The two reporters

from the *Post* are to your left. Go!" The truck driver reached for him like she was going to strangle him. Then Jack said the magic words that made Kathryn and the other two pick up their feet. "Charles sent me. Go!" It was all the trio needed to hear.

Harry Wong and his merry band of black-clad ninjas appeared out of the rain the moment the women took off at lightning speed. "See you got your ass in a sling again, eh, Emery?"

"Nice to see you too, Harry. Get her out of there," Jack said, pointing to the open grave. "I can't hang around here. Here come the shields. You have my permission to beat the living shit out of them. I hit Ted and Maggie with the taser so they'll be coming around soon. Scare the living shit out of them too, OK? Can you handle it, buddy?"

"Piece of cake, Jack. Here, catch!" he said, throwing the tape recorder in the plastic bag toward Jack, who caught it on the fly. "Move your ass, mister, here come the assholes!"

Jack split, knowing he was leaving the situation in capable hands.

Kathryn drove the rental car the way she did her rig—at eighty miles an hour. Her face was grim and tight, the gash on her cheek oozing blood, which she swiped at from time to time.

Isabelle sat in the back seat, a triumphant smile on her face. "We got her! Did you hear her confession? Did you? Damn, that was music to my ears."

Kathryn slammed on the brakes and made a U-turn in the middle of the road. "We forgot to take the stuff out of Rosemary's safe. We have to go back for it."

Isabelle was so happy she started to cry. "I was a little busy there at the end with all that mud sliding into the grave, but I did hear her confess. God, I thought I'd never hear those words. But we left the tape recorder by the grave. Charles is going to be so . . . so angry with us. We were like amateurs tonight. What the hell happened to us back there?"

"The rain, for one thing. Fifteen feet of piled-up dirt that turned into mud is what happened to us," Alexis said. "Hey, we got away. That's the important thing. Trust me, that woman is never, ever, going to be the same."

"Someone call Charles. We're going to need his help in opening Hershey's safe. You do it, Alexis, and for God's sake, Isabelle, stop gloating. We still have work to do."

"Why do you always have to be so mean, Kathryn? I never claimed to be a professional vigilante. If I remember your mission, you almost fainted and couldn't respond. No one said a word to you because we all understood what you were going through. It's not so hard to be nice once in a while."

Kathryn's shoulders slumped. "You're right, Isabelle. I'm sorry. Sometimes I don't know . . . It's hard to be nice. I don't know why that is. I think I've been defensive all my life. I don't know why that is, either. I've never had anyone but Alan depend on me. This is all as new to me as it is to you. I'll . . . I'll try harder to be nice."

Isabelle sniffed. "If that's an apology, I accept."

"Damn good thing. We're here. Since we didn't lock the door, I guess we just waltz in like we belong here."

"I have Charles on an open line, so let's get with it," Alexis said. She shoved the phone in her pocket and motioned to the two women to move closer. "Charles said he didn't send anyone to help us."

"Then who the hell was that person back at the cemetery?" Isabelle demanded.

"Maybe our guardian angel. Whoever he was, he saved the day, or rather, the night. Hey, maybe it was Bobby Harcourt. Did you recognize his voice, Isabelle?" Kathryn asked.

"If you recall, I was dangling over the grave at the time. No, I didn't recognize the voice and it was hard to see the man's face with the watch cap, those things coming out of his ears and those funky-looking goggles. Maybe it was one of those men with the special shields."

"No, not them; Charles would have known. We can talk about this later. We have a job to do, so let's do it and get back to the farm. I still think it was the husband. Rosemary was expecting him," Kathryn said as she opened the front door. "Since we shredded our latex gloves at the cemetery, we can't afford to leave any fingerprints. Hershey probably has some panty hose we can use. Alexis, check out the dresser drawers and don't leave any prints. Isabelle, come with me." Alexis moved off but not before she tossed the cell phone to Kathryn.

Kathryn's hands were feverish as she removed the desk drawer and then the false bottom to reveal the safe. The phone to her ear, she followed Charles's instructions for a full fifteen minutes, stopping only once to push her hand through one end of Rosemary Hershey's panty hose.

"It's not opening, Charles."

"Let me try," Alexis said as she dropped to her knees. "Let's go through it again, Charles. Kathryn

is all thumbs this evening. Slow. I understand."
Twelve minutes later, the last tumbler fell into
place. Alexis sat back on her haunches. "And vic-
tory is ours!" she said triumphantly. "Get one of
those pillowcases and we'll put everything in it."

"I just heard the front door open," Isabelle
hissed, her eyes full of panic. "Oh, God, it's Bobby!
He's going to come up here. Hide!"

"Where?" the wild-eyed women hissed in return.
Isabelle ran to the closet, Alexis crouched down
behind the recliner in the corner and Kathryn was
left to stand behind the open door. She had the
good sense to turn off the desk light before she
scurried to the door.

"Are you here, Rosemary?" Bobby shouted from
the hallway. "What the hell is that smell? No games;
it's late and I'm tired. OK, have it your way. I'm
leaving." The light in the office came on. Bobby
stood in the doorway taking in the scene—the
desk drawer on the floor, the open safe. He made
a snorting sound before he turned off the light.
The women heard him walk down the stairs and
the front door close.

"Now, *that* was close," Kathryn said as she stepped
away from the door and out to the hall where she
waited for Alexis and Isabelle. "If I'm even halfway
correct, I think Mr. Harcourt correctly assumed
Rosemary cleaned out her safe, which he probably
knew nothing about, and took off. That's what I
would think if I was in his place."

"Let's get out of here. God, I cannot wait to get
back to the farm. This has been one hell of a night.
I don't know if I'll ever sleep again. That guy . . .
the one Charles *didn't* send . . . you all believe he
pulled her out, don't you?"

"Yeah, sure," Alexis said.

"Of course. Why else would he let us get away?" Kathryn said.

"But what if he didn't . . . ?"

"Isabelle, shut up. He got her out. I'm trying to be nice here. Don't push it. Rosemary is probably in some five-star hotel right now soaking in a hot tub. She's sipping fine wine and nibbling on chocolate-covered strawberries. Now, wipe down anything you touched and let's go home."

"The tape . . ."

"We're going to let Charles worry about that tape," Kathryn said. "I'm still trying to be nice here, Isabelle. Keep pushing it and I'm going back to being my old nasty, ugly self."

Isabelle clamped her lips shut. Alexis did the same thing.

Kathryn tossed the pillowcase onto the back seat, climbed behind the wheel, backed out of the driveway and headed for McLean.

Forty minutes later, Kathryn signaled to turn into Myra's driveway. A car roared past them and out to the highway.

"Who was that?"

"Probably a friend of Charles. Who else would dare use this private driveway?" Kathryn pulled abreast of the keypad to punch in the code. A plastic bag holding the tape recorder was stuck to the pad with duct tape. Kathryn pulled it off and handed it to Alexis. "I think maybe that guy who just roared out of this driveway was our guardian angel. I don't want to ever talk about this again. Agreed?"

"Agreed," Alexis and Isabelle said in unison.

Kathryn parked the car and got out, Alexis and Isabelle right behind her. "We did it!"

"We did, didn't we?" Alexis laughed.

"We sure did. OK, let's go and tell the others all about it."

Myra held the door wide open. "Welcome home, girls!"

front page was a picture of Rosalind. Her boy-co

Epilogue

Charles stood behind Myra's chair, his hands on her shoulders. His face wore a huge smile. Myra was smiling, too. The others relaxed. Smiles were a good thing.

It was late-morning and they'd celebrated the previous night's events with a gourmet breakfast after sleeping late. Now they were all assembled in the command center waiting to see what Charles had to say.

"Ladies, I have always believed a picture is worth more than a thousand words. Although, in this case there are words to match the picture. Myra, do the honors."

Myra reached down into the canvas bag at her feet. She held up six copies of the *Post,* which she handed out. She could barely contain herself. "And it's *above* the fold!"

The women laughed, sputtered, choked and then high-fived each other. Smack in the middle of the front page was a picture of Rosemary Hershey, covered in mud, dressed in her muddy tutu, holding her tattered parasol as she was helped from the fifteen-foot grave. The caption under the picture said: "Miss Hershey, a well-known Washington, DC architect, was singing and saying she was going to dance for her husband when she inadvertently toppled into the freshly dug grave." The article went on to say that she had been taken to George Washington's psychiatric unit.

"Are we all comfortable in agreeing that Isabelle's case is satisfactorily closed?"

All the women agreed.

"Charles made copies of the tape and sent them to the architectural board, the insurance companies and the lawyers involved in the initial lawsuit. Later today, the contents of the safe will be delivered to Mrs. Myers by a trusted friend. She will now, thanks to you, have a much easier life, and young Tommy's future is secure. The money won't bring back their family, nothing can do that, but I hope Mrs. Myers felt some satisfaction this morning when she read the paper. On the off chance that she didn't see it, there will be one in the packet we'll be leaving with her. Well done, girls. Do any of you have anything you want to add or say at this time?" The women shook their heads.

Isabelle spoke up. "Can I hear the tape one more time? Just the part where Rosemary confessed. I heard it but I was so busy trying not to fall into that grave that I think I missed half of it."

Charles walked back to his workstation to return with the mini recorder. He pressed a button to fast-forward the tape. Isabelle clasped her hands against her chest and sucked in her breath. She closed her eyes and listened to the voice on the tape.

"All right, you bitch! I did it! I stole your designs. I framed you. Now are you satisfied? Get me out of here!"

Isabelle's clenched fist shot into the air. "That'll do for me!" She looked around, her face serious, her voice just as serious. "Thank you all. Thank you all so much."

"It was our pleasure, Isabelle," Charles said. The others nodded, smiles on their faces.

Beaming from ear to ear, Myra said, "Ladies, it's time to choose the recipient of our next mission. Isabelle, choose a name."

Isabelle reached into the shoe box. She handed the folded slip of paper to Myra.

"Alexis," Myra said happily.

"We'll now adjourn and meet here one month from today. Thank you again for all your efforts."

The women laughed as they filed out of the command center, chattering about how they were going to spend the next month. Outside, they hugged one another before they climbed into their vehicles to go their separate ways.

Whether you are new to Fern Michaels's fabulous Sisterhood series,
or have read every book,
you won't want to miss the next adventure of the Ladies of Pinewood!

Turn the page for a special preview of

VANISHING ACT,

a Zebra paperback on sale in January 2010.

Prologue

Five Years Earlier

It was a beautiful restaurant, beautifully decorated with well-dressed diners, discreet service, and ambience that had no equal. It was the kind of restaurant where there were no prices on the parchment menus because if you had to ask the price, you didn't belong in The Palm—or so said the owner. Not the Palm Restaurant in New York. This was the Palm Restaurant in Atlanta, Georgia. On Peachtree Road. A hundred-year-old eatery passed down through multiple generations of the same family. When people talked about this particular restaurant, they always managed to mention *Gone With the Wind* in the same breath.

Plain and simple, it was a place to be seen. Not necessarily heard.

Not that the young couple wanted to be seen. Or heard, for that matter. They didn't. They were there because they were celebrating the possibility of a business venture, and what better place than the Palm? Years from now, no one would remember that the couple had been there drinking priceless wine, eating gourmet food served on the finest china, and drinking superb champagne from exquisite crystal flutes.

The woman was striking, the kind of woman men turned to for a second look, the kind of woman other women looked at and sighed about, wishing they looked more like her. She was a Wharton graduate. Her professors had given her glowing recommendations, assuring all and sundry that she would go far in the world of finance. She believed them implicitly.

The young man looked athletic, the boy next door, clear complexion, sandy hair. Tall, at six-two, a hundred and eighty pounds. He, too, was a Wharton graduate. He also dressed well—and women stared openly; men took a quick look and turned away, vowing to do something about their receding hairlines and paunches.

They looked like the perfect couple, but they weren't really a couple in the true sense of the word. Partners was more like it, but in time they would drift together, not out of passion but out of need.

The man was fearless.

The woman was a worrier.

They were not compatible.

The only real thing they shared was their mutual greed.

The woman held her champagne flute aloft and smiled. The man clinked his flute against hers and liked the sound. A clear *ping* of crystal.

"So, is it a deal or not?" the woman asked.

"It has flaws."

"Every plan has flaws. Flaws can be corrected," the woman said.

"That's true. I'm inclined to go along with it. But I think I need some reassurance."

The woman set down her glass and reached over for her clutch bag. It was small and glittery and gold in color. She opened it. There was only one thing in the small bag. She withdrew the little packet and slid it across the table.

The man blinked, then blinked again as he looked inside the dark blue covers. At first he thought he was looking at a small stack of passports. What he was really looking at was a pile of old-fashioned bankbooks. Something in his brain clicked as he calculated the last stamped numbers. He pushed the little stack back toward the woman. She, in turn, redeposited the bankbooks in their nest inside the clutch bag.

"Well?"

"There's over one million dollars on those books."

"And I did it all myself. Imagine what we could do together. In five years, we could have a hundred times that amount of money. Offshore, of course. You look nervous," the woman said.

The man sipped his champagne. "Only a fool wouldn't be nervous. I'm not a fool. What you're saying is that you require my organizational skills to continue, is that it?"

She hated to admit it, but she said, "Yes, that's what I'm saying."

The man remained silent long enough that the woman had to prod him. "It's risky," he said.

"Everything in life involves risk," she said, finishing her champagne.

The waiter approached the table and poured more. She nodded her thanks.

The man raised his glass, smiled, and clinked it against hers. "All right . . . partner."

"There is one thing," the woman added. The man's eyebrows lifted. "This is a five-year project, not one day longer. We need to agree on that right now. On December thirty-first, five years from now, our assets are divided equally. You go your way, I go my way. If you don't agree to it, there's no reason for us to stay here to eat the meal we ordered. I'll leave now, and you can pay the check."

"Why five years?"

"Because that's my timeline, my deadline."

The man shrugged. "Okay. Should we shake hands or something?"

The woman reached into the pocket of her suit jacket and withdrew a tape recorder that was no bigger than a credit card. She smiled. "It's on record. We don't need to shake hands. Oh, look, here comes our food!"

An hour later, just as they were finishing their meal, the man asked, "Aren't you forgetting something?"

The woman twirled a strand of her hair as she stared across the table at the man she'd agreed to partner with. Her eyes narrowed slightly. "I don't think so." She let go of the hair between her fingers and started to crunch up her napkin and gather up her purse.

"What about the . . . ?"

The woman froze in position. "Do not go there. I presented the deal to you, and you accepted it. There are no other perks. That's another way of saying what's mine is mine. Not yours."

The man wasn't about to give up. "But—"

"There are no buts. Any other operations I have

going on are solely mine. I mentioned them only to show you that the possibilities are endless." She was fast losing patience with her dinner companion. "Well?"

The man still wasn't about to give up. "Can we address this at some later point?"

"No. This is the end of it." She could tell by the man's expression that it was not the end of it. She sighed. Greed was the most powerful motivator in the world. She was on her feet and walking toward the door. *Like I'll really share my little gold mine with someone like him.*

One

The day was hot and sultry, the sun blistering in the bright-blue cloudless sky. Even the birds that usually chirped a greeting when the Sisters appeared poolside seemed to have gone for cover in the cool, tall pines on Big Pine Mountain.

"I can't believe this heat! It's only July, and we're on a mountain!" Alexis said as she fanned herself with the book she'd been reading. "It's a good thing we aren't on a mission. We'd disintegrate."

Nikki stood up, a glorious nymph in a simple, one-piece pearl-white swimsuit, and headed for the diving board. "Don't even say the word *mission*, Alexis. We're on hiatus. My brain has gone to sleep," she shouted over her shoulder.

The Sisters watched Nikki as she danced her way to the end of the diving board. She bounced up, then hit the water, barely making a ripple. A perfect dive that would have been the envy of any Olympic diver who might have seen it.

After Nikki—a glorious bronzed creature—surfaced, she swam to the far side of the pool, climbed out, and walked back to the chair that sat under a monster outdoor umbrella. She immediately started to lather on an SPF 35 sunblock.

Yoko appeared out of nowhere carrying a huge tray, with plastic cups and a frosty pitcher of lemonade.

"What's for dinner?" Kathryn asked.

"Whatever it is, it better be slap-down delicious," Annie warned.

"Then you better get on the stick, my dear, since it is your turn to cook," Myra said with a straight face.

The wind taken out of her sails, Annie got up and headed toward the main building. "Don't you all be talking about my sagging ass while I'm gone," she tossed back.

"Don't worry, dear, when it gets down to your knees it will be time enough to talk about your derriere."

The Sisters giggled as Annie flipped her friend the bird and continued her march to the kitchen.

"Slap-down delicious! I wonder what she'll whip up," Isabelle said.

"Weenies on the grill. Wanna bet? And she'll talk the whole time about how slap-down delicious they are," Yoko said, laughing. "We had weenies twice last week. I hate it when Annie cooks. A very nice shrimp stir-fry with jasmine rice would be nice."

"With a light, fluffy lemon pie or maybe a pineapple cake for dessert," Kathryn said.

"I'd settle for a corned beef on rye with a ton of mustard," Nikki said.

"Well, none of that is going to happen unless we

get up, go to the kitchen, and toss those weenies I know she's going to make down the garbage disposal," Alexis said.

"We could go in and help," Myra said hesitantly.

"We could, couldn't we," Nikki said, making no move to get up.

No one else moved, either.

No one said a word.

Because it was suddenly so silent, the Sisters were able to hear the gears of the cable car as it descended the mountain. Suddenly realizing that the cable car was going *down,* the Sisters looked at one another.

They moved then as one, racing to the main building, where the gun cabinet was located. Within seconds, Nikki had it opened and was handing each Sister her weapon. In bathing suits and bare feet, they ran out of the building, across the compound, and stopped only when Annie shouted for them to wait as she flew down the steps, gun in hand and a string of hot dogs dangling around her neck.

"Jack's in court," Nikki said. "I just talked to him at lunchtime."

"Harry's at Quantico," Yoko said.

"Bert is at the White House having lunch with the president," Kathryn said.

Alexis and Isabelle looked at one another and shrugged before Alexis finally said, "Joe Espinosa is on assignment in Baltimore."

"Lizzie?" Annie asked.

"She's in Las Vegas. She checked in early this morning," Myra said.

"Nellie and Elias went to New Jersey to see Elias's new grandchild," Isabelle said.

"Then some stranger is on his or her way up the

mountain," Annie, the best shot of them all, said. "Wait a minute, what about Maggie?"

"She and Ted went to Nantucket for a long weekend," Nikki volunteered.

"Then it has to be someone who knows us, knows about the cable car, and knows about the switch at the bottom of the mountain," Myra said. "Maybe we should stop the car halfway up until we decide who it is."

"But if someone knows about the car and managed to get it to the bottom, they know about the safety switch inside," Kathryn said. "We should cut the power! As you can see, the dogs aren't real happy. Otherwise, they'd have gobbled those weenies, and Annie would be flat on the ground."

The Sisters looked down at the two dogs belonging to Kathryn and Alexis, then to Annie and her necklace of hot dogs. As the two dogs pranced on and off the platform that housed the cable car when it was inactive, they snarled and pawed the ground.

"C'mon, c'mon, someone make a decision here," Kathryn hissed. "The car is coming up. Now, goddamn it!"

"Wait two minutes and cut the power," Myra said calmly.

Kathryn raced to the platform, her index finger on the master switch. "Tell me when, Myra."

Myra looked down at the oversize watch on her wrist with the glow-in-the-dark numbers. One hundred and seventeen seconds later, she said, *"Now!"*

The dogs went silent, running to their mistresses and panting as though to say, *What now?*

The Sisters looked at one another.

"I suppose we can hold out longer than the person in the cable car. We need to make a decision here," Nikki said.

Annie waved her gun. "Unless there are seven people in that cable car, I'd say we outnumber our visitors."

"Feds? CIA?" Alexis demanded.

Myra shook, her head. "Bert would have let us know if anyone at the Bureau was looking at us. I was thinking more like Secret Service, but even that's a bit of a stretch. It is entirely possible some hunter, some stranger, stumbled over the hidden switch and is just exploring for a look-see."

Annie made an unladylike sound. "If you believe that, Myra, I am going to strangle you with this string of hot dogs."

"At least then we wouldn't have to eat them," Myra quipped.

For the first time, the two dogs seemed to get the scent of the wieners wrapped around Annie's neck. As she broke off some of the weenies and handed them out, she was suddenly their new best friend.

"How long are we going to stand here in the boiling sun?" Yoko asked as she swiped at her forehead with the inside of her arm. "I say we let the car come all the way up but stop it before it hits the pad. Let the passenger swing over the side of the mountain. We'll still be in control."

Myra thought about that for a moment before she looked at Annie and nodded. Kathryn flicked the switch that turned the power back on. They all held their breath as the cable car started upward, the gears protesting at the status change.

Myra looked down at the dogs quivering at her knees. Their ears were flat against their heads, the fur on the nape of their necks standing straight up and bristling, their tails between their legs. A trifecta that could only mean trouble.

Up high, a fluffy cloud bank sailed past, momentarily blotting out the orange ball of the sun. Someone sighed.

Annie looked at her fellow Sisters and liked what she was seeing. Then she looked at their hands. Steady as rocks. She took a moment to wonder how loud the sound would be this high on the mountain if all seven guns went off at the same time. Pretty damn loud, she decided.

Myra licked her lips. "Turn off the power now, Kathryn."

Kathryn turned the switch. The sound of the cable car's grinding gears screeched so loud that the dogs howled. The Sisters rushed to the platform and peered over the side. But all they could see was the top of the cable car and the grille on the side. The identity of the occupant was still in doubt.

"How about if we announce ourselves?" Annie whispered. The others looked at her, their eyes questioning. "You know, a shot across the bow, so to speak. In this case, I think I can shave it pretty close to the grille. If you like, I can shoot off the lock. Of course, if I do that, the person inside *could* fall out. Not that we care, but we should take a vote!"

Knowing what a crack shot Annie was, the Sisters as one decided it was a no-brainer. "Do it, dear. We don't need to vote," Myra said.

Annie did it. Sparks flew, and the roar of outrage that erupted from inside the cable car made the Sisters step back and blink.

"Charles!" they shouted in unison.

One look at Myra's expression kept the guns in their hands steady as Kathryn turned the power switch back on. They all watched with narrowed eyes as the car slid into its nest, the door swinging wildly back and forth.

Two

Charles Martin stood rooted to the floor of the cable car. He dropped his duffel bag and raised his hands as he eyed his welcoming committee with a jaundiced eye. Whatever he had been expecting, this definitely wasn't it. He couldn't remember the last time he'd seen so much exposed bronzed, oiled skin. Nor had seven women ever gotten the drop on him. One part of him was pleased to see that the guns were steady even though they were aimed at every part of his body. He knew Annie could blow his head off in the blink of an eye. Myra would aim for his knee and hit the pine tree fifty feet away. The others would hit their marks, and he'd wind up dead as a doornail. Then they'd bundle him up and toss him off the mountain. *Cheerfully* toss him off the mountain.

He knew they were all waiting for him to say something. Anything that would make this little

scenario easier. For them. Not for him. He hated
the look he was seeing on Myra's face.

Murphy and Grady pawed the ground but
stayed near the Sisters. They could not understand
these strange goings-on. Charles was the guy who
had slipped them bacon, fed them twice a day, and
even gave them root beer on special occasions.
And he was always good for a belly rub before
going to bed. He had a good throwing arm, too,
and would throw sticks for them to retrieve for
hours on end. They whimpered in unison, hoping
for a kind word. They whimpered even louder
when nothing of the kind happened.

Charles had known this little reunion wasn't
going to be easy, but he didn't think it was going to
be quite so devastating. He cleared his throat. "The
way I see it, ladies, is this. I have two choices here.
Three, actually. One, I can pick up my bag and
leave and apologize for this unexpected visit. Two,
I can pick up my bag and go to my quarters, and
we'll pick up where we left off. Three, you can rid-
dle my body with bullets and toss me over the
mountain. Decide, ladies. I'm very tired right now
and in no mood to remain in limbo."

Annie risked a glance at Myra, who seemed to
be in a trance. "An explanation would go a long
way in helping us make our decision."

"As much as I would like to provide one, Annie,
I'm afraid that I can't. Do you know you have a
string of frankfurters hanging around your neck?"

Annie ignored the question. "Can't or won't?" she
snapped.

"Both!" Charles snapped in return.

"You think you can just waltz back to this mountain and pick up where you left off with no explanations? You left us flat, to fend for ourselves," Kathryn screeched, her voice carrying over the mountain. "Your conduct is . . . was . . . unacceptable regardless of the circumstances. We deserved more, Charles," she continued to screech. Murphy reared up and pawed at his mistress's leg. "I don't think so!"

"You want us to trust you, but you don't trust us? That's not how it works, Charles," Nikki said, frost dripping from her words. "Kathryn is right—your behavior is unacceptable."

"My situation is different from yours, Nikki. I have to answer to Her Majesty. In the past, you only had to answer to me. If I could, I would answer all your questions. Unfortunately, I am duty-bound to say nothing."

Myra squared her shoulders and leveled the gun in her hand. "NTK, is that it? If there is no trust on both sides, then it doesn't work. I think I'm speaking for the Sisterhood when I say need-to-know doesn't work for us."

Charles looked at his ladylove and noticed that she wasn't wearing her pearls. Chains with circles draped her neck. Annie was wearing the same set of chains. He didn't like this new look. Myra wasn't Myra without her beloved heirloom pearls. He realized at that moment that things had indeed changed here on the mountain since he'd left.

Isabelle stepped forward. "We found out the hard way that we don't *need* you. Back in the day, we may have *wanted* you because you made it easier with your meticulous planning. We managed two missions. And even though we bumbled our way through them, we are standing here in front of you, guns drawn. On you! There is no reason to assume we cannot bumble our way through more missions. Actually, *Charlie,* we're getting rather adept at meticulous planning."

"You used my people. *My people,* ladies," Charles said quietly.

"*Your people* are mercenaries, Charles. Mercenaries go where the money is. We have the money. I rest my case," Alexis replied.

Charles took his time as he looked from one to the other, then down at his bag. Without another word, he picked up his bag and turned around to flick the power switch that would connect the power to the cable car. All he had to do was get in and then hit a second switch that would send the cable car to the bottom of the mountain. "Then I guess there's nothing more to say. Good-bye, ladies."

Yoko stepped forward, but not before she clicked the safety on her gun. Her hand dropped to her side. "I haven't spoken yet, Charles. I would like you to stay," she said softly.

Charles turned back to face the women. He smiled, and his tone matched Yoko's when he said, "I appreciate your vote, but I can't stay unless it's unanimous."

The women watched in horror as Charles pressed the main switch, not realizing he had just turned the power off. Then he sat down inside on the little bench so he could hold the door closed. When he realized his mistake, he stretched out a long arm to hit the power switch. He was going, leaving them again. Murphy and Grady howled. A lone tear rolled down Myra's cheek.

"Mom, don't let him go. If he goes, he will NEVER

*come back. You have to take Charles on faith. You know
that. Pride, Mummie, is a terrible thing. Hurry,
Mummie, hurry!"*

Myra whirled around as she tried to reconcile what
she was hearing from her spirit daughter and at the
same time saw Charles reaching for the switch that
would activate the cable car and take him to the bottom of the mountain. She literally leaped past the
two dogs and pulled Charles's hand away from the
switch. "We want you to stay, Charles."

The collective sigh behind her told Myra all she
needed to know. The girls wanted Charles to stay
but were willing to send him packing, thinking it
was what she wanted. When she stepped back, she
felt Annie's arm go around her shoulder. It felt so
comforting that she wanted to close her eyes and
go to sleep.

"Will you get rid of those weenies, already?
Charles will be preparing dinner this evening," was
all Myra could think of to say.

Annie laughed as she peeled the string of weenies from around her neck and handed them all
out to the dogs, who were waiting politely for the
rest of their unorthodox early dinner.

Charles stepped out of the cable car and started
to walk toward the main building, the girls following behind. Yoko was the last in line, her head
down.

"Honey, I admire your courage," Annie said to
her.

"I'm sorry, Yoko. I should have been the one to
speak up to tell Charles to stay," Myra said. "It's re-
freshing to see you have the courage of your con-
victions. I don't know what we all thought we were
trying to prove back there," she went on, waving

her hand behind her, "other than to make Charles sweat and punish him in some way. It's my fault entirely. The others thought I wanted to send Charles packing, and they went along with it."

"We need Charles," Yoko said softly.

"Yes, we do," Annie said forcefully.

"I agree," Myra said. "But we are going to have a few new rules this time around."

"Do you believe Charles is not allowed to talk about whatever it was that went on over there by orders of Her Majesty, or was he pulling our legs?" Annie asked fretfully.

"Charles never lies. Rather than tell a lie, he simply says nothing. The fact that he even offered up the explanation makes it all ring true. Whatever went on over there, we are never going to know about it, so we had better get used to the idea," Myra said.

"Does that mean you are moving back into the main house, Myra?" Annie asked.

"It means no such thing. I'm more than comfortable right where I am, in the room next to yours. That's not to say I won't be . . . uh . . . moving back at some point in the future. Then again, I may never move back in. I'm not the same person who followed Charles to England."

"I see that," Annie said, with a twinkle in her eye.

"I see that, too," Yoko added, giggling.

"I wonder what's for dinner," Myra said as she linked one arm with Annie and the other with Yoko.

"Barbara told me to do it," Myra whispered to Annie.

"I know, dear. I actually heard her this time."

"Oh, Annie, did you really?"

"Absolutely," Annie lied with a straight face.

Up ahead, Charles closed the door loudly behind him and walked through the main building that he and Myra had shared for so long. He stopped, dropped his duffel bag, and looked around. He struggled to figure out what was different but couldn't quite hone in on what it was. Everything was neat and tidy. There were fresh flowers in a vase on the coffee table. There was no sign of dust. The windows sparkled.

Charles picked up his duffel bag and walked into the war room. Again, it was neat and tidy. The computers were on; the clocks were working. No sign of disarray anywhere. He flinched at the emptiness. He continued his journey down the hall to the suite he shared with Myra. And that's when he knew what was different. Myra had moved her things out of the suite. He tossed his oversize duffel on the bed and hurried to the closet. All he could see were empty hangers. There were no shoes on the floor. No boxes on the overhead shelf. His eyes burning, he stepped into the huge closet and saw his own clothing at the far end, all enclosed in garment bags. When he'd left, his things had been hanging loosely on hangers. Someone, probably Myra, not knowing when or if he would return, had hung them in zippered garment bags. His shoes were in boxes instead of on their usual shoe trees. He swiped at his eyes before he looked over at the dresser where Myra kept the jewelry box in which she put her pearls every night. The box was gone, the dresser bare, save his own hairbrush and his own small box for cuff links. His things were now encased in a plastic bag. He bit down on his lower lip as he made his way to the bathroom.

It was a large bathroom, the kind any woman would love, and Myra had loved this bathroom, with its built-in Jacuzzi and the shower with seventeen different heads that shot out steaming-hot water from all angles. The vanity held only his things on the right side, again encased in plastic bags. The left side, Myra's side, was bare as a bone. He opened the linen closet to see a stack of hunter green towels that were enclosed in a zippered bag. Myra's fluffy yellow towels were gone, as were all her sundries. Only his remained, encased in plastic. Suddenly he had a hate on for plastic.

His eyes still burning, Charles walked back into the bedroom, and this time he noticed that the comforter on the bed was different. When he'd left, there had been a green and yellow appliquéd tulip spread with matching pillows. Now a darkish green and brown comforter was on the bed, and there were no matching pillows. It looked depressing. He realized then how alone he was. He hated the feeling. He swiped at his eyes again. Sometimes life just wasn't fair. He wondered if it would ever be fair again.

Charles stripped down and headed back to the shower, where he stood under the seventeen needle-spray jets and let them pound the tension out of his body.

Forty minutes later, he was dressed, freshly shaved, and on his way to the kitchen, where he was expected to prepare a gourmet meal, the last thing in the world he wanted to do. A smile tugged at the corners of his mouth when he remembered the string of frankfurters hanging around Annie's neck. Obviously, the girls had been eating things that were quick and easy.

A check of the larder and the Deepfreeze gave the lie to that. Someone had ordered and stocked everything just as he'd done. He took a minute to go to the back door that would allow him to see the garden, which—he knew—would be a disaster. He blinked at the neat, tidy rows of plants. The pole beans were tied neatly, as were the tomato plants. Shiny green peppers in need of picking peered up at him. He just knew there were at least a hundred zucchini under the trailing vines. Cucumbers were deep green and plentiful. The broccoli looked wonderful. He knew it would be tender and savory. Thanks to Yoko and her green thumb.

So his girls had managed nicely without him. He had to admit it hurt to know they had not only survived but prospered. Which then brought up a nasty thought. Did he subconsciously want them to have failed without him? The fact that he even thought such a terrible thing bothered him. Knowing and hearing Isabelle say aloud that they didn't *need* him even though they *wanted* him was almost impossible to accept, but it was a sad reality, and he had no choice but to deal with it. He told himself he just needed patience. Well, his time in England had certainly not instilled patience in him.

As Charles checked out the vegetable bin and the freezer, his thoughts raced. If there was some way he could explain to Myra and the others, he'd do it in a heartbeat. But Her Majesty had looked him in the eye and made him swear never to divulge what had gone on during his stay in England.

He'd promised, and he would die before he would break that promise.

The best he could hope for now was that time would heal all the wounds he'd created. Women, he knew, were, for the most part, forgiving creatures. He corrected that thought. Most women, with the exception of Myra, possibly Annie, too, were forgiving creatures. The only word that came to mind was *endurance*.

And endure he would.

Shifting his thoughts to the matter at hand, he finally decided on his menu—or, rather, his peace offering. He would prepare Shrimp Étouffée. A crisp summer salad from the garden, some of the pole beans in a light, savory garlic-butter sauce, homemade biscuits with soft honey butter. Myra loved his Chinese Almond Rice, so he would prepare that, too, and hope she understood he was making it just for her. For dessert he would make Rice Pudding with Raspberry Sauce and, of course, pots and pots of coffee. He dusted his hands together, satisfied that in the midst of all the turmoil in his mind, he could think of other things.

Charles licked his lips, crossed his fingers for luck, and started to prepare his homecoming dinner.

If you love the Sisterhood series,
but are hungry for a non-Sisterhood story from
Fern Michaels, you're in luck!

Her next stand-alone novel will be
coming from Kensington in May 2010.

Turn the page for a special preview of

RETURN TO SENDER,

the wonderful new bestseller by Fern Michaels.

Prologue

January 13, 1989
Dalton, Georgia

Rosalind Townsend, whom everyone called Lin, held her newborn son tightly in her arms as the orderly wheeled her to the hospital's administration office. A nurse tried to take him from her so she could tend to the business of her release, but she refused to give him up.

After eighteen hours of agonizing labor without any medication, she'd delivered a healthy six-pound eight-ounce baby boy. She wasn't about to let him out of her sight.

She'd named him William Michael Townsend. A good, solid name. She would call him Will.

Like his father's, Will's hair was a deep black, so dark it appeared to be blue. Lin wasn't sure about his eyes at this point. She'd read in her baby book that a newborn's eye color wasn't true at birth. Nothing about him resembled her, as she was fair-haired with unusual silver-colored eyes and milk white skin.

She gazed down at the securely wrapped bundle in her arms and ran her thumb across his delicate cheek. Soft as silk. He yawned, revealing tender, pink gums. Lin smiled down at her son. No matter what her circumstances, she made a vow to herself: she would devote her life to caring for this precious little child.

Lin had spent the past seven months preparing for this day. During the day she worked at J & G Carpet Mills as a secretary. Five evenings a week and weekend mornings, she waited tables at Jack's Diner. Other than what it cost for rent, food, and utilities, Lin saved every cent she made. She had to be conservative, because it was just her and Will. She would allow herself a week off from both jobs so she could bond with her son, adjust to her new life as a mother. While she would've loved spending more time with her son, being the sole caregiver and provider made that impossible. She'd lucked out when Sally, a coworker at Jack's and a single mother to boot, had asked her if she would sit for her two-year-old daughter, Lizzie. In return, Sally would look after the baby on the days that she wasn't working. Lin had agreed because she had to. There were still the days to cover, but Sally gave her a list of reliable sitters she'd used in the past. Dear Sally. Only five years older than Lin but so much wiser to the ways of the world. They were fast becoming good friends. Sally was the complete opposite of Lin—tall, olive-skinned, with beautiful brown eyes that had a slight upward slant, giving her an Asian look. Lin had called three of the sitters: two high-school girls and one elderly woman. She would meet with them later in the week. Lin was sure that if Sally approved, she would as well.

Sadly, there would be no help from Will's father or her parents. Lin recalled her father's cruel words when he learned she was pregnant.

"May you burn in hell, you little harlot! You've disgraced my good name. Get out of my house. I don't ever want to lay eyes on you again or your bastard child!"

Lin had appealed to her mother in the hope she would intervene, but, as usual, her mother had cowered behind her father, accepting his word as law. Lin would never allow a man to intimidate her the way her father did her mother.

Never.

"Miss?"

Lin directed her attention back to the woman behind the administration desk. "Yes?"

"If you'll sign here and initial here." The woman slid a single sheet of paper across the desk.

Lin signed the paper, releasing the hospital from any liability. Since she had no health insurance and refused public assistance, she could only afford to stay in the hospital for twenty-four hours. She'd spend the next two years paying a hundred dollars a month until her debt was paid in full.

The woman behind the desk reached into a drawer and pulled out a thick envelope. "Here, take these. You might find them useful."

Lin took the envelope, peered inside. Coupons for diapers, formula, baby lotion, and anything else one might need. She gave the woman a wan smile. "Thank you."

"You're welcome."

Throughout her pregnancy, she had visited the local dollar store once a month. She'd purchased generic brands of baby items that were on the list of layette necessities she'd read about in the baby book given to her by her obstetrician. Lin didn't have extra money to spend on a homecoming outfit for the baby, so she'd gone to Goodwill and found a secondhand pale blue sweater set. She'd carefully hand washed it in Dreft detergent. Subsequently it had looked good as new. Someday, she swore to herself, her son wouldn't have to wear secondhand clothes.

The orderly wheeled her back to her room, where she dressed in the maternity clothes she'd worn when admitted to the hospital the day before. She ran her hand across her flat stomach. Now she would be able to wear the uniform Jack required, thus saving wear and tear on her few meager outfits. She gazed around the room to make sure she wasn't leaving anything behind. Had it only been twenty-four hours since the taxi had dropped her off at the emergency room? It seemed like a week.

Lin carefully removed the sweater set she'd placed in her overnight bag. With ease, she dressed her son, smiling at the results. Will looked like a little prince in his blue outfit from Goodwill. Briefly, she thought of his father and their weeklong affair. What would his reaction be when he saw his son for the first time? After months of indecision, she'd finally written him another letter two months ago, the first one since she had been on her own, and mailed it to his parents' address in New York, the only way she knew to contact him. She'd begged Nancy Johnson, a girl Will's father had introduced her to, for his phone number as well, but the woman had been adamant about not revealing more of her friend's personal life. She'd told Lin that if Nicholas wanted her to have his phone number, he would have given it to her. The harsh words had stung, but there was more at stake than her raw feelings. She had a child to consider. She'd written a lengthy letter, revealing her pregnancy, telling Nicholas he would be a father shortly after the new year. Weeks passed without a response. Then just last week she'd trudged to the mailbox only to find the letter she'd sent unopened and marked RETURN TO SENDER.

What's one more rejection? she'd asked herself.

Her father hadn't accepted her, either. Her mother had once told her that he'd always dreamed of having a son. At the time, Lin had been terribly hurt, but as the years passed, she learned to set those feelings aside. She'd been the best daughter she knew how to be in hopes of gaining some kind of approval, and maybe even a bit of love and affection from both parents, but that was not to be. When she told her parents about the decision to keep her baby, they were mortified and humiliated. She'd been tossed out of the only home she'd ever known with nothing more than the clothes on her back.

A soft, mewling sound jerked her out of the past. "It's okay, little one. I'm right here."

With the quilt that Irma, Jack's wife, had made for him, Lin gently wrapped Will in a snug bundle. It was below freezing outside. Lin had halfheartedly listened to the local weather report as it blared from the television mounted above her bed. An ice storm was predicted. Meteorologists said it could be the worst in north Georgia history. With only two small electric space heaters, her garage apartment would be freezing. How she wished she could take Will to her childhood home. While it wasn't filled with love, at least it would be warm.

But Lin recalled the torturous evenings of her

childhood. She would rather die than subject her son to such a strict and oftentimes cruel upbringing. Every evening, as far back as she could remember, she'd had to pray while kneeling on the hardwood floor in the living room as her father read from the Bible.

A die-hard Southern Baptist who considered himself a man of God, her father had constructed a pulpit for himself in the center of the living room from which he would gaze down at her with disdain, as though she weren't good enough. Then, as if that weren't bad enough, he'd make her recite the names of all the books of the Bible in order. If she missed one, he would make her start from the beginning until she named them correctly. Once, when she was about seven or eight, she remembered spending an entire night on her knees praying. She'd prayed hard, her father watching her the entire time. Little did he know she'd been praying for his immediate death. Many times she'd wet herself while on her knees in prayer. Her father wouldn't allow her to change her clothes or bathe afterward.

"The devil lives inside you, girly! Taking a shower ain't gonna cleanse your dirty soul!"

She'd winced the first time she'd heard those words. After a while, she became immune to his cruel words. She'd even gotten used to smelling like urine. The kids at school were relentless, calling her Miss Stinkypants. And she would do what she always did when she was hurting.

She prayed.

Every night that she knelt on that cold, hard floor, she prayed for her father's death. Not once

in the seventeen years that she had lived in her father's house had he ever relented on this evening
ritual. She had thick, ugly calluses on her knees to
prove it.

When she left home, or rather when she was
thrown out, she made a promise to herself: she
would *never, ever* kneel again.

Freezing definitely held more appeal.

She checked the room one last time. One of the
nurses waited to wheel her downstairs, where the
hospital's courtesy van would take her and Will
home.

In the lobby, the automatic doors opened, and a
gush of icy air greeted her, smacking her in the
face. She held Will close to her with one arm and
carried her small suitcase with the other. The driver,
an older black man, opened the door and reached
for her bag. "You best hop inside, miss. This here
cold ain't good for the young'un." He nodded at
the bundle in her arms.

Shivering, Lin stepped carefully up into the van.
Thankful for the warm air blowing from the heater's
vents, she sat on the hard vinyl seat and realized she
was still very sore from the delivery. Her breasts felt
as though they would explode. She couldn't wait to
get home to nurse Will. She'd only be able to do so
for the week she was home. Then she'd have to resort
to formula. She'd calculated the expense, and while
it was very costly, she would manage. Unfortunately,
she had no choice.

"Thank you," she said to the driver as she placed
Will in the car seat beside her. When Lin had dis-
covered she was pregnant, she'd been frightened,
fearful of having inherited her parents' harsh and

unloving manner. However, when Will was placed in her arms, the love she felt for him was the most natural thing in the world. Her worries had been for naught.

When mother and son were secure in their seats, the driver made his way through the parking lot. Waiting at the traffic light, he perused a stack of papers attached to a clipboard. "Tunnel Hill, ma'am?"

"Yes, just make a left on Lafayette, then take the second right." Lin hated having to take Will home to a one-room garage apartment. Someday they would have a home with a big yard with flowers, a white picket fence, and lots of trees for him to climb. Will would have a swing set, and she'd watch him play. Yes, she would see to it that Will had a good home, and, whatever it took, she would make sure he had an education.

Lin remembered her father telling her years before that it was foolish for women to go to college, a waste of money. He'd assured her then that he would not contribute to her education, so after she'd preenrolled at Dalton Junior College during her senior year of high school, she'd saved enough money for the first year.

Having spent three terrifying nights alone in a cheap motel after her father threw her out, she'd made her first adult decision. Instead of using the money for college, she'd paid three months' rent on an apartment. In retrospect, her father's attitude had worked out well since it forced her to save for her education. If not, there wouldn't even be a place for her to bring Will.

The driver parked in her landlady's driveway.

She hurriedly removed Will from the car seat and took her bag from the driver. "Thank you. I appreciate the ride."

"Jus' doin' my job, miss. Now scoot on outta here. That ice storm's gonna hit real soon."

"Yes, I know. Thanks again for the ride."

Lin felt rather than saw the driver watching her as he slowly reversed down the long driveway. She didn't feel creepy at all, because she knew he was good and decent and just wanted to make sure she made it inside safely. A stranger cared more about her well-being than her own flesh and blood. Sad. But she smiled at her thoughts. She had the greatest gift ever, right here in her very own arms.

Holding Will tightly against her chest, she plodded down the long drive that led to the garage apartment. She felt for the key in her pocket, then stopped when she heard a whining noise. Putting her bag on the ground, she checked Will, but he was sound asleep. She heard the sound again.

"What the heck?" she said out loud.

On the side of the garage, at the bottom of the steep wooden steps that led to her apartment, Lin spotted a small dog and walked behind the steps where he hovered. Holding Will tightly, she held out her hand. Its brownish red fur matted with clumps of dirt, the ribs clearly visible, the poor dog looked scruffy and cold. He or she—she wasn't sure of the animal's gender—whined before standing on all fours, limping over to Lin, and licking her outstretched hand.

She laughed. "You sure know the way to a girl's heart."

"Woof, woof."

With the ice storm ready to hit, there was no way Lin could leave the poor dog outside. She fluffed the matted fur between its ears and decided that the dog was going inside with her.

"Scruffy, that's what I'm going to call you for now. Come on, puppy. Follow me." The dog obeyed, staying a foot behind Lin as she made her way up the rickety steps while holding Will against her chest.

Unlocking the door, Lin stepped inside and dropped her bag on the floor. Timidly, Scruffy waited to be invited in. "Come on, Scruffy. You're staying here tonight. Something tells me we're going to get along just fine."

Two unwanted strays, Lin thought.

Scruffy scurried inside and sat patiently on the kitchen floor. With Will still clutched to her chest, Lin grabbed a plastic bowl from her single cupboard, filled it with water, and placed it on the cracked olive green linoleum. She took two hot dogs out of her minirefrigerator, broke them into small pieces, and placed them on a saucer next to the bowl of water. "This should tide you over for a bit. I've got to feed the little guy now."

Scruffy looked at her with big, round eyes. Lin swore she saw thankfulness in the dog's brown-eyed gaze.

With her son still clutched in her arms, Lin managed to remove her jacket before loosening the blanket surrounding him. Making the necessary adjustments to her clothing, Lin began to nurse her son. Reclining on the floral-patterned sofa, she relaxed for the first time in a long time. Her son was fed and content. She'd inherited an adorable dog, however temporarily, and she was warm.

For a while, that would do. Someday their lives would be different.

Lin stared at the sleeping infant in her arms. "I promise you, little guy, you'll have the best life ever." Then, as an afterthought, she added, "No matter what I have to do."

One

Friday, August 31, 2007
New York University

Will's deep brown eyes sparkled with excitement, his enthusiasm contagious, as he and Lin left University Hall, a crowded dormitory for freshmen located at Union Square. If all went as planned, Will would reside in New York City for the next four years before moving on to graduate school to study at North Carolina State University College of Veterinary Medicine, one of the most prestigious veterinary institutions in the country.

"I just hate that you're so far away from home. And in New York City, no less," Lin said for the umpteenth time. "With all the remodeling and holiday parties going on at the restaurant, I doubt I'll be able to make the trip north for Thanksgiving. I don't want you to spend your holiday alone."

"Mom, I said I'd come home if I could. And I will. I promise," Will said. "Besides, I'm a big boy now. I just might like spending some time alone in this big city full of hot chicks."

Laughing, Lin replied, "I'm sure you would." She watched her son as they rode the elevator downstairs. Over six feet tall, with thick, raven black hair, Will was the spitting image of his father, or at least her memory of him.

Lin recalled all those years ago when she'd first met his father. She'd fallen head over heels in love while he'd been visiting a friend in Georgia. Briefly, Lin wondered if Will would follow in her footsteps or his father's. She prayed it wasn't the latter, though she had to admit she really didn't know how he'd turned out. But she didn't want her son to take after a man who denied his son's existence. Lin knew he was very wealthy, but that didn't mean he was a good man. Good men took care of their children, acknowledged them.

Three weeks after she'd brought Will home from the hospital, she'd sent his father a copy of their son's birth announcement along with a copy of the birth certificate. She'd shamelessly added a picture of herself just in case he'd forgotten their brief affair. Throughout the years, she had continued to send items marking Will's accomplishments, the milestones reached as he grew up. Photos of the first day of school; first lost tooth; then, as he aged, driver's license; first date; anything she thought a father would have been proud of. Again, all had come back, unopened and marked RETURN TO SENDER. After so many years of this, she should have learned, should have known that Will's father had no desire to acknowledge him. To this very day, she'd never told Will for fear it would affect him in a way that she wouldn't be able to handle. Recalling the hurt, then the anger each time she and her son were rejected, Lin tucked away the memories of the man she'd given herself to so many years ago, the man she'd loved, the man who had so callously discarded all traces of their romance and in so doing failed to acknowledge their son's existence. When Will had turned twelve, she'd told him his father had died in an accident. It had seemed enough at the time.

But as Jack, her former employer and substitute father, always said, "The past is prologue, kiddo." And he was right. She'd put that part of her life behind her and moved forward.

The elevator doors swished open. The main floor was empty but for a few couples gathered in the corner speaking in hushed tones. Most of the parents were either visiting other dorms or preparing for the evening banquet. Will hadn't wanted to attend, but Lin insisted, telling him several of the college's alumni would be speaking. She'd teased him, saying he might be among them one day. He'd reluctantly agreed, but Lin knew that if he truly hadn't wanted to attend, he would have been more persistent.

She glanced at the exquisite diamond watch on her slender wrist, a gift from Jack and Irma the day she'd made her last payment on the diner she'd purchased from them eight years ago. "I'll meet you in the banquet hall at seven. Are you sure you don't want to come back to the hotel?"

Will cupped her elbow, guiding her toward the exit. "No. Actually, I think I might take a nap. Aaron doesn't arrive until tomorrow. It might be the last chance I have for some time alone. I want to take advantage of it."

Will and his dorm mate, Aaron Levy, had met through the Internet during the summer. Though they hadn't met in person, Will assured her they'd get along just fine. They were studying to become veterinarians and both shared an avid love of baseball.

"Better set your alarm," Lin suggested. Will slept like the dead.

"Good idea." He gave her a hug, then stepped back, his gaze suddenly full of concern. "You'll be okay on your own for a while?"

Lin patted her son's arm. "Of course I will. This is my first trip to the city. There are dozens of things to do. I doubt I'll have a minute to spare. Though I don't think I'll do any sightseeing today, since I made an appointment to have my hair and nails done at the hotel spa."

Will laughed. "That's a first. You never do that kind of stuff. What gives?"

"It's not every day a mother sends her son off to college." She gently pushed him away. "Now go on with you, or there'll be no time to relax. I'll see you at seven."

Will waved. "Seven, then."

Lin gave him a thumbs-up sign, her signal to him that all was a go. She pushed the glass door open and stepped outside. The late-afternoon sun shone brightly through the oak trees, casting all sorts of irregular shapes and shadows on the sidewalk. The late-summer air was cool and crisp. Lin walked down the sidewalk and breathed deeply, suddenly deliriously happy with the life she'd made for herself. She stopped for a moment, remembering all the struggles, the ups and downs, and how hard she'd worked to get to where she was. Abundant, fulfilled, completely comfortable with her life, she picked up her pace, feeling somewhat foolish and silly for her thoughts. She laughed, the sound seemingly odd since she was walking alone, no one to hear her. That was okay, too. Life was good. She was happy, Will's future appeared bright and exciting. The only dark spot in her life was her father. Her mother had died shortly after Lin had moved into Mrs. Turner's garage apartment. She'd had to read about it in the obituaries. Lin had called her father, asking how her mother had died. He told her she'd fallen down the basement steps. She suspected otherwise but knew it would be useless, possibly even dangerous to her and her unborn child, if she were to pry into the circumstances surrounding her mother's death. She'd tried to establish a relationship with her father on more than one occasion through the years, and each time he'd rebuffed her, telling her she was the devil's spawn. Her father now resided in Atlanta, in a very upscale nursing home, at her expense. Lin was sure his pure meanness had launched him into early onset Alzheimer's.

Lin thought it was time for her to proceed at her own leisurely pace, kick back, and totally relax for the first time in a very, very long time.

Lin continued to ponder her life as she walked down the sidewalk toward a line of waiting taxis. After ten years of working at Jack's Diner, when she'd learned that Jack and Irma were considering closing the place, she'd come up with a plan. Though she'd skimped and saved most of her life, for once she was about to splurge and do something so out of character that Jack had thought she'd taken temporary leave of her senses. She'd offered him a fifty-thousand-dollar down payment, a cut of the profits, and a promissory note on the balance if they would sell her the diner. It took all of two minutes for Jack and Irma to accept her offer. Since they'd never had children and didn't think they'd have a chance in hell of selling the diner given the local economy, closing the doors had seemed their only option.

Lin laughed.

She'd worked her tail off day and night and most weekends to attract a new clientele, a younger crowd with money to burn. She'd applied for a liquor license and changed the menu to healthier fare while still remaining true to some of the comfort foods Jack's was known for, such as his famous meat loaf and mashed potatoes. Within a year, Jack's was crowded every night of the week, and weekends were booked months in advance. From there, she started catering private parties. With so much success, she'd decided it was time to add on to the diner. In addition to two large private banquet rooms that would accommodate five hundred guests when combined, she added three moderately sized private rooms for smaller groups. The remodeling was in its final stages when she'd left for New York the day before. She'd left Sally, her dearest friend and manager, in charge of last-minute details.

Lin quickened her pace as she saw that the line of taxis at the end of the block had dwindled down to three. She waved her hand in the air to alert the cabbie. Yanking the yellow-orange door open, she slid inside, where the smell of stale smoke and fried onions filled her nostrils. She wrinkled her nose in disgust. "The Helmsley Park Lane." She'd always wanted to say that to a New York cab driver. Though it wasn't the most elite or expensive hotel in the city, it was one that had captured her imagination over the years. Its infamous owner, known far and wide by the well-deserved epithet the Queen of Mean, had been quite visible in the news media when Lin was younger, especially when she'd been tried and convicted for tax evasion, extortion, and mail fraud, and had died just over a week before.

Through blasts of horns, shouts from sidewalk vendors hawking their wares, and the occasional bicyclist weaving in and out of traffic, Lin enjoyed the scenery during the quick cab ride back to the hotel. New York was unlike any city in the world. Of course, she hadn't traveled outside the state of Georgia, so where this sudden knowledge came from, she hadn't a clue, but still she knew there was no other place like New York. It had its own unique *everything*, right down to the smell of the city.

The taxi stopped in front of the Helmsley. Lin handed the driver a twenty, telling him to keep the change. Hurrying, Lin practically floated through the turnstile doors as though she were on air. She felt like Cinderella, and the banquet would be her very own ball, with Will acting as her handsome prince. He would croak if he knew her thoughts. Nonetheless, she was excited about the evening ahead.

She dashed to the elevator doors with only seconds to spare. She'd lost track of time, and her salon appointment was in five minutes. They'd asked her to wear a blouse that buttoned in the front so she wouldn't mess up her new do before the banquet. She punched the button to the forty-sixth floor, from which she had an unbelievable view of the city and Central Park. Lin cringed when she thought of the cost but remembered this was just a onetime treat, and she was doing it in style.

She slid the keycard into the slot on the door and pushed the door inward. Overcome by the sheer luxuriousness, she simply stared at her surroundings, taking them in. Lavender walls with white wainscoting, cream-colored antique tables at either end of the lavender floral sofa. The bedroom color scheme matched, though the coverlet on her bed was a deep, royal purple. She raced over to the large walk-in closet, grabbed a white buttonup blouse, and headed to the bathroom. This, too, was beyond opulent. All marble, a deep Jacuzzi tub, a shower that could hold at least eight people, thick, soft, lavender bath towels and bars of lilac soaps and bath beads placed in crystal containers gave Lin such a feeling of luxury, and it was such a novel feeling, she considered staying in the room her entire trip. She laughed, then spoke out loud. "Sally would really think I've lost my marbles." She'd discussed her New York trip with her, and they'd made a list of all the must-see places. If she returned empty-handed, Sally would wring her neck. She'd bring her back something special.

They'd practically raised the kids together, and Sally felt like the older sister she'd never had. And she'd bring Elizabeth, Sally's daughter. something smart and sexy. She'd opted to attend Emory University in Atlanta instead of leaving the state as Will had. Sally told her she was glad. Not only did she not have to pay out-of-state tuition, but Lizzie was able to come home on the weekends. She would graduate next year. Where had the time gone?

She hurried downstairs to the spa for her afternoon of pampering.

Three hours later, Lin returned to her room to dress for the banquet. The hairstylist had talked her into a pedicure and a facial. After an afternoon of being catered to, she felt like royalty. Of course, it all came at a price, one so high she didn't dare give it another thought, or she'd have such a case of the guilts that she'd ruin the evening for herself and Will. No, she reminded herself again, this was a once-in-a-lifetime trip. As she had explained to Will, it wasn't every day that he went away to college. Besides, she wanted to look her best at the banquet, knowing there would be many well-to-do parents attending with their children. No way did she want to cause Will any embarrassment just because she was a small-town hick who ran a diner. Her accomplishments might mean something in Dalton, but here in New York City she would just be seen as a country bumpkin trying to keep up with the big-city folk, even though her net worth these days could probably match that of many of New York's movers and shakers.

Discarding her self-doubts, Lin took her dress out of its garment bag. She'd ordered it from a Macy's catalogue four months ago. She slid the black, long-sleeved silk dress over her head, allowing it to swathe her slender body. Lin looked at her reflection in the full-length mirror. With all the skipped meals and extra work at the diner, she'd lost weight since purchasing the dress. The curve-hugging dress emphasized her tiny waist. She twirled around in front of the mirror. *Not bad for an old woman,* she thought.

"Shoot, I'm not *that* old." She cast another look in the mirror and slipped her feet into her ruby red slingbacks she'd been dying to wear since she'd purchased them two years ago. Lin remembered buying them on a trip to Atlanta as a prize to celebrate her first million. On paper, of course, but still it was monumental to her, since she'd clawed her way to the top. It hadn't been all rainbows and lollipops, either.

Clipping on the garnet earrings Sally and Irma had given her for her thirtieth birthday, she returned to the mirror for one last look before heading downstairs.

Five-foot-three, maybe a hundred pounds soaking wet, Lin scrutinized her image. The stylist had flat-ironed her long blond hair, assuring her that it was the current style, and, no, she was not too old to wear her hair down. Her face had a rosy glow courtesy of Lancôme and a facial. The manicurist had given her a French manicure, telling her it, too, was "in vogue." After leaving the spa, she returned to her room with a few makeup tricks under her belt. Plus, her hairstylist had sashayed back and forth, showing her the fashionable way to strut her stuff so that she'd be noticed when making an entrance. While that was the last thing on her mind, she'd had a blast with the women, more than she cared to admit. Lin had confessed that she hadn't had time for such things as a girl, but she hadn't explained why.

She glanced at her watch. Six-fifteen. It was time for Cinderella to hail her carriage.

"Get off it!" If she continued thinking along those lines, she would have to commit herself.

Lin visualized her mental checklist. Purse, lipstick, wallet, cell phone, and keycard. All of a sudden her hands began to shake, and her stomach twisted in knots. It wasn't like she would be the only parent there. Unsure why she was so jittery, she shrugged her feelings aside, telling herself she simply wanted to make a good impression on Will's professors and classmates. Plus, she wasn't on her own turf, and that in and of itself had the power to turn her insides to mush.

Instead of exiting through the turnstile doors, Lin allowed the doorman to open the door for her. Discreetly, she placed a twenty in his hand and hoped it was enough. Sally told her you had to tip everyone for everything in the city. Lin calculated she'd be broke in less than a year if she remained in New York.

"Thank you, ma'am," the elderly man said as he escorted her to a waiting taxi.

Okay, that was worth the twenty bucks. She would've hated to chase down a cab in the red heels.

The inside of the taxi was warm. Lin offered up a silent prayer of thanks that there were no strange odors permeating the closed-in space. She would hate to arrive at the banquet smelling like cigarettes and onions.

More blaring horns, shouts, and tires squealing could be heard. Lin enjoyed watching the throngs of people on the streets as the driver managed to weave through the traffic. Lord, she loved the hubbub, but she didn't think she could tolerate it on a daily basis.

Poor Will. She smiled. *Not* poor Will. After the slow pace of Dalton, he would welcome this. It was one of the many reasons he had chosen to attend NYU in the first place. He'd wanted a taste of the big city. Lin thought he was about to get his wish and then some.

Twenty minutes later, the cab stopped in front of the building where the banquet was being held. She offered up two twenties, telling the driver to keep the change.

"Do you want me to pick you up later?" the driver asked as he jumped out to open her door. Lin thought the tip must have been a tad too generous.

"Uh, I'm not sure. Do you have a card?" she asked.

He laughed. "No card, lady, but if you want a return ride, you gotta ask for it."

"Of course. Midnight. Be here at midnight." Now she was starting to *sound* like Cinderella.

"Will do."

Her transportation taken care of, Lin stepped out into the cool night air.